THE OWL AND THE DRAGON

A Bander Adventure

RANDY NARGI

The Bander Adventures

The River's Bane

A Conspiracy of Shadows
In Terror's Thrall
Revenge of the Battle Mage

The Owl and the Dragon

LIBRARY OF CONGRESS CATALOGING-IN-PUBLICATION DATA
Nargi, Randy. The Owl and the Dragon: a Bander novel / Randy Nargi.
pages cm.

ISBN: 978-0-9851943-3-8

to JIM KOEHLER

Thank you for all your encouragement

The Empire of Marion

THE PROVINCE OF
KREED'S KEEP

THE PROVINCE OF VALE

THE TENGAN TERRITORIES

CITY OF
Vale

THE WEST WAY
AND ENVIRONS

MARSTON
HILLS

Names & Places

People

Alford Platt — steward of Lockwell Farms
Arno Lockwell — Lord of Hytwen, master of Lockwell Farms, and husband to Ellia Lockwell
Bander — former imperial investigator, now retired
Borsus Skenn — Creagar Skenn's brother and steward of Ortwen Farms
Creagar Skenn — Lord of Ortwen, cousin to Ellia Lockwell
Dorson — the new marshal in Ortwen
Ellia Lockwell — Arno Lockwell's wife, cousin to Creagar Skenn
Fandott — cook at Lockwell Manor
Felde — mage in Bexden
Fenton Skenn — Creagar Skenn's son, aged 11
Geddis Lockwell — son of Armo & Ellia Lockwell, aged 8
Haddon Fane — a recluse
Harl, Pots, Dessan, Starnery, Tobbler, Barnes — mercenaries hired by Arno Lockwell
Hauf — upper housemaid at Lockwell Manor

Herron of the Black — the Guildmaster in Vale

Iblan — bone carver in Vale and friend to the Guild

Jillen Lockwell — adopted daughter of Armo & Ellia Lockwell, aged 12

Jory — young street urchin in Vale

Kaderly — peddler in Vale whose route takes him south into the Tengan Territories

Lohuin — butler at Lockwell Manor

Lynd — healer in Hytwen

Milnan — Kaderly's son, aged 20

Minch — Hytwen's town marshal

Perras Tul — mage in Vale; an associate of Bander

Raerig — proprietor of the Green Tree Inn in Hytwen

Sangal — gardener at Lockwell Manor

Sittig — renowned blind cobbler in Vale

Valthar — Bander's old friend

Vogan — footman at Lockwell Manor

Wylla — nursemaid at Lockwell Manor

Places

The West Way — the longest Imperial highway stretching east from Sulmos through Vale, Kreed's Keep, Mynwal and then further east into the kingdom of Gadmark

Kreed's Keep — capital city of the province of Kreed's Keep

Marston Hills — a large city on the West Way, west of Kreed's Keep

The Tengan Territories — the vast forested wilderness on the southern border of the Empire of Harion, also known as the Wilderlands

Hytwen & Ortwen — two villages on either end of Lake Teagh, south of the West Way in the Tengan Territories

Bexden — a town between Marston Hills and Vale on the West Way

Vale — the ancient capital city of the province of Vale in the heart of Harion's cattle country

Hamwick — capital city of the province of Hamwick in the center of the Empire

Chapter One

❦

Spring, 1713
The West Way

THEY SAY YOU CAN DROWN IN AN INCH OF WATER—if you happen to be face down and unconscious in a muddy ravine in the midst of a rain storm, for example. I suppose the length of your nose has something to do with it. I knew a man—Geddric—who was nicknamed "The Duck" because of his prodigious nose. Geddric would have been okay in the ravine.

I was not okay.

I was about to die.

I had been drugged, robbed, stripped of my boots, pushed off an embankment, and left for dead. On a forest road in the middle of nowhere. Over a hundred miles away from the nearest town. And technically not even within the Empire's borders.

It had been my own fault. I had been too trusting. Too eager to help.

You'd think after two decades in Rundlun, dealing with

thieves, grifters, and every other variety of criminal, day in and day out, I would have had my guard up. But I didn't. At least not enough.

The two young women and their elderly uncle had played their parts well. I didn't doubt their tale of woe for a moment. And, truth be told, I had been a little lonely. So when we met on the West Way—a half day east of Marston Hills—and they beseeched me to travel with them, to keep an eye on things, I agreed. At least to Vale. At the time I wasn't sure if I'd be heading north from Vale or continuing on to Rundlun.

The women were young. Reeni looked to be fifteen or sixteen. Her sister, Barelle, was maybe two or three years older. The old man, Sambart, was at least twenty years older than me—definitely too old to be on a thousand mile journey. They all had horses, but they were content to slow down in order to travel with me. Even still, we made good progress. Maybe twenty or twenty-five miles that first day. Talking the whole time.

That's probably what threw me off.

People who are trying to deceive you are pretty careful about speaking too much. They are too afraid of a slip of the tongue. But not these young women. They chattered on about their lives in Kreed's Keep, the sad death of their mother, and how they were making the journey to Whill to live with their aunt. They talked about the friends that they left behind and what they imagined Whill to be like. They asked me a lot of questions. And at the end of the day, they cooked for me.

The younger of the two women was an accomplished cook, and she had a satchel so filled with vials of spices it reminded me of a healer's kit. We ate like nobles that first night. I told myself that the food was designed to keep me around for protection, but I was wrong. Dead wrong.

They wanted my gold.

It happened like this.

Around noon on the second day, Reeni became excited while looking at some of the plants that grew on the sides of the West Way. She told us that we were in the lowlands now. And there was a certain kind of mushroom called an ormilla that grew around here. These ormillas were very rare in Kreed's Keep and very expensive. But she thought that we were now far enough away from the mountains that she might be able to find some. And she promised that it would be worth the detour.

I didn't argue. I wasn't in any rush to get anywhere.

We found an old game trail that wound its way south into the Territories. It was barely wide enough for a horse, and it was pretty overgrown, but Reeni skipped down it, certain she'd find her treasure. And the whole time Barelle peppered me with questions about Rundlun. What were the women like? What did they wear? How did they style their hair? Were there really a thousand galas happening throughout the city on any given night?

The old man didn't say a word. Just sat on his horse, hunched like an old gargoyle, hood up to protect his old bald head from the fine drizzle of rain which had started up.

Then Reeni let out a shriek of delight and raced down into a little dark canyon, choked with snaca vines and wet with moss.

She searched along the banks of a brook for the better part of an hour until she found what she was looking for. Then she called the rest of us over to a stand of thin trees. Reeni explained that ormillas liked to grow at the base of these particular trees. And, sure enough, when she dug around at the roots she found a white clump of something that looked to me more like an egg or a stone than a mushroom.

3

Reeni kept digging at the base of each tree in the grove and eventually had a collection of around a dozen ormillas. She was gleeful and said she couldn't wait to start cooking. She said it would be the best thing I had ever tasted and asked if we could make camp here so she could begin her preparations.

By this time it was mid-afternoon, and the rain had increased. I didn't like the idea of lingering in a valley next to a brook during a storm. It was springtime, and we were on the edge of a forest that stretched for a few thousand miles, getting denser and denser until it became a jungle. And even though the temperature was mild, the weather was unpredictable. So I told them to stay with the horses while I scouted around for a more suitable camp site.

I backtracked a hundred yards up the game trail and climbed out of the little canyon. Then I found a clearing at the top of a stone cliff. It was just a couple dozen feet up from where the girls and their uncle waited, but it looked safe enough.

I waved to them and signaled them to join me. Then I went down to help them get the horses up to the clearing.

Within an hour I had built a lean-to against a large boulder and Barelle had made a fire. Reeni collected water from the brook and set a kettle of grain boiling.

While the girls cooked, I tried to engage the old man in conversation, ask him what his trade was back in Kreed's Keep, but all he wanted to do was nap.

The girls worked on the meal, slicing the ormillas into thin slivers and then frying them in butter and spices. The smell was amazing. My stomach began to grumble. I didn't want to torture myself, so I decided to take a walk.

As I wandered through the wet forest, I thought about talent and youth and wondered if I had wasted my early life.

When I was Reeni's age, I had no real skills to speak of.

Except brawling. And being able to adapt. To whatever life threw at me. I learned that at an early age—that was for sure. But I didn't have a trade. I couldn't hunt or fish or grow plants or make horseshoes or even talk my way out of a bad situation. All I really had was my size and my strength.

Even before I reached my sixteenth birthday, I stood nearly six feet tall and weighed 170 pounds. I was stronger than most adults. But I was also reckless. I got into a lot of fights. True, I won just about every fight I got into, but I didn't avoid the ones I could have and should have. It wasn't that I had a bad temper. It was more that I liked challenges.

Now, thirty-five years later, I was wandering the country-side. No home. No profession. No wife. No family. What would my life have been like if I could cook like Reeni, or paint like Malso Jard, or compose plays like Leocald Grannt?

I pushed the questions from my mind. They served no purpose. Instead, I checked on the horses, then returned to the camp to clean my boots. I was halfway done when Reeni announced that the meal was ready. Barelle woke her uncle and the four of us sat on rocks and stumps overlooking the dark little canyon, eating the grain dish. Or, to be more accu-rate, the old man and I began to eat, while the girls looked on expectantly.

The meal was a sort of pottage made with long rice in a creamy sauce. I could taste onions and butter and cheese and shavings of what must have been the ormillas. I inhaled the aroma as I tasted it, rich and fragrant—with almost a floral smell. It was just about the best thing I had ever tasted and I told Reeni so.

She beamed and began to eat small bites from her own dish, chattering on about the history of the ormilla, where it grew, why it was so rare, and every other fact she knew about it.

I asked her how she had come to be such a good cook at

such a young age. It was a natural question, but Reeni fell silent as soon as I asked it. Barelle told me that their mother had been an exceptional cook. Reeni had spent a lot of time in the kitchen with their mother. Right up until their mother became ill and died.

The old man changed the subject. He asked me if I had ever been to a tavern called the Raxton Arms in the Steading. I told him that I did not remember a tavern by that name, but he barely even paused in his narrative. Sambart said that he knew the cook at the Raxton Arms and even did a favor for the man by helping him out when some thugs tried to rob him in the alley behind the tavern. In return, the cook offered Sambart his recipe for gorman stew, which supposedly was such a famous dish that people came from all over the south to try it.

I asked Sambart if he was a skilled chef as well, and he replied that he couldn't even boil water. He also couldn't read, so the recipe he had been given didn't do him much good.

He then launched into another story about the time he had been mistaken for a duke in Pampalon, but at that point, two things were happening. And they were happening very quickly. First, I was finding it very difficult to concentrate on what the old man was saying. Second, the clearing was spinning around me. And then I felt myself falling from the rock and hands pushing me over the edge of the embankment.

My last thought was a question posed to myself. *How could I have been so stupid?*

Chapter Two

✿❀✿

I N THE END, WHAT SAVED ME WAS MY SIZE AND MY STRENGTH. Not strength of will, or strength of character. Just pure physical strength. Specifically, the fact that my body is solid muscle, from head to toe.

I stand six feet, five inches tall. That's about seven or eight inches taller than the average man from the north, and ten inches taller than the average man from the south. Even still, I've met plenty of men who were as tall as me, and some who were taller—though not by much. But tall men tend to be thin. Some as thin as a sapling, long and gangly. Others just moderately thin. But you rarely find a tall fat man—especially one who is my age. Things just don't work that way. The tall fat ones don't last that long. Their heart gives out or their back gives out or something else gives out. Nature favors tall and wiry, like Sambart. Or short and stout.

But I was neither. I was a freak of nature.

I had spent the entire winter rebuilding stone walls at a settlement up north and the early part of the spring hiking along the foothills of the Gondiath Mountains on the edge of a desert, averaging 25 miles a day for a full month. So every inch of my six foot, five-inch body was pure muscle. And muscle is denser and heavier than just about anything else in your body. At that point in the year, I weighed over 250 pounds, more than a stag or a bear.

But luckily for me, Reeni or Barelle, or whoever had poisoned me didn't have a good idea of how much poison it would take to kill me. Either that or they didn't have enough poison to do the job properly.

So they left me. Face down at the bottom of that narrow muddy canyon. Unconscious. Dying. And if the poison didn't finish me off, the waters from the flooding brook certainly would.

At least that's what they thought. But it didn't work out that way.

The pain woke me. It was like being kicked awake.

Retching, coughing, convulsing. Spitting bile and mud in the darkness.

I managed to turn my body and prop my head sideways on a rock before I blacked out again.

The second time I regained consciousness, it was dawn. I was shivering and sweating at the same time. My head felt like it had been run over by a team of oxen. Every bone felt broken. I couldn't tell if the muck I was laying in was mud or my own diarrhea.

After hours in a semi-conscious state, I managed to crawl to the edge of the embankment and prop myself upright. I vomited again and again until I couldn't vomit anymore. And then I passed out. For the second time.

In one of my rare moments of lucidity, I debated with myself whether I should just give up and die right then or there—or whether I should try to live, claw myself out of the muck, get back on the road, and hunt down those girls.

I chose to live.

It was the next morning when I finally made it back to the West Way. They had taken my gold and my boots. All I had was a branch I found that I was using as a walking stick. No food. No water. No knife.

The loss of the gold was one thing. I wasn't happy about it, but I never carried too much gold with me on my travels. Instead, I kept a few thousand regmarks worth of coin and gems cached in hiding places outside of each major city. It was easier that way. I didn't have to carry around my wealth, and I avoided the taxes levied on bringing currency into the Northern cities I visited.

What I really missed were my boots. They were my most valuable possession, worth more than a half dozen horses. They were crafted by Enos Hayes & Sons in Three Rivers, who were probably the most celebrated shoemakers in the entire Empire. The boots were made with soft leather and suede with a fur lining and thick soles. I had worn them for several thousand miles of walking and they fit me perfectly. A man who spends all his days walking needs his boots.

I wanted them back.

And I would get them.

And the girls and the old man. They would pay.

I wasn't sure how I would feel about exacting vengeance upon children. But I'd have no problem snapping the old man's neck. No problem at all.

But first I would have to find them. And in order to do that, I needed to get back on my feet, figuratively and literally. I needed a healer.

I had studied healing myself once—two decades ago. At the time I had thought that since I was so good at inflicting damage—breaking bones, pulverizing faces, and damaging internal organs—that I might as well learn how to put someone back together. Balance out the ledger.

So I sought out a man named Cero Wold. He was a healer who lived way up north in Standon's Gate. It took me a few months to get up there from Rundlun, and once I found him, I needed to pay him a lot even to speak with me. But Cero Wold was a remarkable individual. He had spent the first half century of his life in service to the Mage Guild as an instructor at Delham University. Then he was allowed to retire from the Guild, which is a pretty rare occurrence.

He spent the next twenty years training himself as a healer. But, unlike nearly every other healer in the Empire, Cero Wold approached his training with scientific rigor—the same scientific rigor he had used at Delham University. To Cero Wold, the healing arts weren't some mystical mumbo jumbo. They followed natural principles. And he was willing to share those natural principles. For a hefty price.

Within five minutes of meeting me, he could tell that I would never be a healer. And he told me so. Right after he accepted my payment. It turned out that I could not produce enough excess life force or 'nemia' as he called it. Different people had different capacities. It was something that was decided at birth.

I told him I wanted to learn anyway. Even if I couldn't actually perform the healing arts.

So he taught me, in an abstract sense. I learned about the transfer of nemia from the healer to the patient. I learned about how it circulates through the human body, how it can cluster and repair physical damage much like a team of brick-layers can repair a hole in a wall. I learned how nemia connects every living thing, and how certain herbs and other plants can enhance the flow of it. I learned about poultices and teas and salves and ointments. There were dozens of other things I learned about healing, and although I tried dili-gently to put my knowledge into practice, the best I could do was bind wounds and treat some basic infections.

Trudging along the West Way, being ignored by caravans and riders, I knew that I still had poison in my system and I would remain a weak shadow of myself until I was healed.

And I knew that I didn't have much time.

Chapter Three

❧

ON THE THIRD DAY AFTER I WAS LEFT FOR DEAD, I GOT LUCKY.

A courier riding from Bexden to Marston Hills took pity on me and decided to stop for a few minutes. We chatted, and he shared his canteen of water and a few pebblecakes. He also told me that I wasn't far from a village. Actually, two villages. Hytwen and Ortwen. On either side of a huge lake. Maybe a half day away by horse.

"Don't go to Ortwen," he told me.

"Why?"

"They don't like strangers. Go to Hytwen."

"Are you serious?"

"Yes. They're both within a dozen miles of each other, but I'm telling you, you'll be turned away at Ortwen and then you'll have to backtrack another half dozen miles." He motioned at my feet. "And judging from the looks of you, you don't want to walk an extra step you don't have to."

The courier was right. I wasn't doing well. My feet were cut and bleeding and swollen. And probably even infected.

The rest of me was just as bad. I was tired, starved, and dehy-drated. I needed that healer, and I needed some boots.

"How big is Hytwen?"

"It's a good-sized village, I believe."

That gave me hope that there might be a healer there. The alternative was to continue on to Bexden, a large town right on the West Way with five or six thousand people. But it would take me more than a week to get there at the rate I was going. And I didn't think I would last that long.

I asked the courier what they did in Hytwen, but he didn't really know. Maybe fishing. Maybe farming. He did say that the village was south of the highway which meant that tech-nically it was outside the Empire's southern border. In the Tengan Territories. So I wondered about that. Was Hytwen some sort of independent freehold?

The courier departed, and I was feeling slightly better. My mood had improved considerably because now at least I had a destination.

As I slowly made my way west, every step was painful. But I tried to minimize the pain by resting frequently. I even found a little stream where I sat and soaked my feet for a while. I also foraged when I could, but eating bark and weeds didn't feel very nourishing. I was in no condition to hunt though.

By the mid-afternoon, I was tired enough to seek out a spot under a tree in a meadow adjacent to the West Way. There I slept for a few hours. When I awoke, I felt disori-ented and my legs were cramped.

I continued on my way, though, sticking to the meadow—which was much softer underfoot. But I made sure that I stayed within sight of the highway. I had no intention of missing the turn to Hytwen.

And then for the second time that day, I got lucky.

A little farther north in the meadow, I spied a bush with

clusters of small dark berries. It was a samberry bush, and I tasted one of the new berries. It was a little bitter but safe to eat. At least I hoped it was. Unripe samberries can make you sick and the red ones can kill you.

Samberries grew throughout the south and they were good for reducing swelling of joints and muscles, a condition that I most certainly suffered from. They also were the key ingredient in a healing tea which supposedly helped with rheumatism, though that wasn't something I needed to concern myself with, thank Dynark.

I rested there for a while and collected as many ripe berries as I could find. I ate half of them and wrapped the rest in my tunic. Then I continued west.

It was nearly dark when I heard the clop of a horse. One rider. Moving slowly. Looking for something.

I watched him for a half minute and then he saw me.

"Don't move!" he yelled, and then he rode over.

The man was around forty years old, bald, with a dark complexion. I couldn't tell if he was born that way or just spent a lot of time in the sun. He was dressed in leathers, like a rangeman, and was armed with a long knife and a bow. He reined his horse to a halt right in front of me and looked me up and down.

"Hail, stranger!" he said. "You're a sorry sight, you are. What's your name and where are you coming from?"

I didn't say anything. Just looked at him. Noticed that his clothes were not particularly dusty. That meant he probably hadn't traveled a long distance. He was from around here.

"I asked you who you are, friend. Don't make me ask twice, now."

"My name is Bander. I'm a traveler. From Kreed's Keep. I was drugged and robbed. And now I need a healer and some boots. Is that enough information for you?"

He didn't respond, but it was obvious that he was

thinking through what I just told him. Probably trying to figure out if I was lying or not.

If I hadn't almost died a few days ago and was feeling a little more energetic, I might have pulled the man from his horse and just ridden away. But that wasn't going to happen. Instead, I shrugged and continued walking.

This surprised the man on the horse. He began to follow me and called out, "Where are you going all shoeless and banged up like that?"

"The nearest town. Someone said it was Hytwen."

"Hold up there, friend," he said. "I can get you to Hytwen. But first I need to know something."

"What's that?"

"Did you see a young girl around here?"

The rider eventually told me who he was. His name was Minch, and he was Hytwen's town marshal. Which explained why he was out trying to find the girl. It was his job.

I asked, "This girl, did she run away from her parents?"

"Doubtful. Extremely doubtful."

"Was she abducted?"

His eyes narrowed. "Why would you be saying that?"

"Someone's missing, it's either voluntary or involuntary. If she didn't run away, she was taken. It's been known to happen."

"You do ask a lot of questions," Minch said.

"Yes, I do. How far away from town are we?"

"Five hours, I'd say. Maybe four and a half if we keep up a good pace."

"I'm not going to make it there tonight."

"Don't be so sour, my friend," Minch said. "Let's just see

how far we get, shall we?" He swung off his horse. "Go ahead. You ride. Give those wounded feet of yours a rest."

I looked at the marshal for a moment. He was very trusting. I shrugged and climbed onto the horse. "Aren't you worried that I'll just ride off?"

"No."

"Why not?"

"Three reasons. First off, a man who asks as many questions as you do seems pretty interested. At least interested enough to see for himself what's going on. Am I right? Reason number two: Comet here is damn smart. I whistle a certain way and he bucks you off on your ass. Maybe even gives you a kick for good measure."

"And the third reason?"

He hefted his bow and grinned at me. "I'm not a bad shot. Especially when I haven't been drinking for a while."

"Fair enough," I said. "But since we're going to be traveling for half the night, maybe you could tell me more about this missing girl."

He nodded and then launched into the whole story.

The girl's name was Jillen Lockwell. She was twelve years old. She was the adopted daughter of Arno and Ellia Lockwell, who basically owned the village of Hytwen. Two days ago she went missing in her home, a big manor house on a hill above the village. Her nurse left her momentarily and when she returned, Jillen was gone.

I interrupted Minch. "Did you say that the girl is twelve years old?"

"Aye."

"And she has a nurse? At that age?"

"Yes..." His voice trailed off. I could tell he was struggling.

"I have to tell you something, so's you understand," he said. "She's not like other girls, Jillen."

"What do you mean?"

"She's what you call an 'innocent.' Not right in the head. But that don't matter to the Lockwells. They don't care if she's touched and they don't care that she's not their own flesh and blood. They love that little girl with all their hearts."

I didn't know what exactly he meant by 'innocent,' but I didn't want to press him. Instead, I asked if they had searched the town.

"Of course we did. Me, the hands, and a several dozen mudders went house to house, building to building. We searched every shop, cabin, warehouse, outhouse, shed, well, stable, drying house, barn, anything with a roof."

"Mudders?"

"Workers. Lapp farmers. We call them mudders around here."

I still didn't know what he was talking about. "How big is the village?"

"What do you mean?"

"How many people?"

"Well, it varies, doesn't it? Right now there's about half a thousand of us," Minch said,

"So you're talking hundreds of buildings."

"You're telling me. Took us nearly two days. But for naught. We also checked the lake, a half mile north and a half mile south."

"And?"

"And no sign of her."

"So you started widening the search area. That's why you're on the road."

"Aye."

I thought about all this while I rode. We didn't talk for a while. I had some experience with missing people. Two days was a long time. If Jillen Lockwell hadn't actually run away, she was probably dead. But I didn't say that to Minch.

After a time we arrived at a wide road exiting the West Way due south. There was some sort of sign, but in the gloom of dusk, I couldn't make it out.

"Almost home," Minch said. "Two hours. Maybe less."

"You want your horse back?"

"No. I'm fine."

The road to Hytwen was long and straight and well-maintained. Certainly enough room for a caravan. But what was the cargo?

"You're farmers?" I asked.

"Aye."

"This doesn't look like farmland to me."

"What does it look like then?"

"I get the feeling we're in a pretty dense forest."

"Right you are, my friend."

"What do you grow in a forest? Mushrooms?" The thought of Reeni came back to me in a flare of anger.

"No, we don't grow anything in the forest. Our crop's in the lake."

"Fish?"

"No, lapp."

"What's that?"

"You know what seaweed is?"

"Sure."

"Same thing, but lapp grows in fresh water."

"And you farm it?"

"Oh, yes. You'll see. It's a marvelous crop."

"Who wants seaweed? There's a market for it?"

"Of course there is. Quite a good one in fact."

Minch went on to tell me that lapp was pretty rare. In fact, the lake here, Lake Teagh, was one of only three or four places in Harion where it grew. Something to do with the elevation and certain things about the water.

"What's lapp used for?" I asked.

"A great many things. Food mostly. You can make flour out of it. Medicines. Ink. And other stuff, of course. You'll have to ask Alford Platt. He knows more than me."

"Who's he?"

"The farm steward. Money man. Does all the selling. Arranges the shipments. He can talk your ear off about lapp. The miracle harvest, he calls it."

"Tell me more about Jillen's family."

"The Lockwells. Arno and Ellia. Two children. The younger is a lad named Geddis. He's eight or nine."

"Is he... like his sister?"

"Not at all. He's quite a normal boy. A good boy. Minds his elders. A skilled rider."

"You said the Lockwells own the village."

"The village, the farm, half the lake. Ellia's a Skenn, you know. Her great grandfather built Hytwen, but back then it was called Skenntown."

"Obviously."

"She was an only child, so she inherited everything when her father Erlmander passed. He was a good man. Or so I'm told."

"So her husband got lucky. Married into a wealthy family."

"You won't catch me discussing the private goings on of Arno Lockwell, and you'd best not either, if you please."

I said, "Just trying to get the lay of the land."

We continued down the road in silence for a half hour while I thought about what Minch had told me. Hytwen seemed like a common enough village, like a hundred other small settlements all across the Empire. Started by one family, who grew a business. Could have been cattle, or farming, or plants for dyes, or mining, like the village I spent the winter at.

But one thing seemed odd about this village.

"You said they own half the lake?" I asked.

Minch nodded. "Now that, my friend, is an interesting story."

And then he told it to me.

Ellia Lockwell's grandfather, Bordagar Skenn had two twin sons, born just three minutes apart. The elder was Erlmander Skenn, Ellia's father. The younger twin was named Baylan.

When it came to deciding who should inherit the estate, this presented Bordagar Skenn with a dilemma.

His solution was to divide everything and build another village on the other side of the lake. The elder son, Erlmander, would inherit the village of Skenntown, which was renamed Hytwen. A new village, named Ortwen, was built for Baylan.

The farm was divided as well, with half the workers, half the boats, and half the drying racks sent to Ortwen. A line was marked, and each village had rights to farm their own side of the lake. Furthermore, it was agreed that Erlmander's farm was to sell lapp to the west, and Baylan's farm was to sell lapp to the east.

This all happened forty or fifty years ago. Ellia's father Erlmander Skenn died close to a decade ago. And her uncle Baylan Skenn died four or five years ago, leaving his son Creagar Skenn to inherit Ortwen.

It was an interesting solution. And it seemed fair enough, given that the two brothers had been born so close together. But apparently there was a problem.

Minch told me that relations between the two villages started to sour five or six years ago. It came down to money. Like it always does.

Back when the farm was divided, there was a bit more demand for lapp in the west—especially up north in Laketon and Waterside. But then someone had started another lapp farm in a lake near Brecalle and that had cut into Hytwen's sales. At the same time, as trade with the eastern kingdom of Gadmark increased, so did Ortwen's fortunes.

Soon after the death of Erlmander Skenn, Arno Lockwell approached Ellia's uncle Baylan with the idea of reuniting the two farms, but Baylan Skenn would have none of it. And when the Lockwells made the same entreaty to Creagar Skenn a few years later, he ran them out of Ortwen.

Since then things had been bad between the two villages.

Yesterday, the situation got worse. Arno Lockwell dispatched one of his men to Ortwen to ask if they had seen Jillen. The man came back bloody and beaten half to death with a parchment pinned to his flesh.

It read *Stay Out!*

When I heard that last detail, I said, "That reaction seems extreme."

Minch nodded. "In truth, no one can understand it. But Arno Lockwell is furious. So's Ellia. I mean, Jillen's like flesh and blood." He trailed off.

I remained silent. Something was definitely wrong here, but I needed more information.

We stopped for a few minutes to rest and Minch shared a loaf of bread and some cheese and water. Then we continued onward. The moon was rising and Comet the horse certainly knew his way back home. My biggest problem was staying awake so I wouldn't fall out of the saddle.

Fortunately I managed to keep my eyes open for the next several hours. We passed some pastures and cattle pens for a mile or so. After that we were in the village of Hytwen.

It was bigger than I had imagined it from Minch's description.

We entered on a wide main street lined with two and three story buildings, some of them made of brick. I saw a tavern, a modest inn, a large dry goods store, some other smaller shops. The downtown proper spanned five blocks and then the main street curved to the south. I could smell the lake, but couldn't see it in the gloom. But it felt close.

Minch led us down a narrow side street which ended in front of a squat building constructed from heavy logs. It looked like a miniature fortress, but Minch explained that it used to be an old storehouse and now was the marshal's office. But everyone still called it 'The Storehouse.'

Inside, he lit a lantern and motioned to a single jail cell with a cot and a blanket.

"It's not much, but probably a damn sight more comfortable than sleeping on the side of the road, don't you think?"

"Indeed."

I sat down on the edge of the cot and looked down at my swollen, scabbed feet.

"We'll see to that in the morning," he said.

I nodded and said, "Thank you."

"For what?"

"For everything. The ride, the food, this." I patted the cot.

Minch said, "Don't thank me just yet, friend."

And then he pulled the cell door closed and locked me in.

Chapter Four

THE NEXT MORNING, SOMEONE CAME TO SEE ME, BUT IT WASN'T MINCH.

"I'm Arno Lockwell." The man stood up ramrod straight. He had red hair, a handsome face and smiled a friendly, easy smile that struck me as completely false. He was fit and looked to be older than 40, but not by much. And he wasn't dressed like the lord of the manor. In fact, he was dressed like the men he came in with—like warriors, in leather coats and trousers, armed with short swords. One man held a crossbow. And they all had nice boots.

There were six of them altogether. And Lockwell was the smallest of the bunch even though he was a little taller than average. The other five stood a few steps behind Lockwell, fanned out in a semicircle. I knew immediately that they were mercenaries. They all had the look.

"You must be Bander," Arno Lockwell said.

I didn't reply, but I did untangle myself from the blankets and swung my feet out so I was sitting on the edge of the cot.

"Welcome to Hytwen. Minch told me he found you on

the side of the highway. Half dead, the way he tells it. Gave you some food and told you of our problem."

"Yes. I'm sorry to hear about your girl."

"Well, don't be. We're going to find her." His men nodded in back of him. Arno Lockwell moved in closer. He said, "Now, if you would be so kind as to stand up."

"Why?"

"I'd like to get a better look at you."

I wasn't sure whether I should indulge him or not, but then I thought of the food and the ride and the fact that the man's daughter was probably dead, so I stood up and stretched.

Arno Lockwell looked me up and down for a while. Finally, he asked, "How old are you?"

"Just over a half a century."

"Well, you don't look that old. What's your trade? Guard, gladiator, soldier?"

"Guard. I used to work at the Imperial Ministry of the Axe. I was a Red Shoulder Captain."

At the sound of my old title, some of the men made small noises of disgust. Maybe they weren't fans of the guard.

Arno Lockwell said, "Well, well, well. I'm impressed."

I just shrugged.

"So I have to ask. How did a Red Shoulder Captain manage to find himself shoeless on the West Way?"

"Could have been a spot of bad luck," I said.

"Well, I have to confess that I am a firm believer in making one's own luck."

"Me too."

"I'm glad to hear you say that, Bander, because I'm going to give you the opportunity to do just that."

I wasn't sure what he was talking about, but then he nodded to one of the men who unlocked the door to my cell and stepped in.

The man was not quite as tall as me, but heavily muscled. His head was shaved, and he had arched eyebrows, which made him look angry or diabolical. He played it up by tilting his chin down. Maybe he thought it made him look danger- ous. But I wasn't afraid.

"Here's how's it going to work," Arno Lockwell said. "You and Tobbler will go at it for five minutes—"

I interrupted him. "That's not a good idea."

"Sure it is. Friendly tussle. I just want to see what you're made of, soldier."

"I think you need all the help you can get to find your daughter."

"Don't worry. We got a healer in town. He'll patch you right up. Fix up the feet for no extra charge."

"I wasn't worried about myself."

Arno Lockwell laughed out loud. "Well aren't you some- thing?" Then his voice turned cold and hard. "Have at him, Tobbler."

The man with the eyebrows grinned and nodded at me. "I'll try to make this quick, old man. You'll barely feel a thing, I expect—"

I like it when people jabber away instead of getting right down to business. Especially during a fight.

So while Tobbler was jabbering, I took a long step in and head-butted him. Quick and easy. A snap forward and *bang*: my forehead into his nose. Solid bone versus flesh and carti- lage. No contest.

Tobbler's nose exploded in blood and he went down like a tapestry that had fallen off a wall. He hit the floor hard, which probably didn't do the back of his skull any favors.

I stepped back and took a deep breath. My heart rate wasn't much quicker than when I was sleeping.

"You happy now?" I asked Arno Lockwell.

He didn't answer me. Just motioned to his men to drag Tobbler out of the cell. Then he locked the cell door and left.

When everyone was gone, I laid back on the cot and rubbed my head. It felt a little sore, but I wasn't going to let Arno Lockwell know that. I must have dozed off because the next thing I knew Minch was there unlocking the cell door.

"Well, well, well. You made quite an impression," he said.

I got up and stretched.

"It was a stupid move on his part."

"He was testing you, my friend. He did the same with all of his men."

"Still stupid."

"Perhaps it was, but you earned yourself some time with a healer. And these."

He held up a pair of soft shoes. They were made of deer-skin and stitched up the center in a very simple way. I took the shoes and nodded in thanks. Not as good as a pair of boots, but they were better than nothing.

"Thank you, but I'm really going to need some boots."

"Leather's rare around here. We don't have a lot of cattle."

"Why's that?"

"Forest's too dense. There are a few pastures, but it's a constant struggle to keep them clear."

I knew what he was talking about, and it was worse the farther south you went into the Territories. The vegetation was very aggressive in this part of the world.

Minch gave me some water and bread and smoked fish and waited until I ate. Then we left the building, and he led me towards the main street. He didn't offer me his horse.

The village was buzzing with activity. There were a lot of people on the streets, and carts, and wagons, and horses.

Men, women, and children—everyone seemed to be on a mission.

"No sign of the girl?" I asked.

"No."

"Where are you searching next?"

"We're not."

"What do you mean?"

"I mean, Arno Lockwell's pretty sure he knows where Jillen is."

"Let me guess," I said. "Ortwen."

I had thought about it while lying on the cot. Lockwell's man. Sent back from Ortwen, beaten and bloody. The parchment. *Stay Out!* Seemed like a declaration of war to me. No other way to take it. Arno Lockwell had come to the same conclusion.

"I'm not supposed to talk about it," Minch said. "Sorry."

So I shut up and looked around the village as we walked down the main street. Minch told me the street was called Lake Way. It was wide enough to accommodate teams of horses and caravans and wagons and was paved with cobblestones. The cobblestones looked like a fairly recent improvement and certainly helped with keeping the mud under control.

The buildings that lined Lake Way were mostly shops. In the light of day, I could see a lot more of what was what. There was a big feed and grain building, a barber, mercer, provisioner, bakery, carpenter. One of just about any type of business you'd find in a village this size. But only one of each. No competing bakeries on either side of the street, trying to lure customers away from each other with fresher stretchbread or cheaper prices.

I asked Minch about that and he said that's how it had always been. If there was already a certain type of business in Hytwen, you'd have to wait until the proprietor retired, moved away, or died before you could open a similar business.

"What about taverns or pubs?" I asked.

"That's the exception," he said. "Can't have half a thousand people crowding into a single pub, can you?"

We continued to walk, and I looked down the side streets which intersected Lake Way. To the southwest, they were narrower and lined with residences. To the northeast was the lake itself, visible through alleys and between buildings. Some of the side streets on this side ran down to docks and piers. Others led to a dirt track that ran parallel to the lake's shore. Probably something to do with their seaweed farming operation.

Eventually, we arrived at the healer's house, a sturdy two story brick building that stood beside a tailor's shop and across the street from a weaver. The sign above the door read simply "Lynd the Healer."

Inside we were greeted by a plump woman who turned out to be Lynd's assistant. There were benches along one wall and a door to a back room and a staircase leading up. Besides the woman, there was no one there. I guessed that the citizens of Hytwen were a healthy group of people.

Minch chatted a bit with Lynd's assistant and then she took a look at my feet.

"Are you in pain, good sir?" she asked.

"I have been. I don't really notice it anymore."

"That's not what we like to hear," she clucked.

She went up the stairs and five minutes later returned with a thin man in his sixtieth year with a hawk-like face and a high forehead. He had unruly red hair streaked with grey and a bushy beard. There were crumbs of bread in his beard. I guessed we had interrupted his breakfast.

He introduced himself as 'Lynd the Healer' and then told us to follow him into the back room.

We entered some sort of workroom or laboratory, cluttered with shelves and cabinets full of jars and vials. I saw dried herbs, clay, bone, dozens of different dried roots and branches, seeds, nuts, flowers, and hundreds of bottles of different liquids. A long work table ran against the far wall covered with various equipment, scales, tools, mirrors, candles, and stacks of books. It was an impressive place as well equipped as any healer's workshop I had seen in Rundlun.

I told Lynd so, and he nodded. "I can't just wave my hands and perform miracles. I need all this."

He sat me down on the edge of a cot and asked me to remove my shoes, which stuck a bit to my feet where dried blood and pus adhered to the deerskin.

"I've seen worse," he said.

"Truly? Or is that something you just say?"

"Usually it's something I just say, but in this case, it happens to be true."

He and his assistant washed my feet and then carefully examined every inch. They used a sharp tool to remove splinters and tiny bits of stone from my wounds. Then they worked for an hour, lancing blisters and pustules, stitching wounds closed, and then treating my cuts and lesions with some sort of paste that had a strong, yet not unpleasant odor. It was all stuff I could have learned to do in Standon's Gate, way back when. But then Lynd did something I could never do. He placed his hands on my feet and manipulated the nemia to stimulate my body's natural healing. It wasn't instantaneous, but according to what Cero Wold had taught me, a healer could help the patient's body heal itself thirty or forty times faster than normal.

When Lynd was done, he gave me three cups of various colored potions to drink. Then he told me to return in the morning.

My feet felt noticeably better. Both Minch and I thanked him and then the marshal led me back the way we came. From this angle, I saw a large hill that loomed up behind the village. Perched on the top of the hill was an impressive gleaming white structure, glowing in the morning light.

Minch saw me looking up and told me, "Lockwell Manor. Isn't she a thing of beauty? That's where we're heading now."

I asked if we could see the lake first and he obliged. We walked northeast on Sabon Street, past a greengrocer, and then down to the shore and out on a narrow dock.

The lake was huge, at least a few miles wide and it stretched out forever into the mist, but the water was very shallow. Every fifty yards or so, in a series of straight lines, stone pilings peeked above the surface of the water. Minch explained that rope stringers ran between the pilings and the lapp grew on the rope. They harvested it every six to eight weeks, dried it out on racks on the shore for ten days, then in a special heated drying house for another thirty days.

It struck me that lapp was just about the perfect crop. Light, easy to transport. Probably unaffected by the weather. No plowing. Maybe I should give up my wandering and become a lapp farmer myself. It would have been a halfway appealing idea if I didn't hate the water and doubly hate being on a boat.

I asked Minch how far away Ortwen was and he said that if I got into one of the skiffs and rowed out, I'd go for twelve miles before hitting land again. Ortwen was basically a straight shot to the northeast. He told me that most of the lake was ringed by rocky cliffs so there weren't many other places to build a village. In the old days, before Ortwen, the area on the other side of the lake was a little shanty town of fishermen, but in 1668 Bordagar Skenn bought them out and started building Ortwen.

I considered the idea that maybe some of the fishermen

weren't too happy about that arrangement. Maybe they were holding a grudge and decided to kidnap Jillen Lockwell as retribution. But who holds a grudge for 40 or 50 years?

"We've tarried long enough," Minch said. "They're expecting us at the manor."

Chapter Five

MINCH TOLD ME THAT LOCKWELL MANOR WAS A GOOD MILE FROM THE CENTER OF TOWN. But he took pity on me and we detoured back to the Storehouse. Around the back were some stables with horses owned by the village. We borrowed two and returned to Lake Way, but instead of turning right, we turned left and started up the hill.

We passed a few dozen houses that looked a lot nicer than all the others. Probably belonged to the town elders or something. The road narrowed a bit once we left town, but it was still paved with cobblestones and remained paved all the way up until we reached the courtyard in front of Lockwell Manor. Minch hadn't exaggerated. It was a mile from the village to the manor and whoever paid to pave the road all that way had more gold than he knew what to do with. That type of road work was never seen outside of the big cities.

The manor itself looked to be in perfect condition— almost new. It was a showy three-story structure built in the Habradin style that had been popular among nobles for the past few decades. In fact, if I didn't know better, I'd guess that someone teleported a baronet's home from Duncarden or Pitham's Cross to this rural village.

The grounds were immaculately manicured, with terraced flower gardens, perfect hedges, and topiary. As we rode closer, I saw a pair of gardeners working on the edge of an ornamental reflecting pool ringed with statues.

Minch said, "Look at that, will you? Have you ever seen anything as grand?"

"Lapp must be more valuable than I thought."

"They rebuilt the whole manor house, top to bottom. Wait until you see the inside. It's a sight to behold."

Servants took our horses, and we were escorted into the hall by a stout footman who then departed to announce us. The hall itself was paneled in carved wood with a large fireplace and a double staircase leading up to the second story. The ceiling was easily twenty-five feet high and was decorated with ornate beams. An immense carpet covered a good portion of the floor. I recognized the distinctive woven diamond pattern as a Potenska from Gadmark. Very expensive.

I drifted over to the wall next to the fireplace where a trio of large portraits hung, all skillfully painted. Three men, all related. The family resemblance was clear as day. I read the names on the plates mounted toward the bottom of each frame: Thandric Skenn, Bordagar Skenn, Erlmander Skenn. I remembered that the latter was Ellia Lockwell's father. But there was no painting of the twin brother, the one who founded Ortwen.

The footman returned to the hall and then escorted us up the stairs, through the salon, and into the library. It was a long, narrow room which ended in an oversized ceaon desk, behind which sat Arno Lockwell. He didn't get up, just told Minch he wanted to speak with me alone.

After the marshal left, Arno Lockwell beckoned me to have a seat.

"Tobbler is feeling mighty embarrassed, as well he should."

"I wouldn't say that."

"Why not?"

"Nothing to be ashamed of. The same would have happened to any of your men. Maybe any three."

"I see you have a high opinion of yourself."

"It's well deserved."

He chuckled briefly, then didn't say anything for a few minutes.

Neither did I. It wasn't any hardship for me to keep my mouth shut. I could spend days not saying a word. Unlike most people.

Eventually, Arno Lockwell said, "Well, Bander, you were right about one thing."

"What's that?"

"I do need all the help I can get to find Jillen. And now it seems that I'm down a man."

"Your fault, not mine."

"Perhaps. But I had to take your mettle, know how hard you were. Because I need hard men for this endeavor."

I didn't say anything. Just looked around the library. There were more weapons on display than books, so I'm not sure how it qualified as a library. But the furnishings were certainly expensive, just like the rest of the house.

"Mark me," Arno Lockwell said, as he tapped the desk to get my attention. "I'm offering you employment."

"I'm not looking for employment. I'm retired."

He leaned back. "Really? As far as I can tell, you don't have any gold, and we don't allow beggars here in Hytwen, so perhaps you actually do need a job."

"I don't."

"There's also the matter of your account."

"Account?"

"Healers don't work for free. You've been given room and board, as well. Plus those shoes."

"Boots are what I really need."

"You'll get them. Plus a generous salary."

"What would I have to do in return for the boots?"

"Go to Ortwen. Find out if Craegar Skenn has Jillen."

"I thought you tried that already."

"Barnes wasn't quite up to the task, I'm afraid. You very well just may be."

"I'll think about it."

"Don't think too long. I want you gone by dark."

With that, he sat back down behind the desk and waved for me to leave.

The footman had been waiting outside the door, and he escorted me back through the salon. There was a woman there, finely dressed, tall, with dark hair. Ellia Lockwell, the lady of the house. I nodded politely, but she ignored me.

Then we returned down to the entrance hall where Minch was waiting.

As we departed, I told him that Arno Lockwell wanted me to go to Ortwen.

"Just like the last man?" he asked, his eyes full of concern.

"Apparently I'm a bit tougher than the last man."

"Are you going to do it?"

"I'm going to think about it. He promised me some boots."

A man who spends all his days walking needs his boots.

I asked Minch about Arno Lockwell's men. He didn't know

too much about them, other than that they were mercenaries. Expensive mercenaries.

"Where are they from?"

"Not sure, really," he said. "Maybe Marston Hills. I think Pots is from Kreed's Keep. Why do you ask?"

"I'd like to have a chat with them. Clear the air a little about what happened this morning."

"You sure you want to do that?"

I told him that I was sure, so Minch led me around to the side of Lockwell Manor. There a dirt road wound down to the stable block. As we rode, I saw a large herd of goats grazing on the north lawn. I wondered how the gardeners prevented them from eating all the flowers.

The stable was an impressive long brick building with a tall roof dotted with gables. Adjacent to it was the bunkhouse. It was made of wood but wasn't as fine looking as the stables. It appeared that the horses were more valuable than the hired hands.

"It may be a little rough in there. You want me to come in with you?" Minch asked.

"Not necessary."

"Whatever you say."

I left Minch outside and pushed the bunkhouse door open. Inside was a long room with five cots on the left and five on the right—and a small stove at the end. Four of the cots had men lounging on them. I recognized them all from this morning, but there was no sign of the sellsword who got stuck in the cell with me. Maybe he earned his own room. Maybe he was upstairs at Lynd the Healer's place.

The men all glared at me, eyes as hard as a blacksmith's anvil. I could feel their hostility.

"You've got a lot of nerve coming in here," one of the men said. He was thick and ruddy and looked to be a few years older than the other three men. The leader, I guessed.

I made a show of looking around the room. "I came by to talk to Tobbler. Tell him I was sorry."

"Sorry that you nearly killed him? With some dirty trick...?"

"Yes. I was half asleep. Wasn't thinking clearly. I just reacted. What would you have done?"

The ruddy man sat upright so he was perched on the edge of the bunk and scowled up at me. I could tell he was pondering. Perhaps Arno Lockwell had done the same thing to him.

He finally said, "Tobbler's not employed here anymore. Lockwell sent him away. Maybe you're supposed to take his place."

Lockwell had told me that Tobbler had been embarrassed. He never mentioned sending the mercenary away. But I didn't bring it up. Not just yet. Instead, I checked each face in the bunkhouse. No one looked especially welcoming.

I said, "Arno Lockwell asked me to go over to Ortwen. Assess the situation there."

The ruddy man spat out a laugh. "Good luck with that. You hear what happened to Barnes?"

"I did."

"Well, he was twice the man you are. Fast, and sharp as a stiletto. No way you'd be able to beat him in a fight. A fair fight that is."

"Did he say what happened to him over there?"

"His face is too busted up to talk."

"What about Lynd?"

One of the other men piped in. "Ain't no small town healer good enough to heal those injuries. Barnes got to go to Marston Hills to get patched up. If'n he can afford it."

"Won't Arno Lockwell take care of him?"

"You haven't been paying attention, old man," the ruddy leader said. "Lockwell don't reward failure. You best keep that in mind."

With that, he laid back on his bunk and ignored me. The other men followed suit.

I guess I had been dismissed.

Outside, Minch asked me if I got what I came for.

"In a sense."

"At least you are still in one piece. That's something, isn't it?"

"Never any doubt about that. Just wanted to talk to those boys in there."

"What for?"

"Curious about whether it could have been one of them who took Jillen Lockwell."

Minch lifted an eyebrow. "And?"

"I don't think so. They're not smart enough."

We retrieved our horses from the stables and started to ride up the hill, back towards the manor house. Then I thought of something. "You said the girl was taken from up here?"

"Aye."

I stopped my horse for a second and looked around. I turned him in a slow circle, trying to take everything in.

We were up a few hundred feet and so had a good view of the village and the lake to the northeast. Beyond where the town bordered the lake shore the vegetation grew thick. I could barely make out the rock cliffs farther down the shore.

"Let's ride the perimeter," I said.

We started to the south, past the gardens and walkways, near where the cobblestone road led back to the village. Maybe a hundred yards beyond the road was a steep drop-off into dense brambles, then a dark wood.

"It's like this all around," Minch said. "Like a castle on a hill."

He was right. The top of the hill was about twenty acres of cleared land, but beyond that were rocky ledges and thick foliage. I dismounted and tried to scramble down to the west and soon found myself snared in brush and thick, woody trees with low branches.

With some effort, I climbed back up the stone cliff. My clothes had new rips and tears from that brief excursion.

Minch said, "Look at you. You could have just asked me if I thought anyone would have been able to take the girl down into the wood. That's one of the first things I checked."

I didn't say anything. Just climbed back on the horse and rode north, back towards the stables. I was looking for a foot-path, riding trail, any sort of shortcut down to the village. But I didn't see anything. Minch was right. Whoever took the girl, took her down the main road.

I asked, "What about wagons? Deliveries?"

"What do you mean?"

"I mean, could she have been stuffed into a back of a wagon?"

"I'd need to check with the steward, but the only deliveries they'd get up here are from the village. Foodstuffs, mostly."

"How about strangers in town? Anyone?"

"Besides you?"

"I meant at the time the girl went missing."

Minch thought for a moment. "Hard to say. We get people coming and going from time to time. Mostly merchants negotiating about the lapp."

"And where would these merchants be staying?"

"Only one inn here."

"Let's go."

Chapter Six

THE GREEN TREE INN WAS AN OLD STONE BUILDING WITH VINES GROWING UP ONE SIDE. It rose up three stories and the steep roof was dotted with dormer windows. Inside, the inn was finished with lots of wood. Wood paneling, wood timber beams, wood tables, and a wood mantel over the fireplace. Wood everywhere. But none of it was green.

Minch introduced me to the proprietor, a man named Raerig who was slight of build and had dark eyes. We asked about any strangers staying at the inn over the past three or four days.

Raerig shook his head. "Look around if you want. The last man to rent a room was the warehouse owner from Vale. I can't recall his name, but it's in my book somewhere."

"When was this?" Minch asked.

"Last week, must have been. Five or six days ago at least."

"How long did he stay?"

"Just one night. Met with Alford Platt the next morning, then left."

I asked, "Anything odd about him?"

"Other than his foul breath? No. Nothing I can recall."

We thanked the innkeeper and left. I told Minch I needed clothes, and he took me to a large building two blocks down the street. It was a general store with some clothing from Marston Hills. I got lucky and found breeches and a tunic that I could fit into and that were in better shape that the tattered things I was wearing. We put the purchase on Arno Lockwell's account and I changed into my new clothes right there in the shop.

"I suppose you want a shave and a haircut as well?" Minch asked.

"No, that can wait. Although I don't suppose you have a public bath around here?"

"Of course we do. It's called the lake. But I've got something even better."

We rode down a side street to the Shore Road and then past the docks and piers in an area east of town with lots of farm buildings. There were long rows of lapp drying tables, dozens of beached skiffs, shanties with rope makers and net makers and boat makers, a water tower, and three large warehouses. Two of them looked brand new.

Again, I thought that maybe I should become a lapp farmer. Or, better yet, a lapp farm owner like Arno Lockwell. He's the one who was doing well. Judging from the look of the men working on the ropes and skiffs, being a lapp farmer wasn't how one became wealthy.

I asked Minch where all the lapp was and he said that a caravan had departed less than a week ago. Next harvest wasn't for two weeks. Then there would be the drying and the sorting and the packing. I guess it was just like any other sort of farming. Lots of waiting around.

Minch led me over to a blacksmith's place near the water tower. We chatted with Clanton the blacksmith for a bit. Then he took me around the back where there was a kind of fenced-in pen with raised wooden troughs partially filled with water and all kinds of shiny iron pipes and valves and other mechanisms I didn't quite recognize.

"This is our pride and joy," Minch said. He was beaming.

"What is it?"

"Clanton calls it 'Hytwen Falls.' It's a bit of an experiment right now. You're the first outsider to see it, matter of fact."

"I don't understand."

"I'll show you, then."

He fiddled with some valves and a spray of steaming water shot out of one of the pipes into a trough. Minch stuck his hand under the spray and laughed.

"Feel it."

I did. The water was pleasantly warm. Like a shallow pond on a hot summer's day. I guessed that it had been heated by the blacksmith's forge on the other side of the yard.

Minch said, "Like your own personal bathing fountain, isn't it? We think this will be a big draw for the caravans."

He was right. Someone riding in from Rundlun to here might be on the road for a thousand miles or more. Who wouldn't want to clean themselves off under a stream of warm water?

"Go ahead and take your time, my friend," Minch said. "I'll be back in a half hour or so."

With that, he left me to enjoy the comfort of Hytwen Falls. I cleaned the sweat, and dirt, and dried blood from my skin and hair. The warm water loosened my muscles and soothed my injured feet. It was an incredible experience.

But it didn't last a half hour.

Within fifteen minutes, Minch was back with the horses. And the footman from Lockwell Manor.

"Sorry. Arno Lockwell wants you back up the hill," Minch said. "And I don't think he's happy."

We rode back up the cobblestone road, past the big houses on the bottom of the hill, and the gardens and the goats at the top. I was halfway dry by the time we got to the top.

The footman didn't waste any time. Just brought me directly up to Lockwell's library. This time Minch came with me. As per Lockwell's instructions.

Arno Lockwell stood at his desk. Minch was right. The lord of the manor was not a happy man.

He said, "Bander of Rundlun. Red Shoulder Captain, Imperial Guard."

I remained silent.

"I asked about you," he said. "This morning I spread the word throughout the entire village. Sent my men around to talk to folks. 'Anyone ever hear of a man named Bander?' You know what's interesting? Even in a tiny place like Hytwen, folks are more worldly than you think. Are you following me, sir?"

"Not really."

"Well, I'll cut to the chase then. It turns out, you're famous. A renowned investigator. Pride of the Imperial Ministry of the Axe. At least according to one of our bakers. Olwin apprenticed in Rundlun some years back and knew all about you and your accomplishments. Something to do with some big scandal with the Imperial Ministry of the Shield, a knave stealing weapons or some such. You solved the crime. Then there was the attempted murder of a duke or a baron. You stopped it. Olwin rattled off a half dozen big crimes in Rundlun that you solved. Very impressive."

"He was exaggerating. I was just doing my job."

"I don't think so. I don't think so at all." He moved out from behind the desk and took a step closer. He stretched himself up to his full height—a head shorter than me—and looked me in the eye.

"The question is: why would you keep that a secret? Especially if you knew what we are going through here?"

"You really want the answer to that question, Lockwell?"

He nodded grimly. There was genuine pain in his eyes. I've seen that look many times before. So I decided to be completely honest with him.

"Fine. It's true that I was the Imperial Investigator. And yes, it's true that I solved a lot of cases. And I guess it's true that I have some sort of reputation. But the reason I didn't mention all of that is because if you knew all that, you'd be affected by something that could destroy you. You and your family."

"You speak in riddles."

"Hope," I said. "If you knew who I was, you'd have hope. I would have given you hope."

"What's wrong with that?"

"It's a completely unrealistic feeling. That's what makes it so dangerous. You look at me and think 'the Empire's most accomplished investigator is here in my village, just as a horrible crime has occurred. He can solve it. He can get my daughter back.' But here's the thing. I can't. It's a false hope."

Arno Lockwell shook his head. "That makes little sense. Why would you say that?"

"Because it's true. There's no other way to look at it. I've had to deal with dozens of abductions, including the Walding Kidnapping. In nine out of ten cases, the victim is dead within twenty-four hours. Jillen was taken three days ago. You haven't been contacted by anyone. No one has demanded a ransom. She's gone. That's the truth of the matter."

He didn't say anything, just returned to his desk and slumped down into his chair.

"Listen," I said. "I know what you are going through. And the fact is, I have already done some investigating here—"

"What?"

"Ask Minch. I've been interrogating everyone I meet. I've been studying the terrain around this house, looking for escape routes. I've been checking on strangers who may have been here when Jillen was taken."

He sat up and something played across his face. Probably a glimmer of hope. The last thing I wanted.

I continued, "You need to understand something. Anything I do, any questions I ask—I'm just doing it because it's in my nature. Like an instinct. I almost can't help myself. But here's the thing. Deep down, I don't believe I can find your daughter. I really don't. So you need to put that out of your mind. The absolute best case scenario for you is that I'm able to give you some answers about why this thing happened. There's always a reason why."

"Are you quite finished?"

"Pretty much."

"Well, sir, that was a fine enough speech. But, I'll tell you something about me. I'm not the kind of man who will be put off. Not by you, nor by anyone else."

He stood up again.

"I'm still going to hire you. But not to go to Ortwen. I want you here, doing whatever you can do, digging into whatever you need to. Find Jillen."

I started to speak, but he raised his hand and cut me off.

"I heard what you said. I know you're setting my expectations. But I don't give a damn. Find Jillen. Find answers. Do what you do."

He turned to Minch and said, "This change of plan affects you too, marshal. You're the one going to Ortwen tonight."

I saw the look on Minch's face. It was the look of someone who had just received a death sentence. But the man just nodded and said, "Yes, sir."

Arno Lockwell summoned his butler and told him that I

would have complete access to the house and the staff. And then he dismissed all of us.

The butler was a wiry man with a bird-like nose and sharp, dark eyes. His name was Lohuin, and he spoke quickly like someone who was used to being cut off and so had to rush to get his message across.

I told him I wanted to interview the staff and I would start with him. He led me to a smaller office on the other side of the building. Minch didn't want to stay. He said he needed to prepare for his mission tonight. So it was just me.

I learned that Lohuin had served the Lockwells and the Skenns before that. He'd been employed here at the manor for over 40 years. He knew every member of the staff and told me that they were all beyond reproach. With one exception: Wylla the nursemaid. But he didn't want to say anything more about her. He wanted me to make up my own mind.

I asked him the usual questions. Did the Lockwells have any enemies? Was there any bad blood between Lockwell and anyone connected with the family? I asked if there was someone who had requested a favor or gold. Any business rivals who recently surfaced? Was any member of the staff let go?

He informed me that the answer to all my questions was 'no'—except for the last one. But again, that concerned Wylla. And he remained reticent about her.

I told him that I appreciated his sense of decorum and his desire to protect the staff, but I didn't have the time nor the inclination to indulge him any further.

"Tell me about the nursemaid now or I'll break your arm," I said in a low voice.

It was a fair offer and Lohuin took the least painful option. And so I heard the story of the nursemaid Wylla.

It turns out that she wasn't always a nursemaid. In fact, she had been the wife of the previous village marshal, a man named Unferd. But Wylla and Unferd had marital problems. She was unable to bear him children. And maybe because of that, he strayed. Right before his 30th birthday. He ran away to Vale with the mercer's daughter. The Lockwells felt sorry for Wylla so they took her in to look after infant Jillen and be her wet-nurse. But, by all accounts, the Lockwell's kindness wasn't enough to prevent Wylla from becoming more bitter and troubled over the years. She had no friends, she was often irritable, and there were rumors that she had taken to stealing from the family. Her position had become more and more tenuous. The incident with Jillen was the last straw. Wylla had been dismissed two days ago. But, in the opinion of Lohuin, she should have been imprisoned. And he speculated that she very well might be imprisoned soon enough.

I thanked him for his candor and told him that I needed to interview Wylla for myself.

"I thought you might," he said. "But you won't find her here at the house."

"What do you mean?"

"The mistress won't have her anywhere near young Geddis. Wylla's staying at the inn until Master Lockwell decides her fate."

That didn't make much sense to me. If Wylla was a real suspect, why was she allowed freedom of movement? She could flee at any time.

I asked Lohuin who else had seen Jillen Lockwell that morning. "Did the girl spend time with her mother?"

"No, Mistress Lockwell is a busy woman. And that day she was scheduled to meet with her dressmaker."

"Who else saw Jillen that morning?"

"Several of us, I'd expect. Certainly the pantry staff. And Vogan, the footman, would have served young lady Jillen her morning meal."

"Anyone else?"

"I can check with Mrs. Hauf. She's the upper housemaid."

"Do that," I said. "In the meantime, let's find Vogan."

The footman was easy to find. He was downstairs in the main hall. Unlike Lohuin, he was eager to speak his mind.

"That Wylla's been nothing but trouble if you don't mind me saying."

"How so?" I asked.

"Always in a foul mood. Never a kind word for no one."

"Did she mistreat Jillen Lockwell?"

Vogan shook his head. "She wouldn't dare. Besides, everyone loved young lady Jillen."

"Even Wylla?"

"Aye. Even her."

"And how did Jillen seem when you served her that morning?"

"Fine. Same as always. Quiet."

"So, that morning was just like any other morning? No visitors? No arguments? Nothing out of the ordinary?"

"I cannot think of anything amiss, sir."

I asked him a few more questions and received a few more lukewarm answers. Nothing to get excited about. Then I found Lohuin again and asked him to take me to the room where the nursemaid had last seen Jillen.

We returned to the second floor and Lohuin took me to a small light-filled chamber in the southeast wing of the manor. He called it 'the nursery' but it was more of a parlor. The room was nicely appointed and filled with things that might occupy a child's time: various toys, an art easel, a bookcase filled with books, and a harp.

"Any secret passages?" I asked.

"None that I am aware of, sir."

There were three tall windows. I peered out and saw that the room overlooked a formal garden below. None of the windows opened, and besides, it was a good twenty feet to the ground below.

I walked over to the fireplace and inspected it.

"Has this been used since Jillen was taken?"

"No," Lohuin said. "The room has not even been cleaned. It's just as it was three days ago."

The soot in the fireplace had not been disturbed. No one escaped the room by climbing up the chimney. I walked the perimeter, tapping on wooden panels and checking behind the drapes. A trained thief could have done a much better job detecting potential secret passages, but I was reasonably sure that there were none to be found.

There was only one way in or out, and that was the door through which we had entered. I retraced my steps and exited the nursery into a long north/south corridor. At the south end was a staircase that led down to the main hall. There were five other rooms along the corridor. Three were various storage or sitting rooms and of no particular interest. The other two were bedrooms: Jillen's and Wylla's.

We started with Jillen's room. The walls were plaster, tinted a pale yellow. There was a low bed and a small wooden case filled with more toys. Everything was neat and clean, and nothing seemed out of place.

Across the hall was Wylla's bedroom. This was another story. Everything had been ransacked. The bed had been stripped of blankets and had been pulled away from the wall—as had the small table and chair. There was a wooden chest with a simple lock, but the chest was open and empty.

"Not much to see here," I said.

"Yes, Wylla took her clothes and other possessions when

49

she departed. The master instructed us to search the room, but as you can see, we found nothing."

We left the bedroom, and I followed the corridor north. It ended in a seating area surrounded by a large set of floor-to-ceiling windows covered with fine satin drapes. These windows did open, but it was still a twenty-foot drop to the garden below. I checked the frame of the window for the kind of scratches a grappling hook might leave but didn't see anything of the sort.

Just to be on the safe side, I checked the three other rooms. One was filled with old furniture, draped in clothes. I checked underneath everything. Children are small and it's not inconceivable that Jillen could have been hiding under a table with a shroud on it. But I didn't see anything that led me to believe she was in there.

The next room was empty except for cleaning supplies: mops and buckets and brooms and dust pans. No secret passages.

The final room on the corridor was another sitting room, with a trio of upholstered chairs and a few side tables. Not much of anything else.

Sometimes places tell you things, other times people do. Right now, I wasn't getting anything from the places I had inspected. Maybe I'd have better luck with the people.

Chapter Seven

I DIDN'T.

After leaving the nursery wing, we returned to the ground floor and then Lohuin escorted me below to the servants' area. I spoke to the cook, both housemaids, and the hall boy. All the women expressed a similar opinion about Wylla: she kept to herself, was aloof, and had an angry, bitter demeanor. The hall boy told me she had always treated him well, and he didn't think she was a bad sort.

From what I could piece together, Wylla would usually rise at dawn, dress, and prepare herself for the day. An hour later, she would rouse Jillen, dress and groom her, and then take her down for her morning meal. After that, they would walk the grounds for an hour if the weather was nice, and then Wylla would bring Jillen up to the nursery where she would take her lessons. After that, there was another meal, another walk, more lessons. Every once in awhile, there might be a visit from another child, or a trip into the village. Then dinner, washing, and bed. It turned out that Jillen did not see her parents often—nor her 8-year-old brother Geddis, who mostly spent his time with his unofficial tutor the stable master.

The day that Jillen Lockwell was taken didn't seem to be different in any way. One of the housemaids had seen Wylla and Jillen return from their morning walk. The hall boy saw them in the nursery later that morning. No one noticed any strangers on the property.

Lohuin told me that he needed to get back to his duties, so I decided to walk through the manor one more time by myself.

I started downstairs, poked through the kitchen, larder, scullery, laundry, and servants' hall. Then I made my way upstairs, peering into drawing rooms, vestibules, dining parlors, sitting rooms, storage rooms, salons, and library rooms. I wanted to get the layout of the house right in my mind. I wanted to understand the entrances and exits, public areas, private areas, and hiding places.

After nearly an hour of wandering through the house, I found myself in the upstairs gallery, a long, bright room that connected the east and west wings. It was filled with paintings, gilt-wood armchairs, and other artwork. A line of glass doors opened up to the gardens to the south.

I slowly walked along the gallery, looking at the paintings. They were mostly landscapes and mythological scenes. One might have been by Rassuno, in which case it was extremely valuable. I noticed that the plaster was faded in odd shapes which didn't quite match the outlines of the painting's frames. Maybe Ellia Lockwell had recently redecorated.

Returning to the nursery, I considered the timing of Jillen's disappearance. The hall boy said he had seen Jillen Lockwell and Wylla two hours before noon. That was the last time anyone besides Wylla had seen Jillen. An hour later, Wylla appeared downstairs frantic. Jillen was gone.

In my mind, I broke the problem down to its basic

components. There was a girl and a nursemaid supposedly looking after the girl. They were in the house, in a second story room with one exit. Sometime between an hour and two hours before noon, the girl went missing. That was it.

There were a hundred ways it could have gone down. If it were me kidnapping her, I'd be patient. With a house that large, it would have been easy to hide the girl in an unused room. Then smuggle her out under the cover of darkness.

A voice broke me out of my reverie.

"You're the Imperial Investigator?"

I turned to see Ellia Lockwell there in the doorway. She was wearing a pale lavender gown with a high collar and her hair was elaborately pleated. Her face was powdered and painted, and she looked the farthest thing from a grieving mother.

"Yes, my lady. My name is Bander."

She held her hand out, and I walked over and took it.

"I am Ellia Lockwell."

She smelled of rose oil and I noticed that she fidgeted with a finely crafted silver pomander on a chain that hung from her neck.

I said, "I'm doing everything I can to find answers."

She nodded but didn't say anything. Just fidgeted.

"May I ask you about Jillen?"

"I loved her very much."

"Of course," I said. "I don't mean to be indelicate, but I understand that Jillen is not like other children."

"She is an innocent if that is what you're asking."

"How so?"

Ellia Lockwell walked to the window and glanced out. Then she turned and said, "She is twelve years old, yet if you observed her, you might think she had the mind of a five-year-old."

"I see."

"But she was a contented girl. She never complained."

I didn't say anything.

After a few moments, Ellia Lockwell said, "If that is everything, I need to attend to my duties. I sincerely hope you are able to find Jillen."

I bowed my head, because it seemed like the right thing to do, and she glided from the room.

Ellia Lockwell struck me as an odd woman; not at all what I expected. She seemed to possess a remarkable fortitude in the face of her tragedy. Either that or she simply did not care.

I wound my way back to Arno Lockwell's library, but he wasn't there, so I decided to go back into the village.

Everything pointed to the nursemaid.

I returned to the Storehouse and looked for Minch. He was nowhere to be found, so I brought the horse back to the stables. Then I walked along Lake Way, past the barber, past the bakery, past the mercer, Lynd the healer, the tailor, the dry goods store, a pub, and walked right into the Green Tree Inn.

Raerig the innkeeper was there, cleaning out the fireplace.

"Remember me?"

He stood up slowly, bent the kinks out of his back, and said, "You were here with Minch."

"I'm working for Arno Lockwell now. He hired me to find out where his daughter is."

"I hope you find her, sir. Everyone in this village loved young lady Jillen."

I nodded. "So I need two things right now. A meal—on Arno Lockwell's account—and I need to speak with Wylla, the nursemaid. Can you help me with those?"

"Of course. Sit yourself down in the Boar Room. I'll send

the girl in with an ale and some food." He pointed to a doorway on one side of the fireplace.

"Thank you."

"Wylla's out now, but she'll likely be back soon. I'll let you know when she returns."

The Boar Room turned out to be a decent-sized room with three long tables and its own fireplace—over which was mounted the stuffed head of a huge boar. There were tapestries on the walls and a trio of colorful rugs under each table. All in all, much more finely appointed than the outer common room. This was probably where Hytwen's upper class was served. I'm not sure why Raerig put me in here. Maybe because there was no one else seated here, and he thought I might want to speak to Wylla in private.

I sat down in a sturdy, high-backed chair and waited for the serving girl. In the meantime, I thought about what I might say to Wylla. By all accounts, she was an unpleasant person, and I didn't doubt it. Especially since everyone but the hall boy held her in low regard. Most often, people of the same station can judge each other with a fair degree of accuracy. Wisdom of the flock.

The serving girl came in with a large tankard and set it down on the table in front of me. But she wasn't a girl by any means. She was a full grown woman, maybe in her fourth decade, buxom and strapping with thick hair that hung in a mass of unruly copper-colored ringlets. Maybe the innkeeper's wife. If so, he was a lucky bastard.

"May I bring you some pottage, good sir?" Her voice was warm and husky and she smiled slightly at me. As she turned, I noticed that her nose had been broken at some point. It didn't detract from her appearance any. If anything, it gave her even more character.

"What kind of pottage?" I asked.

"Fish pottage, of course." Her smile widened. "That's

mostly what we eat here. Have you not noticed the large body of water yonder? Our lake?"

"Yes, of course. I was just hoping for turkey on the menu."

"Of course, turkey's on the menu! Just not here in Hytwen. You'd have to go to Bexden or even farther west to find some turkey."

"I don't think I'd last that long. Fish pottage it is then."

"Very good, sir. I'll bring you some bread and a roasted yam as well if it pleases you."

"It would please me." My stomach was rumbling at the talk of all this food. The last meal I had was nearly eight hours ago, and I hadn't quite recovered from being starved for three days.

The serving woman nodded at the tankard on the table and said, "If you wouldn't mind, I'd be obliged if you told me what you thought of that ale. It's a new cask and a new recipe."

"And I am to be your taster?"

"Truth be told, I just had a flagon myself." She moved a little closer and nudged me conspiratorially. "Don't tell Raerig, though! He'd throw me on the street for sure."

"And how did you like it?"

"Figg's best yet. Though it does have a bit of a bite to it."

I was naturally still a little leery of a woman urging me to taste food or drink, but I didn't think I'd be poisoned in an inn. At least not intentionally. Besides, I liked this girl's smile. So I sniffed the ale and inhaled a deep earthy smell.

"It's not made with seaweed, is it?" I asked, with a smile of my own.

"What, you mean lapp?" She laughed again. "Never heard of lapp in ale. Still, not a bad idea. Maybe I'll see if Figg's about and you can tell him the recipe."

I took a drink of the ale. It wasn't bad. Not the best I ever tasted, but dark and malty. And not watered down. I told her so.

"My compliments to the brewer."

She smiled again and left to fetch my food. I took another swallow of ale and decided it tasted better than I originally thought. I slid my chair back and stretched my legs out and thought about the mechanics of the abduction.

I didn't know how tall Jillen Lockwell was, or how much she weighed, but I could easily toss a twelve-year-old over my shoulder and carry her as far as I needed to, but not everybody could carry a child for a long distance. And the manor was nearly a mile from the village—down a hill.

So that left a few options. Either Jillen was transported by cart or wagon or coach or even horse—if she was unconscious. Or someone coerced her to accompany them by foot. Either that or she left willingly—under her own power.

Minch said that he didn't think that she was capable of running away, but maybe he was wrong.

The serving woman entered the room with a tray and told me, "I hope you have an appetite to match your impressive size, good sir!"

"In fact, I do."

She set down the tray. On it was a large bowl of the pottage, an impressive hunk of bread, and two roasted yams. It was all as promised. Better, actually—by a yam. There was also another flagon of ale—which I didn't order. I still had half of mine remaining.

"That's for me," she explained as she sat down on the bench to my left.

"I thought you said that your husband didn't want you drinking while you were working."

"Husband?" She tilted her head. "You mean Raerig? He's not my husband."

"My mistake."

"I'm not married. Turns out no one wants me." She made an exaggerated pouting face and then took a swig of ale.

"I find that hard to believe."

"'Tis true. I'm too old, or too big, or too strong. Whatever, I chase men away like flies."

"Don't you mean attract them like flies?"

"Who in their right mind attracts flies? You shoo them away, don't you?"

"Whatever the analogy, I don't think it's quite accurate."

"You're sweet." She leaned into me playfully. Perhaps she had imbibed more than a little taste of the ale. She asked, "So, if you don't mind me asking, what are you doing in our fair village?"

"That's a long story."

"I have time."

I took another drink of ale. "I'm trying to help. With what happened to Jillen Lockwell."

She said, "It's so sad. We're all wondering, who could have done such a thing?"

I didn't say anything.

"Are you one of Arno Lockwell's men perchance?"

"Not really."

"But you are working for him?" She pushed in a little closer.

"More like I am working for myself."

And then for the second time in less than a week, I let a woman get the best of me.

In a flash, she had a knife pressed against my inner thigh —at exactly the right place to sever the large artery there.

"How about you tell me who you really are?" she said in a low, threatening voice.

Chapter Eight

MAYBE I COULD HAVE SMASHED MY LEFT ELBOW INTO HER FACE BEFORE SHE CUT ME. But I doubted it. I'd be moving at least twelve inches. She'd be moving one.

So I relaxed and said, "My name is Bander and I really am trying to find out what happened to Jillen Lockwell."

"Where are you from?" Her voice sounded completely different. Flatter. More ominous.

"Most recently, from Kreed's Keep." I kept my voice even and calm.

"Is that where Arno Lockwell hired you?"

"He didn't hire me. The marshal found me on the road and took me in. Ask him yourself."

"You're a vagrant?"

"No, I'm retired. I used to be the Imperial Investigator in Rundlun."

She barked out a laugh, and I felt the knife press tighter against my thigh. "You expect me to believe that? An Imperial Investigator just happens to be wandering around in the middle of nowhere?"

"Why not? I have to be somewhere. And the West Way isn't exactly the middle of nowhere. I was traveling from Kreed's Keep to Vale. Look, I've answered your questions, so how about you get that knife out of my groin?"

"Not quite yet, big boy. Why are you looking for Wylla?"

"I want to ask her some questions. Everyone up at the Lockwell place seems to think she was involved in Jillen's disappearance."

"So they sent you to bring her back up the hill?"

"No."

"Right, because that would be dumb—sending the new man who doesn't even know what Wylla looks like..."

She slowly moved the knife off my leg and slid herself away.

Then she said, "I'm Wylla."

A thousand thoughts crowded my head just then, but the one that stood out was a feeling of admiration for the woman. She played her part expertly. I had no clue. No clue whatsoever.

I said, "You don't look like a nursemaid."

"I wasn't a very good one." She stood up and headed for the door. "You can finish your meal. But then I want you out of here. You understand?"

"I still need to talk to you."

"No, you don't. Trust me on this. You don't want to talk to me."

And then she was gone.

I took another spoonful of pottage. That was really the only thing I could do. Besides blame myself for being so stupid.

No, that wasn't right.

I wasn't stupid. I didn't miss anything because there was nothing to miss. Wylla simply duped me. As I thought about it, I decided the only thing that might have given me pause was her flirtatious behavior. But to be fair, such behavior was not at all unusual coming from a serving woman at an inn. Or was I just flattering myself?

After I ate the rest of my meal and drank the ale, I departed the inn. I didn't see Raerig on my way out, which was good news for him since I was thinking about breaking his arm for deceiving me.

Outside, the streets were alive with activity. But it was the reverse of the morning. Instead of going someplace, everyone was coming back. Shops were closing, carts were being stowed, lamps were being lit, and horses were being watered. I could tell by the looks I was getting that there weren't many strangers in town. I definitely stood out.

I was still thinking about Wylla, but I needed to go back up to the manor and ask Lohuin more questions. I wanted to know if there had been any carts or wagons leaving the top of the hill after Jillen disappeared. And I also wanted to know why he didn't warn me that Wylla was a homicidal cutthroat. But he would probably be serving the family dinner and wouldn't want to take the time to speak with me tonight.

So I made my way back to the Storehouse, but instead of walking along the main street, I took a left just before the baker's place onto a narrower residential street called Rank Street. There I saw a mix of two-story and single-story homes. Some were good-sized, but many looked like they were one room cabins. Probably where the lapp workers lived. I noticed that a lot of them looked uninhabited. Like no one had lived there for months, or years even.

I turned to the southeast on a slightly wider lane that ran parallel to the main street. A carefully painted sign identified the lane as "Valley Road" and I could see why. A few hundred yards away loomed the big hill upon which Lockwell Manor perched. This part of the village was definitely in a valley.

Valley Road continued for four blocks, lined with more

homes and more cabins, and then it dead-ended into the Storehouse.

I pushed open the door and there was Minch. It looked like he had finished his evening meal and was now enjoying a bottle of something that I could smell from the doorway.

"Solve the crime, have you?" he asked.

"Not yet." I walked into my cell and sat down on the cot.

"Why not? You are the Imperial Investigator, aren't you?"

It was pretty obvious that Minch was well on his way to being drunk.

He said, "You might have mentioned that little fact to me. Now Lockwell thinks I'm an idiot. A bloody idiot."

"What are you drinking?"

"It does not matter. You shan't be having any."

"I don't want any. I'm just curious."

"Uskbow. Well-aged. Worth a pretty coin. Been saving this bottle for years, but seeing as this is my last night on Tomira, might as well enjoy it, right?"

"What are you talking about?"

"You heard Lockwell. I'm going to Ortwen tonight." He took another swig of uskbow. "I told you what happened to the last man that he sent over there."

"Yes."

"Well, it appears that now it's my turn. And I'm not nearly as sturdy as Barnes." He rubbed his eyes. "I just don't know what Lockwell's thinking. The village needs a marshal. Am I that expendable?"

I didn't say anything. Just stretched out on the cot and looked up at the ceiling.

Minch said, "Perhaps he's going to offer you the job. You want to be the marshal, Bander?"

"No."

"It's not a bad job, when all's said and done. Not a bad job at all."

"I told you, I'm not looking for a job."

"Then why don't you just leave? No one's forcing you to stay."

"I need boots."

Minch laughed bitterly.

"Besides," I said. "I really do want to figure out what happened to Jillen Lockwell. I spoke to the nursemaid a little while ago."

"Did she confess to you?"

"Not exactly. Although she did almost gut me like a fish."

"Wylla's a strange woman. Not right in the head. Ever since her husband left her."

"Yes, the butler told me about that. Did you know the previous marshal?"

"Unferd, yes. Didn't care for the man. I heard he's living in Kreed's Keep now. With a girl from the village."

I told him about Wylla's ruse at the inn and he laughed at me.

"You do need to watch yourself around her. She's not your typical nursemaid. She'll fight any man in town and beat three-quarters of them. In fact, many folks say that she'd make a better marshal than me."

Wylla reminded me of a woman I used to adventure with who was now an officer in Waterside's Ministry of the Axe. Big, strong, wouldn't take any rot from anyone. I liked that.

Minch went over to a cabinet and removed another cup. He filled it with uskbow and slid it across the table towards me.

"I changed my mind," he said. "This isn't your fault. Not really."

"Thank you, but I don't want it."

"Why? This is very fine uskbow. Probably much finer than you've ever had. Enjoy it."

"I need to keep my wits about me tonight," I said.

"Tonight?"

"I'm going with you. To Ortwen."

"Why?"

I shrugged. "The way I see it, it's a two-man job."

Minch didn't say anything, but I could tell he was relieved. Very relieved.

"Here's what we need," I said. Then I listed a bunch of things, ranging from burnt wood to blacken our skin, to an iron pry bar, to weapons: a long knife for him, and a short club for me. I also asked for a wax tablet and then we sketched the layout of Ortwen, based on what Minch remembered of it. Unfortunately that wasn't much.

I asked him who might have a better idea of how Ortwen was laid out, and he told me about an old-timer named Fardigson who was one of the men who helped build Ortwen way back when.

"Let's go see him," I said.

So we did. We left the Storehouse and Minch's expensive bottle of uskbow and walked down Valley Road, almost to the end. We turned on an even narrower street called Pritchard that was lined with a bunch of houses on either side. Some were like the small cabins I had seen earlier, but others were larger and built with a bit more imagination.

We stopped in front of an older two story house with a steep gabled roof and exposed rafter beams. There were carved wooden brackets under the eaves and a spacious covered porch in front.

Minch knocked at the door, and after a time an old man answered. Fardigson was a good thirty years older than me, but his eyes shone bright and it was obvious that his mind was still keen.

Huddled around his table, we examined the sketch of Ortwen by the light of a half-dozen candles.

"Pretty good," Fardigson said. "But you got the center all wrong. This thing was my idea. A market square, but in the shape of a wheel, you see? With spokes. Better than a single main street. Especially when you've got limited acreage to work with."

He made a bunch of corrections on the plan and then pronounced it good.

"Where's the guardhouse?" I asked.

"There isn't one in town," Fardigson said. "Only one road in. Winds like a snake. The guardhouse is a quarter mile down the road. You'll hit it before you see the town."

"No, we won't."

"'Course you will. Between the cliffs and the brambles, there's no way to get in besides the road."

"We're not taking the road. We're taking the lake."

"What? Are you daft?" Minch shook his head. "That will take us all night."

"You said Ortwen was straight across the lake. Ten miles."

"Twelve," Minch said.

"So, twelve. That should take us three hours. We'll take turns rowing."

"We'll be exhausted. It's much easier to ride."

"Did Barnes ride?"

"Of course he did."

"So let's not do what Barnes did."

We left Fardigson's place and returned to the Storehouse. There I spent time memorizing the map on the tablet while Minch collected the rest of our gear.

Then we slept for a few hours. At least I did. Minch looked like he was too agitated to sleep.

When I woke at midnight, he was awake. We gathered our equipment and then made our way to the lake shore. Minch found us a flat-bottomed skiff and checked it for leaks, cracked oars, or anything else that might slow us down. We certainly didn't want to be in a sinking boat five miles from shore. Even if the lake was shallow.

Then we loaded our gear and Minch also grabbed a long pole which would help us maneuver once we got close to our destination. Under the light of a bright moon we set off.

~

I took the first shift of rowing. I hated the water and hated being in a boat, but I did like to row. There was something comforting about the rhythmic motion of pulling the oars through the inky water.

The air was cool and clouds drifted across the moon. Even with the clouds, it wasn't so dark that Minch couldn't navigate. He pulled a spyglass from his bag and peered through it.

"Where did you get that?" I asked.

A spyglass—or perspective glass as they were sometimes called—was a rare and expensive device. You wouldn't expect to see one in a small village.

"It's Arno Lockwell's," Minch said. "He lent it to me when I was checking the road."

"Well, that will come in handy."

"Yes, as long as I don't lose it."

"Any other surprises in your bag?"

He pulled out the half empty bottle of uskbow. "Just my old friend. Ready for a snort, then?"

"No. But save me some. For later. We'll celebrate once this is all done."

"If you don't mind, I might do a little celebrating in advance." He took a swig.

I said, "Suit yourself. Just don't fall overboard. If you do, you are on your own."

After about an hour and a half we gingerly switched positions. Minch got the oars, and I got the spyglass. He was a competent rower and what he lacked in raw power, he made up in technique. I could tell he had been rowing all his life.

The spyglass was an intricate affair of carved wood and brass rings and eyeholes and lenses. When I looked through it, I was a little disappointed that it didn't work better. I was able to see farther, but the image was very dark.

We continued across the lake for another two hours or so, and then we closed in on the far shore and Ortwen. Minch used the pole and guided us into a little rocky cove a hundred yards away from the village and we got out, stretched our legs, and pulled the skiff onto shore.

As we gathered our equipment, I noticed that Minch was planning to leave his bottle of uskbow in the skiff.

"For our victory celebration on the way home," he explained. "Just as you said."

I took the bottle and tucked it into my shoulder bag along with the pry bar. "Just in case we need to celebrate earlier."

We used the burnt wood to darken our skin and Minch donned a dark cloth cap to cover his bald pate. Then we began to pick our way across the rocks along the shore and towards the village.

The biggest thing I was worried about was dogs. I could handle human watchmen, but canine guards were another matter altogether. But Minch had told me that if Ortwen was anything like Hytwen, there probably wouldn't be many dogs in the village. The few dogs around would be on the outskirts of town, at the ranches and farmsteads—instead of near the lake. I hoped he was right.

We approached the village from the west, making our way past drying racks and warehouses. We didn't see anyone, man or beast. Of course, it was very late. Four hours past midnight, which was my preferred time to infiltrate enemy territory. Long ago, the healer Cero Wold had told me that four hours past midnight was the time that humans were least responsive, and therefore most able to be surprised. I didn't understand why, but over the years I had seen for myself that he was correct.

Moving from shadow to shadow, we passed more warehouses, then a boat builder's workshop, and then we arrived at the canal. The old timer Fardigson had explained that when they built Ortwen, they ran into trouble with all the rocky cliffs. The main road in and out was so twisty that long wagons couldn't make it through without getting banged up or stuck. So they decided to barge the lapp out on narrow riverboats down a ten-foot wide creek that ran through a canyon north of town and then rejoined the main road three-quarters of a mile later. The creek had to be widened and dredged, especially through town. So they shored it up and made it into a canal which ran from the lake's shore, around the northern perimeter of the village, and then off to the northeast.

There was a decent-sized bridge spanning the canal a hundred yards to the north, so that's where we crossed and snuck our way into the center of the village. Just as Fardigson had described, Ortwen was built like a wagon wheel with a circular marketplace in its center and six spoke roads leading off.

Even in the half-light of the moon, I could tell that Ortwen was a very different village than Hytwen. The buildings were much newer; the entire village was less than 50 years old. And while Hytwen had room to stretch out, Ortwen was constricted by tall, rocky cliffs that boxed it in against the lake shore. As a result, the buildings were built taller and closer together. And many of the structures were built of stone, probably mined from the surrounding cliffs.

Our first target was Ortwen's version of the Storehouse: a marshal's office and jail in the northwest quadrant of the village. We found the building easily enough, but what caught us off guard was the fact that the marshal was awake and standing right outside, not a dozen feet from the front door.

Chapter Nine

THE MAN WAS FACING AWAY FROM US, URINATING IN A DITCH THAT RAN BETWEEN TWO BUILDINGS. He was tall, maybe my size, and well-muscled, but he was obviously half asleep. Either that or drunk because I watched him sway as he pissed. A lantern rested by his feet. I guessed he was not coordinated enough to hold the lantern at the same time he did his business.

I took a few rapid steps toward him, walking on the edges of my feet to minimize the noise. It didn't matter. He didn't turn around until I spoke.

"I hope you are not peeing on those boots," I said.

As he started to turn, I stepped quickly towards him, covering the six feet between us in two steps. At the same time, I swept the club up in a quick fluid motion. I swung it clean and true in a diagonal motion which caught the man right beneath his jaw. I didn't apply enough force to decapitate him, or even shatter his jaw, just enough to snap his head back. He teetered upright for a moment, then collapsed in a heap and was still.

His boots looked like they might fit me and he had been kind enough not to urinate on them, so I pulled them off his feet. Spoils of war.

Minch said, "You don't mess around."

I whispered, "You think there's someone else inside?"

"How should I know?"

I motioned for him to stay and then I picked up the lantern and lurched in through the door, mimicking a half-asleep man returning from taking a piss.

The marshal's office here in Ortwen was a little bigger than the Storehouse in Hytwen. Basically one long room with two cells at the end. They were both empty, but one of the cells served as the marshal's sleeping quarters. The cell door was chained open, and the cot looked more comfortable than the one next door.

I stuck my head outside and told Minch that it was all clear. He entered the office and looked around.

"Damn. Look at this. Finer accommodations than mine."

"Yes, but he lives here."

Minch nodded. "They don't have as many buildings as we do. Need to make the most of what space they have."

"So do you think this man was the one who beat Barnes nearly to death?"

"Could be. He looks like a brute. Kind of like you."

"I'll take that as a compliment."

"We going to kill him?"

I said, "No reason to. He's not waking up for a good long time."

We had discussed that if Jillen Lockwell was here in Ortwen, she'd likely be imprisoned in a cell. To the best of Minch's knowledge, these were the only cells in town. So now we had to move on to part two of our plan: infiltrate the lord of Ortwen's home. That was the other place we thought Jillen Lockwell might be.

Moving silently, we left the marshal's office and circled around to the north, sneaking along a stream which served as a drainage ditch that protected the last row of houses from the runoff from the cliffs above them. Directly north of the center of the village was Creagar Skenn's home.

Unlike the Lockwells, Creagar Skenn did not live in an opulent manor house on a hill. For one thing, there was no room in the village for a big house. For another, according to what Minch knew, Ellia Lockwell's cousin was a frugal man with a profound distaste for anything that seemed ostentatious.

We stood in front of a blocky and compact two-story stone house. It had a covered entrance with four wooden pillars, and the house itself was maybe thirty feet square. There were eight windows on each side—all dark—and a door in the front and a door in the back. It was a simple, functional building with little ornamentation.

Waiting in the shadows, we listened for dogs or guards but didn't hear anything. The area was quiet but probably wouldn't stay that way for much longer. Dawn wasn't far off.

I decided to go in. But not through the front door.

The back of the house had a small yard that was not fenced. There were some plants growing, maybe a small garden. I couldn't really tell. But there was an outhouse, set back 40 or 50 feet away. And that meant that the back door would probably lead to a hallway with a staircase to the living quarters not too far away. And if Jillen Lockwell was here, there would be a good chance that she'd be locked in one of the upstairs bedrooms.

I did a quick calculation based on the number of windows and the space needed for a staircase. I figured that there would be a minimum of six rooms upstairs, and as many as nine. That was a lot to check, so I thought that I had better get going.

Carefully I pushed at the back door. It was unlocked and reasonably quiet. I waited in the hall for my eyes to adjust. Shafts of moonlight stabbed through the darkness here and there. Just enough to allow me to see where I was going.

The back of the house had a kitchen and a larder to my left, a staircase to my right, and a hall that presumably led out to the sitting room and the front of the house.

I slowly crept up the stairs, making sure I stepped on the edge of the stairs closest to the wall where they were least likely to squeak—especially under my weight. Upstairs I counted seven doors along the hallway that ran the length of the upper story, from north to south. Thankfully, the wood floor was covered with carpets. But it still creaked and groaned as I walked on it, so I needed to move carefully.

There was no way around it. I was going to have to open each of the doors. I started with the closest door, directly to my right as I stood on the top landing, and pushed it open as carefully as I could. It opened into a small store room.

The next room was a bedroom. Asleep on her back, was an older woman who snored loud enough to wake the dead. That was just fine by me. Her snores would mask any sounds I might make. I briefly wondered who the woman was. She could have been Creagar Skenn's mother. Or his wife's mother. Or another relative. According to Minch, Creagar Skenn only had the one child. Plenty of room in this house for relatives.

Of course, the older woman might be a maid or a cook or a nursemaid—if Creagar Skenn kept servants. He might not. Or the maid or cook or whoever might live in her own house. A lot of possibilities.

The next two bedrooms were vacant, but I didn't know that until I cracked the doors of each room and peered in. So far my luck had held, but the longer I stayed in the house, the more I'd risk having a confrontation. I needed to hurry.

At first, I thought that I might just check each door to see if it was locked. They wouldn't leave a prisoner in an unlocked room. Unless she was chained.

The next door was at the south end of the hall, directly opposite the storeroom. I was betting that it was another storeroom—and I was correct. It was filled with old chests and some artwork.

Two rooms remaining. By process of elimination, one should be Creagar Skenn and his wife's bedroom, and the other should be his son's bedroom.

I eased open the furthest door on the east side of the hall and peeked in. Sure enough, there was a boy sleeping in the bed. He was older than I thought. Maybe ten or eleven. And he was stirring.

"Father?" he called quietly, half asleep.

When you're infiltrating a house, encountering children is almost as bad as encountering dogs. Both are loud and unpredictable. So I froze. It was still dark enough that Creagar Skenn's son might not see me. Especially if I remained motionless. People's eyes are good at detecting an object in motion, not as good as picking out something standing perfectly still.

I was hoping that the boy would just go back to sleep, but he didn't. He groggily slid out of bed and teetered towards me.

Less than two seconds. That's how much time I had to make a decision.

I could try to run down the stairs. That would cause the child to wail and scream. I was sure of it. Everyone in the house would be chasing after me in less than a minute.

Option two involved hiding in the storage room next door. I knew the room had a window, so even if the boy woke the entire household, I was reasonably sure I could escape through the window and drop down onto the roof of the covered porch and make my way to the ground. The problem with that was noise. Some men can drop and land on their feet, making no more noise than a cat. Thieves, burglars, doldar, and the like. But people in those professions usually don't weigh over 250 pounds. If I dropped to a rooftop, it would sound like a stag clomping around up there.

Once the alarm had been sounded, escape would be impossible. There would be nowhere to go. We certainly couldn't row our way free of any pursuers.

The third option was the worst in nearly every way, except for one. It might just work.

So when the boy stepped out into the hallway, I grabbed him off his feet and clamped my hand over his mouth.

He tried to scream anyway like I knew he would, so I pinched his nose closed. I kept it closed until I felt his little body go limp.

Chapter Ten

CREAGAR SKENN'S SON WASN'T DEAD. Although if I had misjudged even by a few seconds, he very well might have been. I released his nose so the boy could breathe normally, but kept his mouth pinned closed.

Then, with the boy cradled in my arms, I made my escape.

Minch shook his head in disbelief as we quickly strode away from Creagar Skenn's house.

"Do you know who that is? Do you?" he whispered.

"Yes."

"Well, then, you're not in your right mind. Not at all."

"Later."

We returned to Ortwen's marshal's office. The big lawman was still unconscious, right where we left him.

The kid must have woke up and seen the unconscious marshal and probably recognized the man because the boy started crying and trembling in my arms.

I dragged him inside the office and told Minch to find a

scrap of cloth. Then I swung the boy into a chair and said, "I'm going to uncover your mouth now. You will not make a sound, okay? Nod if you understand."

He nodded.

I slowly released my grip on his face but kept my hand close in case I needed to shut him up in a hurry.

"Very good," I said. "We're not going to hurt you. As long as you do exactly what we say. Nod if you will obey."

He nodded again.

"Now what's your name, boy?"

"Fenton. Fenton Skenn."

"Good, Fenton Skenn. You are a brave lad. I know it must be tough, being taken from your house like this."

"Who are you? What are you going to do to me?"

"I promise that I won't hurt you. I'm just going to ask you some questions. We'll start there. Okay?"

Fenton Skenn didn't say anything. His face twitched, and he was trying not to cry again.

"Do you know who Jillen Lockwell is?"

"She's my cousin. But I don't really know her."

"Have you seen her recently? Is she here visiting?"

"What do you mean?" Fenton Skenn looked genuinely confused.

I asked, "When was the last time you saw her?"

The boy thought for awhile, then said. "I can't really remember. When I was little, I think."

"But you haven't seen her in the past three days?"

"No."

I believed Fenton Skenn. It didn't mean that Jillen Lockwell absolutely wasn't here in Ortwen. But if she was here, she was being kept somewhere more remote.

"Are you going to kill me?" Fenton Skenn asked.

"Of course not. Why would you say that?"

"You look like a murderer."

"Do yourself a favor, kid. Forget what I look like."

I took the strip of cloth from Minch and tied it around Fenton Skenn's mouth. He struggled and tried to cry out.

"Calm down," I told him. "I'm going to lock you in the cell. You're a smart boy and would never scream, so the gag is just in case. I'm sorry about all this, but it's just the way things have to be. Someone will be by to release you in an hour or so. And by that time, we'll be long gone. On our way back to Kreed's Keep."

Once his parents discovered that Fenton Skenn was missing, they'd likely come here to the marshal's office to organize a search party. Then they'd find the boy, and hopefully, the lad would tell them his abductors were going to Kreed's Keep. If all went well, Creagar Skenn would try to find us on the road and never even look on the lake. We had to get out of here now. But we wouldn't be leaving empty-handed.

We bound the hands and feet of the unconscious marshal and then I threw him over my shoulder and we snuck back to the skiff. Then we set off back across the lake.

Halfway back the sun began to rise. It lit up the mist in a soft glow of light. Our prisoner woke up, and I explained to him that his presence was requested in Hytwen. I also suggested that he not make trouble lest he finds himself tossed overboard. It didn't matter if the water was shallow if you were trussed up like a dead deer.

He nodded but didn't say anything. Maybe he was resigned to his fate. Maybe he couldn't speak too well after what I had done to his jaw. Either way, the return trip was uneventful.

It was well before noon when we arrived back on Hytwen's shore. We walked the prisoner through town and to the Storehouse. We gave him some water and then locked him in the cell I had slept in the night before.

Outside, I conferred with Minch and we decided to take shifts guarding Ortwen's marshal. Minch assured me that the cell itself was secure. Indeed it looked sound, but I really didn't want to take any chances.

Minch said, "I'll take the first watch. You can sleep in my house." He told me how to get there.

I didn't argue because I was dead tired. I told him that I would return in a few hours and then set off to find Queen Street where Minch's cabin was.

The cabin was a modest structure at the end of the street, and there was not much inside except for a bed, a large fireplace, some chairs, and a well-built table. I didn't need the table or the fireplace, but I did make use of the bed. I stripped off my clothes and examined the boots I had seized from our prisoner. They were a bit tight. Still, they were better than the flimsy shoes that were still in my satchel. And they were much better than going barefoot. That was for sure.

I reminded myself to visit the healer Lynd later today. I didn't want to risk an infection on my feet and my hands were blistered from nearly four hours of rowing.

Then I thought about the mission and judged that it had been a partial success and that was certainly much better than no kind of success.

And then I fell asleep.

I slept for three hours, then I woke and used Minch's outhouse.

The noon sun was out, and it felt warm on my back as I headed back towards the Storehouse. For the first time in a while, I was feeling pretty good. I just hoped that Minch didn't fall asleep during his guard duty.

But when I walked inside, Minch wasn't there. Neither was the prisoner.

There wasn't any sign of a struggle. The cell door was unlocked, and the cot looked like it had been slept in. I saw the chair where Minch had probably sat for the past three hours. It wasn't tipped over. There was no blood anywhere.

I went round back to the stables, but the horses were right there in their paddock where they were supposed to be.

That was strange. I didn't think Minch would take it upon himself to let the prisoner go. Unless, of course, he was ordered to by Arno Lockwell. Maybe a diplomatic solution had been reached.

But all that in three hours? It didn't make sense.

And then another thought struck me and I quickly saddled up one of the horses and galloped up the hill. I rode past Lockwell Manor down the other side of the hill towards the stables.

But I was too late.

The bloody body of Ortwen's marshal was there, tied to a pole in one of the dry lots. Standing around him was Minch, Arno Lockwell, and one of the mercenaries, the ruddy looking man I had spoken with in the bunkhouse. The mercenary held a whip which glistened with the prisoner's blood.

I rode closer. The bloody man tied to the pole wasn't moving.

"Well done, Captain!" Arno Lockwell said. "Well done, indeed. Minch told me all about the raid."

I dismounted and said, "You weren't supposed to kill him."

"Why not?" the ruddy mercenary said. "After what he did to Barnes?"

"Do we know that for sure?" I asked. "Did you interrogate him?"

"A little," the mercenary said.

In a quiet voice Minch said, "He denied everything."

"Of course he did," Arno Lockwell said. "Creagar Skenn's devils are a resolute bunch. But that won't save them from my wrath."

I glared at Minch. I would deal with him later. But now I turned to the mercenary. Moved close, so our faces were nearly touching. I could smell his fetid breath.

"The prisoner was mine," I growled. "Mine to interrogate. Mine to execute if that's what I chose. You understand that?"

Arno Lockwell stepped forward. "Point of fact, the prisoner was mine. You're working for me, Captain. Just like Harl. Just like everyone else in this town. I wonder if you comprehend that. I do hope so."

I shut my eyes and breathed. I wanted to break his arm. Maybe rip it right from the socket and club him to death with it.

Instead, I said, "I want to talk to your butler again. I need to know about any carts going in or out of the grounds since Jillen was taken."

"Very well." He walked over to his own horse.

I stared at the mercenary Harl for several moments before mounting up. He stared back defiantly.

Arno Lockwell led the way, and I rode after him. Minch didn't have a horse, so he followed by foot. The mercenary stayed put. Maybe to clean up the mess.

I rode up next to Arno Lockwell and asked, "Do you really want a war with Ortwen?"

"If that's what it takes to get Jillen back, then yes. But I doubt it will come to that. They took one of my men, I took one of theirs. It appears we are now even."

"They didn't kill your man."

"Might as well have. He's of no use to me now."

We arrived at the front entrance of the manor and dismounted. The footman opened the doors and then left to attend to the horses. I told him to leave my horse up here. I wasn't going to be staying long.

Arno Lockwell clapped me on the shoulder and said, "Thanks to you, Captain, we showed Creagar Skenn that we can strike at his child at any time. Although I would have preferred that you had taken young Fenton as a prisoner. Still, I expect you've put the fear of Dynark into Creagar Skenn. He will back down and return Jillen. I am certain of it."

"And if not?"

"If not, we'll burn Ortwen to the ground. I've got more men coming in from Marston Hills. They'll be here tomorrow. I suggest you prepare yourself. We're going to strike once they arrive."

He strode away, up the stairs.

I went the opposite direction, down to the servants' hall. It was empty. As was Lohuin's office.

"What're you doing in here, then?" a voice called. It was the cook. She stood in the doorway. Her hands were white with flour.

"I'm looking for Lohuin."

"He's not here."

"I can see that," I said.

"Then why are you lingering in his office?"

"Do you know where he is?"

"Maybe I do."

I just stared at her. Hard. I was still angry about the prisoner.

"He's upstairs," she said, with a frown.

"Where?"

"Gallery, I reckon. Moving everything about again."

As I left the office, I saw a back staircase that I hadn't noticed before. I followed it upstairs and found myself in a vestibule adjacent to the dining hall. The staircase continued up to the next floor. I walked up and soon discovered that I was down the hall from the nursery wing. It made sense. Servants needed to go up and down between floors. This was clearly the servants' staircase. At least one of them. Who knew how many there were in a house this large?

I continued down the hallway towards Jillen Lockwell's room but stopped when I heard the sound of a child crying.

Chapter Eleven

I PUSHED THE DOOR OPEN, HALF EXPECTING TO SEE JILLEN LOCKWELL HERSELF. Instead, I saw a young boy sprawled on her bed, clutching at one of her toys. He was startled when I entered the room, but he quickly recovered and wiped his tears away.

"Who are you?" he asked, as he sat up. He was small and had red hair. Obviously the Lockwell son.

I said, "My name is Bander. Who are you?"

"No, I meant who are you who thinks he's permitted in my sister's bedchambers?"

"Well, I'm allowed to be anywhere I want to be. According to your father's wishes. You are the son, right?"

"Yes."

"I'm an investigator. You know what that is?"

"I think so."

"I figure out mysteries, solve crimes, that sort of thing. At least I used to."

The kid's eyes widened. "Truly?"

"Truly."

"And you're going to find my sister?"

"I'm trying to. What's your name?"

"Geddis Lockwell."

"Well met, Geddis Lockwell. May I ask you some questions?"

"I guess so."

"When's the last time you saw your sister?"

He scrunched his face up in thought for a moment and then said, "Four days ago, I think."

"Where?"

"She was walking with Wylla. I was coming up from the stables."

"Do you remember what time of day this was?"

"In the morning some time."

From interviewing the staff I knew that Jillen Lockwell had been seen in the dining room for her morning meal an hour or so after dawn. A housemaid had also seen her returning from her walk with Wylla a few hours after that.

"Did you see your sister after she came back from her walk? Later that day?"

"No."

"Any strangers show up that day?"

"No."

"What about any carts or wagons? Deliveries?"

"You think someone took Jilly away in a wagon?"

The boy was quick.

"Maybe," I said. "I'm trying to think of all the possibilities."

Geddis nodded.

"Do you think your sister would ever run away? On her own?"

"Never," he said.

"How can you be so sure?" I asked. "Plenty of children run away—even if for an hour. I used to run away every other week."

He smiled. "Yes, I've run away. Always came back though. But Jilly would never. I don't think she could."

"Why?"

"She'd be too afraid."

"Afraid of being punished?"

"No, just afraid. Of being away from home. Of being alone. Getting lost. Jilly's afraid of everything."

I decided to ask him about Wylla. It would be interesting to see if he disliked her as much as everyone else did.

"What do you think of Jillen's nursemaid?"

He came right out and said it. "She's a bad woman."

"What do you mean?"

"I don't know. Just bad. Horrible."

"Strict?"

"Yes, strict. Mean. Cruel. Bad."

His eyes locked with mine.

"Really bad," he said.

"Like how?"

His hand went up to his mouth, like a man about to stroke his beard.

"Lots of different ways," he said. "She wasn't nice. To me, or Jilly."

"Give me an example. How wasn't she nice?"

"She... took things."

"Stole?"

"Yes, she's a thief. An evil thief."

Geddis Lockwell was lying.

Unlike my experience with Reeni and Barelle, there were certain things about the boy that tipped me off. He stared at me without blinking as if he had been coached to look me in the eye. In fact, I think his whole performance—with the tears and the lies—had been orchestrated. But I decided to play along and see what he might tell me.

"What did she steal?"

"What did she steal?" he repeated, stalling for time to think. "Lots. She stole a lot of things."

"Like what?"

He leaned back. "Ummm... valuables. Gold. Silver, I think."

"I see."

"She was a really bad person and I feel safer with her gone."

Yes, he was definitely instructed what to say.

I thanked the boy and told him if there was anything else he remembered about the day Jillen went missing, I wanted to hear from him. And Minch would know how to locate me.

Then I left him and went to find Lohuin. The butler was indeed in the gallery, balancing on a chair, taking measurements of the space above the fireplace.

"I need to ask you some more questions," I said.

He looked down his nose at me for a moment, then said "Very well, sir." Slowly, he stepped down off the chair.

I told him I wanted to know about wagons, carts, or carriages coming or going starting on the day Jillen was taken.

He thought for a moment and then said, "Nothing that day, if I recall. We may ask Mrs. Fandott, but I believe it was two days ago that she sent Vogan to the market. Sometimes she goes herself. Sometimes they go together."

"What about anything out of the ordinary? Surely, you receive merchandise from Marston Hills."

"Of course, and Vale as well. Even from Rundlun a few times a year. But no shipments have arrived in the past week here at the manor."

This wasn't promising. I felt reasonably sure that whoever took Jillen Lockwell must have taken her by wagon. Maybe bribed a driver. Maybe drove themselves.

"How does Ellia Lockwell get into the village?"

"Vogan drives her in the carriage."

I asked, "And does anyone else use the carriage?"

"Lord Arno from time to time, but that's usually if he is journeying away from the village."

The carriage house was probably down near the stables, so I could go inspect the carriage when I was done here, but I had one more question for Lohuin.

"Who haven't I spoken with? That I should speak with?"

He raised an eyebrow. "I don't quite understand the question, sir."

"I've spoken to the household staff, Arno Lockwell, his wife, Geddis, the hired guards—"

"They're not actually guards."

"Mercenaries, whatever you want to call them. I want to know whom I am missing?"

"I told you the last time we spoke, sir. Wylla the former nursemaid. She knows something. Most certainly."

"I spoke to her already."

His eyebrows got even higher. I thought they might fly off his head.

I said, "And I plan on speaking with her again, but who else is connected to the Lockwells?"

"Sir, every single person in Hytwen serves the Lockwells in one fashion or another. This is their village, their farm."

Their farm. That reminded me that Minch had mentioned a man involved with the farm's finances. The marshal had described him as 'the money man.'

"Tell me about the man who actually sells the lapp.

"Alford Platt?"

"Yes." That was the name Minch had mentioned. "Who is he?"

"He's the farm steward, of course."

"Where can I find him?"

"He has a home at the bottom of the hill. Often he comes up to meet with Master Lockwell."

"I'll visit him at his home. And I'll need a letter of introduction."

Lohuin looked at me quizzically. "We're not that formal here, sir."

"That may be so, but I still want that letter. I want it very clear that Alford Platt should answer my questions. See to it at once. Send it down to his house."

"Begging your pardon, sir, but I'm employed by Master Lockwell, not you, and I have other duties to attend to."

Anger swelled up within me. Again.

"My duty is to find out what happened to your master's daughter."

I stepped over to the fireplace and snatched up the fire iron. I gave it a swing. The weight of metal felt good in my hand.

"So you can either do what I ask, or I'll break both your arms. Your choice."

Lohuin's face drained of color.

"Of course, sir."

"One hour. Send a man down to his house to deliver it personally. Or I'll be back."

I left the manor but kept the fire iron.

I returned to the stable block and debated with myself about stopping off at the bunkhouse with my fire iron. Maybe have a little sit down with Lockwell's mercenaries. Especially the one named Harl. That struck me as a good idea. Therapeutic, even.

But the bunkhouse was empty. No sign of the men.

I looked in the stables. No one there either. Nor any horses. They were out in the pasture.

I walked from building to building, room to room. There

was a game larder, a storage room, a tack room, and finally the carriage house. It contained an old wagon and a new carriage. The latter was spotlessly clean, polished to an incredible shine. The body panels were made of lacquered wood and the interior was richly upholstered. It was an expensive coach, no doubt about it. Very expensive.

I set to work.

I examined every inch of the carriage. In and out. Up and down. I was looking for anything I could find. A scrap of cloth, hairs, blood.

But I didn't find any of that.

I also didn't find any hidden compartments.

I examined the wagon just as thoroughly. It had a plain bench up front and a flat bed with slatted rails. The wood was ancient, sun-baked and bleached a light grey. There had been no effort to paint it or adorn it in any way. It was a simple wagon. Probably used mostly for hauling hay. And I found lots of traces of hay, but I didn't find anything that made me think that a young girl had been anywhere near this wagon.

It was a few hours past noon by this time, and I was getting hungry. I wondered if the cook might feed me if I asked nicely. I walked back up to the manor and then down to the kitchen. The cook, Mrs. Fandott, was still in there baking.

I'm not sure if it was because of my polite demeanor or if it was because of the fire iron, but she scrounged up some cold meat and bread and a jar of cool water.

"You can sit over in the servants' hall if you want," she said.

"I'm fine here." I stood at one of the long tables in the kitchen and ate as Mrs. Fandott baked.

"Were you originally employed here by Ellia Lockwell's father?"

"Aye, Master Erlmander Skenn was a good man, may Dynark take his soul."

"And did he build this house?"

"The original, he did. It was much smaller. Not nearly as grand."

"So the Lockwells built most of this?"

"Yes, indeed. Brought woodworkers in from Vale. Tile workers in from Kreed's Keep. If you're curious, you should ask Mr. Lohuin. He knows all about it."

"Maybe I will. When did all this happen? The expansion, I mean."

"It didn't happen overnight if that's what you're asking. The work started maybe five years ago. And they just finished up last spring. Although if you ask Mister Lohuin, he might say that it will never truly be finished. But you didn't hear that from me."

I thanked her for the food and went to the look for my horse. I found him grazing along the back of the house, near the gardens. There was a gardener pulling dead leaves from beneath a row of shrubbery. I think he was one of the men I saw working here yesterday. Lohuin hadn't mentioned the gardeners, but it seemed like they were always out working on something.

As I got closer to the gardener, I waved a greeting. "May I have a word?"

He stood up, and I saw that he was a very tall, gaunt man with sunken eyes and creased skin the color of leather. It was hard to determine his age, but he wasn't a young man. Not by any means.

I introduced myself and told him that I was working for Arno Lockwell trying to find out what happened to his daughter.

He looked down and mumbled, "Bad business."

I asked him his name.

"Sangal."

"And how long have you worked at the manor?"

"Long time."

"When do you start in the morning?"

"Sunrise. Just after."

I asked, "Who's the other man who works with you?"

"Bollar. But he only works when I need him."

"And the day Jillen Lockwell went missing. were you working?"

"Yes."

"Where?"

"The Ring Garden."

"What's that?" I asked.

"Big flower garden in the east gardens. Shaped like a circle."

"And what were you doing?"

"Digging out the goldenbelles."

"What?"

He said, "Mistress Lockwell didn't care for the goldenbelles, so we had to dig them all out and plant alber lilies instead."

"So Bollar was with you?"

"Yes."

"Did you see anyone else that morning?"

He nodded. "Saw the staff coming in. Saw Jillen and Wylla on their walk."

"Any strangers?"

The gardener thought for a moment. "No."

"Can you show me where you were working?"

"I suppose so."

He led me around to the east side of the house. There was a sunny garden made up of concentric rings of white flowers. A statue of a deer rose up in the center and pathways radiated out like spokes of a wheel. I strolled through the garden,

turning in every direction. I had good views of the cobblestone road that wound back towards the village as well as of
the east wing of the manor.

"Did you happen to notice any carts or wagons or
coaches?"

"Nope."

"You sure?"

"Aye."

Not a very talkative fellow. I told him if he remembered
anything else to contact Minch. Then I walked back to the
back of the house to find my horse.

I set off down the hill back towards the village, thinking
about all the dead ends I was running into. No one had seen
anything. There were no strangers on the grounds. No
deliveries.

A girl couldn't just vanish into thin air.

Unless she had been teleported out by a mage, of course.
And that was highly unlikely.

There were only a few thousand mages in the entire
Empire, and most of them were stationed in cities and large
towns where the Guild had a presence. You'd never find one
in a small village like Hytwen. But still, it was worth asking
Minch if any mages ever came through town.

At the bottom of the hill, as I was entering the village
proper, stood a row of stately homes. Each was a fraction of
the size of Lockwell Manor, but I could tell that a lot of effort
went into their construction. They were all tall structures,
with a stone first floor and then two more stories that were
timbered and plastered. Each had a steep roof with turrets
and other decorative elements.

I knew which house was Alford Platt's because the Lockwell's footman was waiting at the door of one of them.

"Mr. Alford Platt appears not to be at home, sir."

I noticed that the footmen held a scroll case.

"Is that the letter of introduction?"

"Yes, sir. From Mr. Lohuin, sir."

"I'll take that and wait for Alford Platt. I'm sure you are eager to return to your duties."

"As you wish, sir."

He surrendered the case and began to walk away.

"Wait," I called. "Take my horse. I won't be needing him."

"Are you sure, sir?"

"Of course. No sense in walking all that way."

"Thank you, sir."

When the footman departed, I knocked on the door myself. There was no answer. I walked around the perimeter of the house and looked in the windows. All was quiet, and no one stirred within. At least, as far as I could tell.

The back of the house had a small, well-tended vegetable garden. There was a shed and an outhouse. And, of course, a back door to the house. The door was locked, but the lock was old. It took me less than a minute to pry it open.

I left my fire iron in the bushes and entered the house. The first thing I did was to call out—just to make sure no one was taking an afternoon nap. No one responded.

The first floor was a warren of rooms, but I eventually found what I was looking for: Alford Platt's office. It was a dark room with heavy curtains and a desk carved from some mottled Wilderlands wood I didn't recognize. There were bookshelves packed with bound journals, a low cabinet, and some upholstered chairs that were expensive-looking, but worn.

I opened the curtains enough to let a shaft of light shine in on the bookcase. Then I got to work inspecting the journals. They contained pretty much what I expected: sales records, accounts, inventory, prices, employee records. They went back thirty or forty years at least.

There was a man who I used in Rundlun for this sort of

thing. His name was Marting, and he had a brilliant mind for numbers and noticed every single detail about nearly everything. Marting could spend an hour or two with these ledgers and know exactly what was what. It might take me days. And I didn't have days.

It turns out that I didn't even have minutes.

There was a sound at the front door: the *thunk* of a lock being released. And then the door began to swing open on squeaky hinges.

Chapter Twelve

HERE WAS NOWHERE TO HIDE IN THIS OFFICE. And there were no other exits. I strode over to the windows and saw that they did not open.

I was trapped.

So I did what I usually do in situations like this. I found an area that was out of the doorway's line of sight, and I backed right up and flattened myself against that wall. And then I froze. Like a statue. And waited.

I heard someone moving down the hallway. An older man, and not very fit, judging by the sounds of his shuffling and labored breathing.

He walked deeper into the house, away from the office and away from me.

Maybe he was planning on walking upstairs and taking that nap. That way I could resume my study of his ledgers in peace.

No such luck.

After some banging about in what was probably the

kitchen, the shuffling sound got closer, and I heard the man muttering to himself. Something about fleas.

I raced over and sat down behind his desk and swung my feet up like I owned the place.

"There you are," I said as he appeared in the doorway.

He must have jumped a good six inches, which was no mean feat for a man of his girth. Alford Platt was short and round, with a jowly face. His hair was almost white, and he had a huge tangle of bushy side whiskers which gave his head a pyramid-like shape.

"Who, sir, are you? And what in blazes are you doing in my house?" he sputtered.

I indicated the scroll case on his desk.

"I'm investigating the disappearance of Jillen Lockwell and I have some questions for you."

He snatched up the scroll case and withdrew the letter and read it quickly.

I stood up and walked over to him. I towered a good foot above him. "Listen, I don't have much time."

"You haven't told me who you are."

"My name is Bander, and I used to be the Imperial Investigator."

His eyes widened briefly in recognition. He had probably heard my name when Lockwell asked about me.

"I still don't understand why you felt you could take the liberty of trespassing in my house," he huffed.

"There is a chance that whoever took Jillen Lockwell had business dealings with her father. Maybe lost some money. Maybe was a rival. I was told that you know everything about the farm's finances."

"Of course I do." He shuffled around the desk and sat down.

"So, tell me. Who is most likely to want to hurt Lockwell?"

He thought for a few moments and said, "I don't know... Master Lockwell is a fair man. He has never cheated his customers or his employees."

"I don't believe that. No one is perfect."

"Of course not, but Lockwell Farms has a sterling reputation. As did Skenn Farms before it."

I decided to try another angle.

"How successful is the business?"

"What do you mean?"

"It's a straightforward question."

"Not really. The success of any business changes from month to month, week to week. Sometimes even from day to day."

"So you are saying that Lockwell Farms isn't successful today?"

"I'm saying no such thing, sir. I am simply stating that we measure success over certain time periods. Since the business was founded in 1616, it has been quite successful."

"What about over the past year?"

"Fortunes rise and fall, from year to year."

"I ask you again, has the business been successful over the past year?"

Alford Platt frowned at me. "No, but that is not unusual."

"What about the year before that?"

"Have you not been listening to what I've been saying, sir?"

I was losing my patience. "Successful, yes or no?"

"No, but—"

I stopped him there.

"Someone told me that the market for lapp has changed. Is that true?"

"Changed how?"

"Demand has shifted. Geographically. From west to east. Is that true? Does the east buy more lapp?"

"Yes, a bit."

"And have shipments west decreased?"

"Perhaps..."

"And isn't it true that Ortwen has the exclusive right to sell to the east?"

"Yes, that has been our longstanding agreement. There is quite a bit of demand still in the west. I don't want to paint—"

I cut him off. "But less than there used to be?"

"Again, it depends on which time periods we are calculating sales."

I decided to switch to another line of inquiry. "Tell me of all the construction projects around the village."

"What do you mean?"

"New cobblestones on the streets, the new warehouses, the expansion of Lockwell Manor."

"Why shouldn't the Lockwells make improvements?"

"I didn't say they shouldn't. I just wonder if it was prudent. Given the state of the business."

"I'm not sure what you are insinuating, sir."

I could tell by his expression that I had hit a nerve.

"Let's go back to my original question. Who is most likely to want to hurt Lockwell? Who are his enemies?"

"I told you that I didn't know."

"What about Ortwen? Creagar Skenn?"

He shrugged. "From a purely business perspective, it would be better for both farms if we could unify again. Like in the day of Bordagar Skenn."

"Why? Less competition?"

He started to nod, but then caught himself. "There isn't any competition now, but—"

"I know, you said that there's a 'longstanding agreement.' But I have a feeling that maybe some buyers haven't been honoring the agreement, right? Maybe you got a contract from someone in the east who didn't like Creagar Skenn's terms?"

"More likely the other way around," he muttered, under his breath.

"Fine. So maybe your counterpart in Ortwen—"

"That would be Creagar Skenn's brother Borsus."

"He's their farm steward?"

"Yes."

"And he's making deals in the west. Maybe undercutting you?"

"We have our suspicions."

"And what are you doing about it?"

"We've had meetings. Master Lockwell has tried to resolve the issue. But Creagar Skenn is a headstrong man if I may say so."

"Headstrong enough to kidnap his sister's child?"

"That's for you to determine, isn't it?"

With that, he stood up and told me to see myself out. Then he shuffled out of the office.

I had a lot to think about and a lot of questions for Minch.

I returned to the Storehouse, but Minch wasn't there. Maybe Lockwell had sent him on another secret mission. But since I knew where Minch lived, I decided to check his cabin.

I made my way down Valley Road. Off to the left loomed the hill on top of which Lockwell Manor perched. I couldn't see the big house from down here, but I pictured Arno Lockwell and Ellia Lockwell gazing down upon their minions.

Minch answered the knock on his door and let me in. He smelled of drink.

"I know what you are going to say. Don't bother."

"So you're a mind-reader in addition to being the village marshal?"

"I couldn't help it. Lockwell showed up with Harl and they just took the prisoner. I didn't have any say in the matter. None at all, Dynark's good truth!"

"How did they know that we even had a prisoner?"

"Are you daft? Nothing happens in Hytwen without Arno Lockwell knowing about it. Someone saw us drag the man through town and sent word up the hill. Maybe it was ten people who sent word. You want something to drink?"

"No." I sat down. "I just came from speaking with Alford Platt."

"Did he try to sell you some lapp, the old blowhard?"

"No, but he did try to sell me a story of a profitable business, more or less. He suggested it might be more profitable, however, if the two sides of the lake came together."

"Never going to happen, my friend. Not in a million years."

"Because of Creagar Skenn?"

"Aye, because of Creagar Skenn."

"What if Creagar Skenn was out of the picture?"

"Then his brother would be in charge."

"What if all the Skenns were out of the picture?"

"What are you getting at?"

"I'm not sure yet. I just think that there's more to this whole thing than meets the eye."

Minch refilled his goblet.

I asked, "You ever get any mages come through here?"

"Mages? In Hytwen? Never. Not since I've lived here, at least. Why?"

"I've interviewed everyone at the manor—including the gardener. No one saw anything out of the ordinary. No strangers. No wagons—"

"Wagons? You think that's how she was smuggled out? By wagon?"

"That would make the most sense. But someone would have seen something. Or heard something. Even in the middle of the night."

"Where does the mage come in, then?"

"He doesn't. But if you told me that there was a mage in town the day Jillen Lockwell vanished, it would be a different story."

"Well, there wasn't any mage. Did you talk to Mistress Lockwell?"

"Matter of fact, I did."

"Did she share her theory?"

"No."

"She thinks Wylla did it."

I nodded. "So does the household staff. And the son."

"Mistress Lockwell is convinced of it. She wants Wylla hanged."

"You still do that here?"

"Haven't for a long time."

"Does Ellia Lockwell have any evidence?"

"That's the thing," Minch said. "She has plenty of evidence that Wylla was up to no good. They found certain stolen items locked in the chest in Wylla's room."

"So Wylla's a thief?"

"According to Mistress Lockwell she is. In fact, the plan was to dismiss her from service at the end of last month."

"So what happened? She was still working the morning Jillen Lockwell disappeared."

"Well, apparently Arno Lockwell intervened. He thought it would upset his daughter too much if they sent away her nursemaid."

"He doesn't strike me as one who coddles his children."

"Yes, well, there may be another reason. You didn't hear it

from me, but rumor has it that Wylla was Lockwell's mistress when she first came to work for them. Maybe he still cared for her."

I wasn't convinced. Arno Lockwell didn't seem very sentimental. But all roads seemed to point back to Wylla.

I told Minch that I was going to have another talk with her.

"Good luck," he said. "Keep your stones protected. That's all I have to say. She's a wildcat."

I left Minch's cabin and walked down Queen Street into the center of the village. It was still a few hours before dusk and I decided to make one stop before looking for Wylla. I made my way back to the home of Lynd the Healer.

I knocked several times. And then he finally opened the door.

"Come back tomorrow. I'm tired," he said.

"I may not be here tomorrow." I pushed my way in.

"Why's that?"

"I'm not doing a particularly good job of what I was hired to do."

"Find out what happened to Jillen Lockwell, you mean?"

"Yes. Arno Lockwell may dismiss me."

"Not sure I can help you with that."

"Did you ever try to heal her?" I asked. "Jillen Lockwell, I mean."

He shook his head. "Well beyond what I can do."

"But they brought her to you, right?"

He didn't answer. Instead, he said, "Sit down. Take off those boots."

I did as he asked and he inspected my feet.

"No infection. Healing quite well, actually. I'm going to get you something."

He disappeared into the back room and emerged a few minutes later with a small clay jar.

"Rub this salve on your feet before you sleep."

"What is it?" I asked.

"That's my secret. And I want the jar back before you depart the village. Agreed?"

"Agreed. Now tell me about Jillen Lockwell."

He stood up. "They adopted little Jillen as a newborn. She was Arno Lockwell's niece. His brother's little girl. But his sister-in-law died in childbirth and the brother went insane and supposedly was going to kill the baby. Luckily his brother's ranch hand saved the little girl, but the brother ended up killing himself. So the Lockwells took little Jillen in."

I shook my head. A tragic story.

"For the first few years of Jillen's life, she seemed more or less normal. Quiet, but normal. It wasn't until she was two or three years old, the Lockwells knew that she was different."

"How is she different?"

"She's in her own world. That's the best way I can describe it. It's difficult to get her to talk to you, even though she's very bright."

"Her brother said she was very fearful."

"I wouldn't know about that. The times I examined her, she seemed fairly calm. But as I said, in her own world."

I didn't have any real experience with children—other than being one myself. But that was half a century ago.

"Do you think she might have run away from home?"

Lynd said, "I have no idea, but I doubt it."

"Why do you say that?"

"The world around her seemed to have no fascination for Jillen. Whenever I saw her, she exhibited no curiosity about what was going on around her. Really, no interest at all."

"So you don't think there would be anything out there that might call to her?"

"Exactly."

"But what if she wasn't drawn to run away?"

"I don't understand."

"What if she was trying to escape something? That might be a good reason to run away."

"As far as I could tell, she had a happy life. I doubt she was beaten or even harshly disciplined. I never saw any evidence of mistreatment."

I thanked Lynd for the salve and took my leave. I still had a lot to think about.

Chapter Thirteen

I WALKED DOWN TO THE SHORE OF THE LAKE. I was hoping to see a fleet of skiffs returning for the day, hauling their catch of lapp onto the rocky beach. But I didn't see anything like that. I saw one old timer fishing. That was it.

"Any luck?" I asked.

"Nope."

"That's too bad."

"It's still early," he said.

"For the fish?"

"For the eels."

I didn't say anything.

"They come out at night," he said.

"The eels?"

"Yes."

I didn't even know that people fished for eels. I had eaten eels, of course, but never really thought about how they might have ended up on my dinner plate.

"You out here every day?" I asked.

"Pretty much. Gets me away from the wife."

We stood in silence for a few minutes. I watched the birds skim the surface of the lake, snapping up insects. The air was starting to cool as the sky darkened.

"Were you here fishing the day Jillen Lockwell went missing?"

"Nope. I just fish in the evenings. After work."

"So were you here that evening?"

"Yes. And the evening before. But no, I didn't see her wander into the lake. People have been asking me that a lot."

"What about any strange boats?"

"What do you mean?"

"Well, I'm guessing that you probably recognize the lapp farmers."

"Mudders," he said. "We call them mudders."

"Sure, mudders. You know them, right?"

"Some of them, I do. But they all come in well before I'm here."

"So you didn't see any boats coming or going that night?"

"Not much reason for someone to go out on the lake at night. Unless they were up to no good."

I didn't know if he was referring to my midnight excursion last night.

Just then there was a splash and the fisherman's rod bent.

"Here we go!" he said with a grin. He quickly coiled his line around his hand and—after a brief struggle—brought his quarry into shore.

It looked like a big silver snake as thick as my forearm. It was maybe six feet long. The fisherman dispatched it with a club.

"Catching's starting early," he said. "Must be the clouds."

I looked up. He was right. The sky was murky. Grey clouds swirled over our heads.

"Good luck with your fishing," I said, as I walked away.

"And yours as well."

Lake Way was getting crowded, and it looked like a good portion of the populace was headed to either the Green Tree or one of the other taverns that were within a few blocks of the inn. I didn't know whether that would bode well or ill for my chances of speaking with Wylla again.

As I walked down the expensively cobblestoned streets of Hytwen, a scenario formed in my mind. Ellia Lockwell and her husband inherit Hytwen and the lapp business. And like anyone who comes into a fair amount of wealth, they start spending. New streets. New manor house. Ostentatious carriages. Expensive rugs and artwork. A staff of mercenaries. Entire gardens replanted on a whim.

But running a lapp farm maybe isn't as easy as they thought. Especially if the market's changed.

So they cut back. Maybe sell some artwork. Maybe employ fewer mudders, or whatever they're called.

Time passes. There's no big boom. No lapp windfalls. No return to the glory days. Those empty lapp farmer cottages are still empty. Hytwen's population is still half of what it used to be under Ellia Lockwell's father.

But something doesn't add up. The artwork is back in the manor gallery. And the manor house keeps expanding. Along with the gardens. The Lockwells still had money. They just weren't getting it from their business.

I had seen this same pattern a million times.

Desperation coupled with unrealistic optimism.

There were people who preyed on that.

Moneylenders of sorts. But I just called them gangsters.

And all of a sudden I knew what happened to Jillen Lockwell.

I could see it clearly now. Arno Lockwell had borrowed gold.

Maybe from someone in Kreed's Keep. Maybe Rytho Marr. Maybe Lavallan. Or someone like them. The kind of men who would loan you money, then charge you a tremendous amount of interest. Interest that accrued every day until the interest was more than what you originally borrowed.

And what happened if you didn't pay?

Then things might get broken. Like your wagon. Maybe a warehouse might burn down. And that would make it more difficult for you to repay your loan.

And then the interest would continue to grow.

Rytho Marr's enforcers would pay you a visit. If you were lucky, they might break your arm. If you were unlucky, they might rape your wife.

And if you still didn't pay?

They'd take a close look at your children.

And you didn't want that to happen.

But I was afraid that is exactly what did happen to Arno Lockwell. He dealt with the wrong type of people and got in too deep. Jillen Lockwell paid the price.

Which meant that right now she was either dead or disfigured. Or sold into slavery.

I needed to get back to Alford Platt and make him talk. He would certainly know if Lockwell Farms owed money to a gangster.

My reverie was interrupted by a cry for help.

It was a woman's voice, and it came from the alley behind the Green Tree Inn. I raced over.

They alley wasn't much of an alley. Behind the inn was a low stable block. Between the two structures was a narrow dirt track. About thirty feet in, two men stood over a woman. I recognized all three of them.

The woman was Wylla and the two men were two of Arno Lockwell's mercenaries: the thick ruddy man named Harl and a swarthy brute.

Wylla lay in a heap on the ground, badly beaten. Blood gushed from her nose and half her clothes had been ripped from her body.

The brute—I think his name was Starnery—kicked at her. The other man, Harl, was pulling down his breeches. It was pretty obvious what was coming next.

"What do we have here?" I spoke in a loud, aggressive voice—the voice I used to use when I was a Red Shoulder Captain. I had perfected the commanding tone, edged with menace. It was a voice backed up by the full might of the Imperial Ministry of the Axe. And it chilled most people to the bone.

But not these men.

"You want some of this, you got to get in line, friend," Harl said. "We done all the work."

"I can see that. Is this the infamous nursemaid I keep hearing about?"

"Aye. She's a right terror."

Starnery said, "Bitch cut me pretty good."

I saw what he meant. He had a serious gash on his forearm.

"Don't you mind," Harl told him. "It'll all even out in the end, I promise."

"Well, here's the thing," I said. "I'm taking her."

"That's fine, but we're going first," Harl said.

I said, "You don't understand. The way I see it, you owe me a prisoner. Seeing as that you whipped mine to death before I got a chance to interrogate him."

Harl laughed. "It don't work that way, Captain." He spat out my title derisively.

"Normally, I take a certain amount of pleasure in debating those who are clearly dumber than me, but I'm in a bit of a rush this evening, so I'll give you three seconds to get out of here."

"Or what?"

"Or I will break your arms. And his."

Starnery laughed.

Harl said, "We saw what you did to Tobbler, laying into him before the fight even started. It was a cowardly move and it won't work on us."

"Last chance," I said. "Leave now with all your limbs in one piece, or leave later with them in pieces. Your choice."

I was watching Harl's eyes, so I knew what he was going to do next. He made a big show of hitching his breeches back up, shrugging his shoulders, and then starting to turn like he was giving up.

But then he exploded towards me, with a ferocious clubbing punch aimed right at the side of my neck.

If he had connected, it would have been bad for me. Very bad. But luckily I knew what was coming.

I spun and caught his arm with both hands.

And then we kept on going. Past the empty air where my head had been. I guided him down towards the ground.

He had put a lot of energy into the punch and therefore there was a lot of momentum.

I just helped that momentum along, until Harl's arm was fully extended and I was standing behind him, one hand on his wrist, the other on his upper arm. He stumbled forward and then I twisted, leaned in, and wrenched his arm from the socket.

He fell to the ground, screaming in pain, but I wasn't done.

I kneeled hard on his arm. *Snap*. It broke like a piece of dried firewood.

Starnery froze, just staring in shock. I could tell that he finally saw me for what I was. A predator. An avenging force of nature. Chill and dread and mayhem. And I was coming for him next.

He tried to run, but he didn't get far. And twenty seconds later I was standing over him, watching him writhe in pain from his own broken arm.

"Now that you men know that I am a man of my word, I'm going to make you another promise. If you aren't gone from Hytwen in the morning, I'll snap your necks and throw you in the lake. Are we clear?"

Harl just groaned, so I gave him a little kick on his ribs with my new boot. Maybe I broke some more bones, maybe not. But he managed to answer me.

"Yes, we'll go. Just stop."

I nodded and went over to Wylla.

She was upright and had a crazy smile on her face.

"Get me out of here," she said.

"Can you walk?"

"Probably not."

So I carried her out of the alley.

Chapter Fourteen

I TOOK WYLLA TO LYND THE HEALER. It wasn't far, and she wasn't heavy. But I did have to pound on Lynd's door for a while before he opened up.

"You again?"

"She's hurt." I pushed my way in.

Lynd recognized Wylla, but at this point, she was nearly unconscious, so she probably didn't even know where she was.

He told me to bring her to the back room. I carefully set Wylla down upon the same cot where Lynd had healed my feet yesterday.

"What happened?" Lynd asked as he examined her.

"She was beaten and almost raped. By Lockwell's men."

"Almost raped?"

"I convinced them it wasn't a good idea. In fact, they'll be leaving town for good—although they might try to stop in here to get their broken arms patched up before they leave."

"I see."

"How is she?" I asked.

"So far, I'm not seeing anything too bad. She's a tough bird."

I watched him as he cleaned her wounds and checked where she had been kicked. No bones were broken, which was good, but getting pounded on the head wasn't something you couldn't recover from instantly. Even with a healer's help.

After the wounds were cleaned and dressed, Lynd ministered to her, laying his hands upon her.

Then he said, "She'll need to sleep for a while, but she should be okay."

"Fine. I'll stay with her."

"That doesn't necessarily help the healing process."

I shrugged. "I don't have any other place to be. Also, if those mercenaries show up..."

"Let her sleep for the night. After that, she should be conscious and able to walk by herself. I'll be upstairs if you need me."

"Thank you."

I watched him go and then found another cot on the other side of the room.

I pulled it closer to where Wylla slept. I put some salve Lynd gave me on my feet and my blistered hands and then left the jar on his workbench. I lay down, shut my eyes, and within two minutes I was asleep.

Some time in the middle of the night, Wylla cried out in her sleep. I snapped awake and checked on her. She was awake too.

"Where am I?" she said. Her voice was hoarse and low.

"The healer's place. You're going to be fine."

"Thank you," she said. "For what you did for me."

"It needed to be done."

"I think I misjudged you. You're not like them at all."

"I'm better."

She tried to laugh but was still in pain. Then her face

darkened, and she sat up. "We need to leave. Lockwell's bringing in more mercenaries."

"I know."

"He's not going to let this go. He won't be allowed to. You know that, right?"

I didn't say anything but sat up myself. We were right across from each other. Three feet away.

"He's not who you think he is," Wylla said.

"What do you mean?"

"I mean, he is a slave. Her slave."

"Whose?"

"Ellia Lockwell's."

"I don't understand."

"She controls everything. Everything about the farm. Everything about the village. Everything about his life."

"I don't know about that."

"What?"

"I'm not saying that you are wrong. I just didn't see any evidence of that."

"Then you didn't look hard enough. I've been with the family for more than ten years. I've seen everything. Ellia Lockwell pulls the strings. Everyone around here is her puppet."

"What about you?"

"What about me?"

"Were you her puppet?"

"Of course not."

"And what was your relationship with Arno Lockwell?"

She laughed softly. "Are you asking if I bedded him?"

"I was told that you were his mistress."

"Well, I wasn't. Arno Lockwell prefers men. If you're looking for his mistress, you'll find him in the bunkhouse."

I wondered if she was telling the truth.

"Did the Lockwells owe money?" I asked.

"Of course they did. The business was failing. And she was spending like a duchess. Did you see the manor?"

"Yes."

"Did you see her clothing?"

"Just what she was wearing."

"Her dressing room is bigger than this house. They owed a lot of money."

"To whom?"

"I don't know exactly."

"Did you ever seen strangers at the house?"

"All the time. There were a lot of business arrangements made. People would come as far as the capital."

"Did you ever overhear anything?"

"No, they'd usually keep all the servants well clear of the library. Why are you asking about all of this?"

"I suspect that it was one of their creditors who took Jillen."

Wylla was silent. She looked down. Finally, she said, "You're wrong. It wasn't a creditor."

"How do you know?"

"Because I took her."

I was dumbstruck.

Wylla continued, "I had to. To save her life."

I stared at her. There wasn't enough moonlight coming in to discern her expression, and I wished there was because I needed to find out if she was lying, telling the truth, or if she was simply insane.

"Tell me more."

She shook her head. "We don't have time. We need to leave now."

"Why now?"

"Because soon Ellia Lockwell will know what you did to those men. She'll know that you saved me. And she'll believe that we are in league."

"What does it matter?"

"She'll convince her husband that we need to be silenced."

"I'm not afraid of Arno Lockwell."

"Me neither, but we'll be outnumbered. He's claiming that Jillen is in Ortwen. He's raising a squad of mercenaries to get her. Just as easy for them to get us first."

I remembered what Lockwell had told me. More sell-swords were on their way from Marston Hills. They would be here today. Wylla was right. We didn't want to be around when they arrived.

"Where's Jillen?" I asked.

"Safe."

"That's not an answer."

"It's the only answer you're going to get from me—for now at least."

"So you're asking me to trust you?"

"I'm asking you to help me."

I stood up. Maybe Wylla was lying, but I didn't get that impression. She seemed genuinely afraid. But then again, she had deceived me before—at the inn.

"Just tell me one thing," I said. "How did you get Jillen Lockwell out?"

"I didn't get her out. She got herself out."

"What do you mean?"

"She teleported."

I sat back down on the cot, considering what I just heard. If it was true, it would explain a lot.

"She's a mage?" I asked.

"Of course not. She's a child with an affliction."

"Who can teleport...?"

"Yes."

It normally took years of tutelage for a mage to learn how to teleport. But there were some people—locestrae—who had kind of a native magical ability. Some of them could even travel using a form of teleportation. But locestrae were very rare and were more-or-less hunted by the Mage Guild, who branded them unlicensed practitioners of magic.

"Is she a locestra?" I asked.

"I don't know what she is. But she does have certain... abilities."

"I want to know everything."

Wylla said, "You will. I promise. But first, we have to get free from here."

I told her I knew where some horses were and asked her if she thought she could ride. She said she would try. Then we slipped out into the pre-dawn gloom and immediately turned down Rank Street to Valley Road. I didn't want to take any chances by traveling down the main street.

It was dark and cold and damp, but the moon peeked through the clouds enough so that we were able to make our way to the stables behind the Storehouse.

I was in luck. Both horses were there. I had been worried that the footman had kept my horse up at the manor, but maybe one of the staff rode him down after they had finished work for the evening.

Without delay, I saddled up the horses and helped Wylla on to hers. Then we quietly rode back the way we came, along Valley Road. Wylla led the way, but it looked like she was heading north, away from the main road out of town. She explained that there was a chance that Lockwell had posted sentries at the entrance to the town. We'd circle around and meet up with the main road a little further out.

As we left Hytwen, the only living thing we saw was a family of deer, foraging in a field near a farm. We rode as fast as Wylla could go and made pretty good progress. Three and a half hours later, we hit the West Way. And as far as I could tell, we hadn't been followed. I half expected to see Harl and Starnery riding up in back of us. I did, after all, threaten to kill them if they didn't leave by morning. But we saw no one.

So here at the crossroads, we had a decision to make. East towards the city of Marston Hills where we'd most certainly pass a squad of mercenaries heading to Hytwen. Or we could go west towards Bexden, a large town with five or six thousand people. Either way, we'd be heading towards places big enough to lose ourselves in. But both places were probably two days ride from here. A day and a half if we rode hard, which didn't seem like an option.

But Wylla had another destination in mind.

"I know a woman named Leshea. She runs the Stag. Do you know it?"

"No."

"It's a coaching inn. The Stag & Pennant, if you want to get fancy. It's thirty more miles west, but I think I can make it."

"And how will we pay for this inn?"

"I told you. I know Leshea. You'll approve of her. She's like me."

"Insane?"

Wylla laughed, but then grimaced in pain.

We rode in silence for another few hours. I had a lot to think about. Most of it concerned Wylla. I didn't know quite what to make of her, but she had a strength about her that I admired. Maybe she was an insane mythomaniac, maybe not. I had a feeling that I was going to find out—one way or another.

At around noon we dismounted and led the horses to a brook to drink. We didn't have any food, so I told Wylla that I'd forage. I came back with some mace rushes I found in a swampy area where the brook overflowed into a meadow. I broke off the heads, which weren't ready to eat this early in the year, and washed the thin roots, which were.

Wylla had never eaten a mace rush before, but soon she was munching on a root and grinning.

"I guess being a vagrant is good for something," she said. "We won't be starving, at least."

"I'm not a ranger by any means. I can't track. I'm a mediocre hunter."

"But you spend a lot of time in the wilderness?"

"Not really. I spend a lot of time on roads. And the rest of the time in towns and cities."

"Why?"

"Why not? Harion is a big land. I've been traveling for a little over a year, and I've only seen a fraction of it."

"And why don't you settle down?"

"That's a lengthy tale."

"Good. We have a long way to go, and I'm easily bored."

Chapter Fifteen

❧❧❧

AS WE RODE, I GAVE HER AN ABBREVIATED VERSION OF MY LIFE STORY. A misspent youth. Then a decade as a professional adventurer. Next two decades in the service of the Imperial Ministry of the Axe. Then mustering out a little over a year ago. And now a vagrant—as she termed it. Or wanderer, if you wanted to call me something a bit more romantic.

"So, I'll ask you again," she said. "Why not settle down?"

"I settled down for twenty-two years. I had a house on Kesley Square in Rundlun with a maidservant. I had friends. I attended parties. I mingled with the wealthy and powerful."

"Did you have a wife?"

"Almost," I said. The memories of Ceronne came flooding back. It had been over a dozen years since I had lost her.

Wylla could tell I didn't want to talk about that topic, so she changed the subject.

"Where did you learn to fight? Were you a gladiator?"

I laughed. "Hardly. I'm a street brawler. Always have been. Since I was a young lad."

"You get into a lot of scraps back then?"

"Of course I did."

"I bet you tormented the other children. You did, didn't you?"

"Sometimes," I said. "Sometimes they tormented me. Or tried to."

We rode a bit longer in silence. Then it was my turn to ask the questions. And I told her so.

"We're well away from Hytwen. Now it's time for you to talk."

"What would you like to talk about?" She smiled at me. "My pretty eyes perhaps...?"

She was acting like the barmaid at the Green Tree again. But I was not about to let myself become distracted.

"I want to know your whole story," I told her. "Start from when you first came to Hytwen and finish when you took Jillen Lockwell."

"You sure you want to hear all that? You might get bored and fall off your horse."

"I'll take that chance."

So she told me her story. Haltingly. Leaving out a lot of details. But I persisted and asked a lot of questions and made her go back and explain things. And eventually, I got a narrative which felt like the truth, more or less.

Wylla was born and raised in Thalas, a good-sized town north of The Steading. And she really had worked as a barmaid—when she was much younger. She met a man named Unferd, and they fell in love. Unferd found work as the marshal of Hytwen and she decided to leave her family, which caused a lot of anger and grief. Wylla was basically disowned by her father.

But she didn't really care. She was in love with Unferd. They left Thalas and traveled for nearly a month to reach Hytwen, the tiny village on the edge of the Tengan Territories where the two of them started a new life together. And that life was good for nearly ten years—except for the fact that she discovered that she was unable to get pregnant.

One day, Unferd announced that he was done being the marshal and done with Hytwen. It was too small, too provincial. There were no challenges for him here. Life was boring. Stultifying even. He needed to leave.

"Fine," she had said. "Where shall we go next?"

He had looked down at the ground and said, "We are not going anywhere. I need to be alone."

Which had turned out to be a lie. Because after all the tears and screaming and then blaming herself, Wylla eventually found out the truth. Unferd had impregnated a girl in the village and wanted to start a new life with someone younger and more fertile.

She was despondent for weeks, verging on suicidal. She couldn't go home to Thalas and face her family. She was too old to find another husband. So she went on a drunken rampage in town, fighting any man she could find, especially any friends of Unferd. Then she tried to run away for a while and live in an old cabin in the forest south of Hytwen, but she nearly starved to death after a few months.

Raerig from the Green Tree Inn and some of the other workers there finally persuaded Wylla to return to the village, back to her old home. The neighbors talked, of course, and soon the entire village knew her business—including the Lockwells.

Arno Lockwell himself visited her and expressed his sympathy. He told her that he was taking in his infant niece whose mother had died. He said that they required a wet-nurse, and he offered Wylla the job. With no other prospects and no way to support herself, she accepted the position and moved into Lockwell Manor. Ellia Lockwell was cold and aloof to her from the first day. It soon became clear that

Arno Lockwell had prevailed upon his wife to bring Wylla on.

And so she was thrust into the role of nursemaid with no preparation, no instruction, and no advice—neither from Ellia Lockwell nor the other staff.

Right from the start Wylla could tell that Jillen was a withdrawn child. Yet, Wylla doted on her and eventually, Jillen seemed to respond.

It took nearly three years for the little girl to smile at Wylla. And then four more years before Jillen uttered a single word to her.

For all intents and purposes, Jillen appeared to be feeble-minded—an idiot. At first, her parents had been frantic at Jillen's apparent condition. They sought out healers and experts in every corner of the Empire.

But as the years passed, they came to accept the fact that their adopted daughter would never be a normal little girl. Ellia Lockwell began to spend less and less time with Jillen—and more time with her son Geddis who was younger than Jillen and normal in every respect. It seemed that the Lockwells were grudgingly grateful for Wylla's presence. Someone was caring for their adopted daughter, so they didn't have to see her.

Then about three years ago, when Jillen Lockwell turned nine, Wylla began to notice some strange behavior. Very strange behavior. Jillen began to talk to people who weren't there.

When Wylla asked Jillen who she was speaking with, the little girl explained that she had made a new friend named Norrah. According to Jillen, Norrah was a girl about Jillen's age who lived between the walls of Lockwell Manor.

Wylla had asked some of the mothers in town if their children ever spoke to imaginary friends and was told that it was fairly common. Just a sign of an overactive imagination. Jillen would grow out of it.

But she didn't.

And then six or seven months later, Wylla noticed that Jillen was doing another strange thing.

She was making things move without touching them.

A latent magical ability. Undeveloped for sure, but it had to be magic.

"You saw this yourself?" I asked.

"I just said that I did."

"What did she move?"

"That first time? Stuff around the room. Toys. A plate of honeycakes."

"Why isn't she in Delham right now?" I asked.

It was the law of the land. Any child exhibiting magical ability was required to register with the Mage Guild. Then these children would be evaluated and most likely taken to Delham University to begin training. The Imperial Ministry of the Wand took this very seriously. Anyone attempting to defy or circumvent the law was strictly dealt with.

Wylla said, "I didn't tell anyone."

I shook my head. "You know the penalties for defying the Guild?"

"Of course I do. Are you going to turn me in?"

"No, but someone else will. I'm surprised there isn't a Guild representative in Hytwen right now."

"No one knew about Jillen. Except me."

"That doesn't make sense. Surely her family witnessed her abilities. Or the household staff."

"No," she said. Then she paused for a moment, considering. "At least not at first. But that's why we had to leave."

"You're not making any sense."

"Let me finish the story and then you can judge."

Wylla went on to tell me that Jillen's most recent ability

was teleportation. Only the girl didn't know it was tele-portation.

"What do you mean?" I asked.

"Jillen called it 'walking through the walls.' And she thought it was normal. I mean she genuinely wondered why I didn't do it as well."

"So she would just teleport around the manor?"

"Yes, the manor, the grounds."

"And no one noticed?"

"I did. And I made her promise not to let anyone else see her do it."

"Describe what she did."

Wylla shrugged. "There's not much to describe. One minute she was there. The next minute she was gone. Across the manor, upstairs, downstairs. All in the blink of an eye."

"Did you ever see her appear?"

"Certainly. I saw her vanish. Then appear moments later. Out of thin air. My heart just about stopped the first time I saw it. I've never been around magic."

"And how long has this been going on?"

"The teleportation? A year, maybe a little less."

"She can control where she's going?"

"I think so. I mean she never got trapped or had any problems if that is what you're asking."

I thought about that for a few moments. Teleportation was an advanced skill. You get it wrong and you could find yourself embedded into a tree trunk or a mile underground or in a plane of existence where there's nothing to breathe. Every year, a handful of neophyte mages perished while trying to teleport. The idea that an untrained girl just picked up the ability naturally was astounding.

"Tell me how and why she teleported away last week. Was she angry at her parents?" I thought about my original theory that Jillen Lockwell had just run away from home—like any normal child.

"She teleported away because I convinced her to. I had to. To save her life."

"From whom?"

"Ellia Lockwell."

"Her mother wanted to kill her?"

"Not exactly." Wylla sighed. "So when I told you that no one besides me knew of Jillen's abilities, that was true. Up until about two months ago."

"Someone found out?"

"Yes. Ellia Lockwell. It was a stupid thing. I had to go into the village. Pick up a new frock for Jillen. Normally, Vogan does that sort of thing. Or maybe even Mrs. Hauf. But I asked to go. I wanted to be the one to surprise her with it. So I arranged for Adelina to watch Jillen."

"Adelina?"

"The under housemaid. She's an earnest girl. I have nothing bad to say about her."

I tried to remember if the inverse was true. Probably not. Just about the entire staff had gone to great lengths to convince me how despicable Wylla was.

"So before I left for the village, I reminded Jillen that she wasn't to use any of her abilities in front of anyone but me. And that included Adelina."

"She agreed, but she became upset—like she didn't want me to go. I asked her what was wrong, and she told me that Norrah had said something bad was coming."

"Norrah's the friend who lived in the walls?"

"Yes. Anyway, Jillen said that Norrah was trying to warn her about a man that was going to come and take her away."

"What man?"

"She didn't know. And that made her even more frantic. She just called him 'the Dragon.'"

"Why?"

"I don't know, but it gets stranger. I eventually calmed her down and assured her that there was no Dragon man coming to the manor and that I would protect her—no matter what. And then I departed. When I returned from the village, I was met by Mr. Lohuin who took me directly to Ellia Lockwell's sitting room. She had been waiting for me. I walked in, not knowing what was happening, and she interrogated me for close to two hours."

"About what?" I asked—although I had my suspicions.

"While I was gone, Ellia Lockwell got it in her head to visit with Jillen. Mind you, the woman had spent maybe a total of five minutes with the child over the past month. She wanted nothing to do with her. Yet, on that day, for some reason, she went into the nursery and there she caught Jillen moving her doll."

"With her mind?"

"Yes. And then she wanted to know everything from me: what else could Jillen do, how long had she had this power, everything."

"What did you tell her?"

"Nothing. Nothing at all. I played dumb. Said I didn't know what she was talking about. I tried to make it seem like I was shocked."

"I'll wager you had no trouble with that," I said.

"Actually, I didn't. And maybe that's why she didn't terminate my employment right then and there. But the fact is, Ellia Lockwell never spoke of the incident again."

"That's surprising."

"Indeed."

"What happened with Jillen?"

"The girl was beside herself. She was convinced that she had done a terrible thing. She apologized to me over and over and cried herself to sleep every night for weeks after that."

I thought for a moment and then asked, "Does Jillen love her mother?"

Wylla didn't answer right away. But then she said, "She thinks Ellia Lockwell is beautiful and elegant. But I don't know if I would say that Jillen loves the woman. Mostly, I think she is afraid of her."

"What about her father?"

"That's a different relationship altogether. Arno Lockwell certainly cares about Jilly. But I think he's afraid of her." Wylla wrinkled her nose. "No, that's not the right word. Not afraid really. More like upset by her."

"I don't understand."

"He would never say this aloud, but I believe Arno Lockwell is upset by the fact that Jillen isn't a perfect little girl—a normal little girl."

I asked Wylla to continue with the story. I was eager to hear how all of this led to Jillen being kidnapped by her own nursemaid.

She went on to explain that life in the manor went back to normal, more or less, for a few months or so. Then a strange visitor appeared at the manor.

"What kind of strange visitor?" I asked.

"He was a mage."

"Minch told me he's never seen a mage in all the time he's lived in Hytwen."

"I don't think the mage spent time in the village. I think he rode directly to the manor on his big black charger."

"Riding a black horse doesn't make someone a mage."

"No, but the fact that he departed without the use of a horse might."

"What do you mean?"

She said, "I mean that he rode in on a horse and when he departed, his horse stayed behind. The Lockwells still have it."

"So how did he leave the manor?"

"He either didn't leave. Or he teleported away," Wylla said. "I suppose he might have snuck away on foot—in the middle of the night—but I doubt it."

I rode a little closer to Wylla. I didn't want to miss a single word of what she would say next.

She said that the man showed up at night on the black charger. He was tall and gaunt, forty or fifty years of age, a sharp face like a hatchet, thin hair pasted back on his scalp, and close-set eyes. He wore a blood red cloak.

"You're very observant," I told her.

"That face is burned into my memory," she said. "Anyway, that night Arno Lockwell was gone—off to Marston Hills, I think. Ellia Lockwell sent all the servants away—"

"Including you?"

"No, I had to attend to the children. So I had both Jillen and Geddis in the nursery. But Jillen was thirsty and so I took the little stairway down to the kitchen to fetch her some warm milk. On the way back, I heard voices in the dining chamber."

I remembered the servants' staircase and the alcove off the dining chamber. I had been there myself.

Wylla continued, "I just waited there, hidden from view. And I heard what they were talking about. Not everything. But enough to get the gist."

"Which was?" I asked.

"Ellia Lockwell was going to sell Jillen."

Chapter Sixteen

"A T FIRST SHE WAS HAGGLING OVER THE PRICE," WYLLA SAID.

"I'm not going to ask how much."

"A lot. It was enough to lift the Lockwells out of debt and allow them to continue living their lavish lifestyle."

"Disgusting."

"The mage was fairly agreeable. He sounded like a real slimy sort though."

"Did you hear his name?"

"No. I don't think even Ellia Lockwell knew his actual name. But here's something. You know what she called him?"

I shook my head.

"She called him 'the Dragon.'"

"You're not serious."

"I know what I heard. This was the man Jillen Lockwell was terrified of."

I wasn't sure what to make of this. "Are you sure this wasn't an official visit from the Guild?"

"Does it sound like it was an official visit? It was odd from the start. Very secretive. Especially with the servants being sent away. Even Mr. Lohuin. That had never happened before. In any case, they were negotiating the time and terms of the arrangement, going back and forth on a number of points. But then Ellia Lockwell said that she wanted something more. I could actually hear the greed in her voice."

"Let me guess. Something to do with Ortwen?"

"You're quick—for a vagrant. I was worried about the children, so I didn't stay to hear the details, but Ellia Lockwell demanded that this Dragon help them with their Ortwen problem."

Right from the start, I had a feeling that Arno Lockwell had seemed overly eager to go to war with Ortwen. Now I knew why. His wife had stacked the deck with a mage.

"Did he try to take Jillen that night?" I asked.

"No. Not at all. He didn't even come up to see her. You'd think he'd want to inspect the merchandise, so to speak. But no. The next morning, the mage was gone. But his horse remained in the stables. I saw it with my own eyes."

We rode in silence for a few minutes while I pondered what Wylla had shared. This explained a lot. Especially the ebb and flow of the Lockwell's fortunes. And it explained why Ellia Lockwell was hostile to Wylla. I was certain she suspected that Wylla knew of Jillen's abilities. So Ellia Lockwell concocted a scheme to explain Jillen's absence and get rid of Wylla in a plausible way. Plus she could tie Jillen's alleged abduction to Ortwen. Make it seem like Wylla was in league with Creagar Skenn. That would justify an attack on the neighboring village. Then after their mage laid waste to Ortwen, the Lockwells could unify the two farming operations.

All for the price of a little girl.

I breathed out hard, trying to clear those vile plans from my mind. Then I asked Wylla about the day Jillen vanished and where she was now.

"I won't tell you where she is just yet. I want to make completely sure we are safe. But I will tell you how Jillen escaped."

Wylla rode closer and said, "After the night when the mage appeared, I thought about the situation a lot. I couldn't let Jillen be taken away. I knew she was in danger. And I knew it could happen at any time. That mage could show up without warning and just take her. And Jillen knew it. She knew all about the Dragon because Norrah had warned her about him."

I thought about that for a moment. On the surface, it seemed like nonsense: an invisible friend warning a young girl that she is going to be sold to a mage. But as I thought about Jillen Lockwell and her affliction, it made sense. I knew that there were women who had very unusual abilities that allowed them to seemingly know of future events. Women like the Witches of Melikti. A young girl trying to make sense of such abilities might create the fiction of an invisible friend who would try to help.

"So Jillen Lockwell knew this mage was coming?" I asked.

"Yes. She told me that Norrah told her that the Dragon was coming back. And this time he was going to take Jillen away. So I had to put my plan into action."

"And what was that?"

"After the mage's visit I started taking Jillen down to the village's caravan circle."

I had seen the area she was talking about. It was a wide roundabout ringed by warehouses, near where the blacksmith was. The caravans could load up and easily turn around in order to leave the village.

Wylla explained that she and Jillen Lockwell had gone down there every day for weeks. No one questioned the excuse that the girl was curious about the wagon train and wanted a new place to play. In reality, Wylla was ensuring that

Jillen was familiar enough with the caravans so that she could teleport there when the time came.

The plan was for Jillen to teleport out of the manor before the mage arrived. She would teleport to wherever the caravan was.

"But how did you know that the caravan would have departed from the village before the mage arrived?"

"It had already left," she said. "I knew the schedule. I knew roughly when the Dragon would return—"

"Thanks to Norrah."

"Thanks to Norrah, indeed."

"And the caravan was already on the road when the mage was supposed to return?"

"Yes. And, in case you are wondering, he did return. Four hours after Jillen went missing, the mage showed up at the manor. But it was too late. Jillen was free."

"I have a few more questions. First, what was your plan after Jillen teleported away? She would be a stowaway on a trade caravan, right? But how would you find her?"

Wylla grinned. "That was the genius of this plan. The caravan would stop for the night at a coaching inn—"

"The Stag & Pennant. That's why you want to go there."

"Exactly. My friend Leshea is looking out for Jillen. She'll keep her safe until we get there."

It was a good plan, I had to admit. Except for one thing.

"But what happens when the mage gets there first?" I asked.

"What?"

I sighed, knowing that what I was about to tell Wylla would devastate her.

"There is a fairly common spell called 'divination.' Mages can track people by collecting scraps of hair or clothing."

"No!" Her face drained of color.

"Any competent mage would have just gone up to Jillen's bedroom and—"

Before I could finish, Wylla spurred her horse and galloped away like a madwoman.

It was late afternoon by the time we reached the Stag & Pennant—or what was left of it. The coaching inn had been burnt to the ground.

A handful of confused travelers milled about. They had planned to stay at the inn for the night, but instead found collapsed walls and scorched timbers.

No one knew what had happened here. And there didn't seem to be any signs of survivors. But that didn't stop Wylla. She raced through the grounds, screaming for Jillen and Leshea.

I inspected what was left of the inn. It was difficult to tell for sure, but it looked like the structure had burned several days ago. That made sense if what I had feared had happened: the mage had been here and had taken Jillen Lockwell by force.

It was a bold move. And not very smart.

Destroying an inn and killing innocent bystanders was a highly visible action and the kind of thing that gave mages a bad name. The Guild wouldn't tolerate it. Once they found out about this, they'd send their own people—battle mages probably—to hunt down the rogue mage. But I knew, from long experience, that the Guild moved slowly. And I had a feeling that Wylla would have no tolerance for that.

The sun began to sink down beneath the tree line by the time Wylla returned to the horses. It was far too late to find another place to camp. Besides, we were in need of food and water.

I told Wylla as much and she nodded then went off to speak with a group of riders who traveled with a wagon. She returned a half hour later with some bread and a flask of water.

"How did you get that?" I asked.

"You don't want to know."

"Will they come after us?"

"No, not at all," she said grimly. "Unless we want breakfast."

We took the horses upwind a few hundred yards and tied them up in a small grove of trees. We had no bedrolls, no way to make a fire, and no tents. Setting up camp was a simple as collecting some rushes and piling them under a tree.

Wylla sat down and held her face in her hands. I could hear her sobbing quietly.

I wanted to tell her that we would find Jillen Lockwell and find the man who took her, this Dragon. I wanted to tell her that everything was going to be fine and that we would avenge the death of her friend Leshea, I wanted to tell her all those things, but I couldn't. I couldn't lie to her.

So I just held her. All night long.

Chapter Seventeen

A NIGHT OF SLEEP HAD NOT CALMED WYLLA. Not at all. I had watched her toss and turn in the night, and when she finally woke, she had a strange look in her eyes. Like a caged animal.

"I want to kill him," she said. "I want the mage dead."

"We don't even know where he is. He could be anywhere."

"He's in Vale."

"Why do you say that?"

"He has to be. That's where Ellia Lockwell found him. Vale's the only place she's traveled to recently. That's where she must have met him."

I thought for awhile. Vale was aboutn 400 miles away. And I didn't think Wylla would be able to make that journey with her injuries. Besides, we didn't have much to go on besides Wylla's quick glance at his face. Not even a name. Just an epithet. *The Dragon.*

Over 60,000 people lived in Vale. It's an ancient city. One of the first in the Empire, probably. Lots of places to hide. Especially if you were a mage—a mage who stole children. It would be impossible to find him.

"We should set off," Wylla said.

But I didn't move. I was thinking about something Wylla told me yesterday.

"You said that Ellia Lockwell negotiated for the mage's help."

"Yes. As part of the price for Jillen, he agreed to aid them in the attack against Ortwen."

"Which must have happened last night," I said. "The mercenaries arrived yesterday. They struck Ortwen in the middle of the night. We should have been there."

"You want to go back?"

I shook my head. "We'd never make it in time—even if they decided to delay the attack until daylight. But we have to do something."

"Yes," Wylla said. "We have to kill the Dragon."

"That's not going to help Ortwen."

"I don't care about Ortwen. I just care about Jillen. And maybe you. A little."

I couldn't tell if she was serious, but I had another thought. "How far is Bexden?"

"From here? Maybe a day and a half. Why?"

"There may be some mages in Bexden. The Guild doesn't have a hall there, but I think one or two mages might be stationed in the town anyway."

A glimmer of hope played across her face. "Will they help us find him?"

"That's a good question. The Guild certainly won't tolerate a rogue mage destroying villages and inns, murdering people, and abducting children. They will hunt him down, for certain."

Wylla noticed my expression. "But..?"

"But it's going to take a while. Years maybe. The Guild is notoriously bureaucratic. They make the Imperial Council look like a bunch of Vrenian Raiders."

"Jillen doesn't have years."

"Agreed. And, maybe I exaggerated a bit. The Guild will move as quickly as it can. But they are very methodical. And, truth be told, not very good at investigative work."

"And you're better?"

"Yes." I wasn't bragging. It was a statement of fact.

"Then why do we even need the Guild?"

"Lots of reasons. To begin with, they may know who this rogue mage is. That's the best case scenario."

"You call that a best case scenario? One of their own?"

"You're right. It would be a bad situation for the Guild. Embarrassing at the least. But maybe good for us. Maybe good for a head start in finding the Dragon."

"So what's your plan?"

"We ride to Bexden. I'll make contact with the Guild. Report what we know—"

"Are you insane? If the Guild learns about Jillen, won't they just lock her up and throw away the key?"

She had a point. As far as the Guild would be able to tell, Jillen Lockwell was a rogue mage as well. And she would indeed be locked up. Probably in a relorcan cell in the bowels of Delham University. Who knows what would happen to her?

I said, "We'll figure out something to say. I don't want to endanger the girl either." I motioned towards the destroyed inn. "There are a lot of people dead because of this rogue mage. He needs to be reported and brought to justice."

Wylla said, "I agree about the bringing to justice part."

"Then let's go."

"I need to do something first." Wylla began to walk towards the ruins of the inn. I began to follow her, but she asked me to stay with the horses. So I found a shady spot with a view of the West Way and waited.

I wanted to keep my eyes open for looters. Word was

probably getting out about the Stag & Pennant and I fully expected a small horde of looters to show up very soon and begin picking the ruins clean.

I also wanted to see if any Shielders appeared. Kreed's Keep's Ministry of the Shield regularly patrolled the West Way from the capital to Bexden, so it would just be a matter of time before they investigated. It was surprising that they hadn't yet arrived.

But neither the looters nor the Shielders showed up while I was waiting. But after nearly an hour Wylla returned. I could tell she had been crying. Fresh tears ran through the grime on her face.

"You find what you were looking for?"

She didn't answer right away. Instead she held out an amethyst ring with an ornate silver setting. It had been blackened by the fire.

"It used to be mine," she said. "Unferd gave it to me when we were married. When he left, I gave it to Leshea."

I didn't say anything.

"Don't think I'm being sentimental," she said. "It's worth something and food's not free in Bexden."

We saddled up and started to ride east.

Chapter Eighteen

I T HAD BEEN SLOW GOING FOR TWO DAYS. The horses were tired and Wylla was in no shape for a long journey. And we had to stop and forage along the way.

There had been one other coaching inn a day and a half west of the Stag & Pennant, but it was full and not very tolerant of travelers who couldn't pay. Still, we relayed the news of what had happened at the Stag & Pennant, but they had already heard of the tragedy from other travelers heading west.

We saw plenty of caravans and couriers on the highway, but no one wanted anything to do with us.

As we rode, my plan solidified. I'd seek out a mage in Bexden, report about what had happened, and ask they contact Perras Tul in Vale on my behalf. Perras Tul was a mage I knew. He wasn't exactly a friend, but he did owe me a few favors. I'd request that Perras Tul meet us in Bexden then teleport us to Vale so we could report to the Guild Master there. That would at least save us a couple of weeks of travel.

I told Wylla my plan, and she agreed that it was worth a try.

A half day away from Bexden, we finally encountered a half dozen Shielders wearing the colors of Kreed's Keep and riding east towards us. It was their job to stop for travelers, so they listened to our report. I didn't mention the rogue mage or the magical attack on the inn. I just told them that the inn had been burned to the ground and there were some dead bodies and the whole thing looked suspicious.

"Duly noted," the commander said. "We'll investigate, rest assured of that." He asked a bunch of questions and then told me his name and asked us to inform Captain Hanton, his counterpart in Bexden, of what we had seen. Then they rode off.

"I like how you played that," Wylla said. "You didn't give them too much."

"I'm glad you approve."

By the time we arrived in Bexden, it was late afternoon. I had only been here once before and I barely remembered it.

There are several towns along the West Way, all fairly similar. They all funnel goods and raw materials from the surrounding area into caravans. Some have warehouses. Some have stock yards. And the ones without farms or mills or warehouses tended to focus on extracting money from the caravans in other ways. Harlots. Gambling halls. Pubs.

Bexden was a large town in its own right. Five or six thousand people at least. So they had a bit of everything. The town sat right at the border of the provinces of Kreed's Keep and Vale. Which is why there was a large Shielder presence there.

We rode down a dusty, wide, long main street called Highgate. It curved north off the West Way. And if I remembered correctly, Highgate would curve back down again and intersect the West Way on the far western edge of town. It was designed to accommodate the caravans. Easy in. Easy out.

The street was lined with warehouses, stables, caravan courts, and coaching inns. Most of the carters and warehousemen were hurrying to finish their work for the day, and there were a fair number of people on the street.

Wylla knew the town well, so she led us north on another main thoroughfare, Market Street, into the center of Bexden. The buildings here were all low and long—most not more than two stories tall. Many had balconies over covered porticos. Everything was constructed of wood, and I could tell where parts of the town had burned down and had been rebuilt.

"I need to find someplace to sell my ring," Wylla said.

"This is not the place to sell it. Wait until we get to Vale. Or better yet, keep it. I know some other ways to get gold."

"You want to rob a caravan?"

"Something like that."

In truth, one of the best ways to get some gold was to steal it. But instead of robbing just anyone, I stole exclusively from thieves.

Thieves were the ideal target because they couldn't run to the guard and complain that they had been robbed. The only downside was that sometimes I'd steal from a criminal who was part of a larger gang. Then the entire organization would be looking for me. And that was just as bad as dealing with the city guard.

One thought I had was to wait until the middle of the night and see if I could spot someone sneaking out of a building with gold or jewels that they had stolen. A man climbing down the side of a building is an easy target. Especially if he is focused on the window he just climbed through and not someone attacking from the ground.

My second option was to see if I could find someone

trying to sell either stolen merchandise or some kind of high value contraband. Maybe ghir. Maybe charfit. Or even dream oil brought in from Gadmark. Most towns along the West Way—including Bexden—did not have tax gates, so anyone could bring anything in or out of the town without much scrutiny. But certain substances like charfit were controlled by Imperial law. Not that there was an Imperial presence here in Bexden. No sign of that at all.

When I told Wylla my plan to liberate some gold from a criminal, she wrinkled her nose. Clearly, she was not impressed.

"That will take too long. I want a bed now—not tomorrow morning."

"And do you have a better idea?"

"Matter of fact I do," she said. "Don't worry. You'll get used to it."

I smiled at her. "Very amusing."

"How confident are you that your mage friend will actually teleport us to Vale?" she asked.

"Fairly confident," I said. "Between the news we bring and the debt he owes me, I can't see him refusing us."

"Good. Then our answer is simple. We sell the horses."

I couldn't argue with her logic. It would be fairly easy to sell the horses, and even if we got just half of what they were worth, we'd certainly have enough gold for a week or so of room and board.

We asked around and a few people recommended a ranch just north of town. It wasn't far. We rode out and after some haggling with the owner, traded the horses for more gold than I thought we'd get.

By the time we walked back into town, the sun was low in the sky. It was nice to have some coins in my bag. It got me thinking about a pair of new boots or at least fixing this pair so they'd fit better.

Wylla found us an inn near the center of town, on Alfrun Street. It was an older structure, three stories with a court-yard. Blocky and built of weathered stone. It looked like a miniature castle. The sign in front read "The Drovers Inn" and apparently it used to be the main stopping point for cattle drovers back when Bexden was a cattle market.

"I need rest and food," Wylla said. "But not necessarily in that order."

Before we ate, I wanted to find a mage and also make my report to the city guard. Wylla decided to wait for me in our room, so I came along with her to inspect it. The room was on the second floor, at the end of an upper hallway. It was cramped, but there was a window.

"It's not the Palace of the Winds, but good enough for me," she said.

"I'll try to do better next time."

"See that you do." Wylla flopped down on the bed. "Now move along and hurry back so we may dine together like civilized people. I'm going to rest."

"Yes, madam," I said. "But bolt the door behind me, if you please."

"Why? Are you actually worried about me, Bander?"

"Not really. I know how formidable you are." I smiled back at her. But she was correct. I was worried about her. And I planned to return as quickly as I could.

I left the inn and followed Market Street north until I encountered a bored city guardsman. He became slightly more alert when I asked where his office was, and even more alert when I mentioned 'Hanton'—the name of the captain the Shielders had given me. The guard offered to take me to see Captain Hanton.

I had been heading in the wrong direction. The office was in an old barbican on the south edge of town. Captain Hanton was nearly out the door when we arrived. And he didn't look too pleased that I was keeping him from his evening meal.

I quickly made my report, but he kept trying to interrupt me.

Finally, he asked, "Where was this inn again?"

"Fifty miles east of here. Stag & Pennant. Surely you know of it."

Hanton shook his head. "Citizen, if it don't roll in on a caravan or kick up a cloud of dust while stampeding, I don't know anything about it."

After I repeated the entire story again, he began to take some notes in a thick logbook. Then he said, "We'll get word to Kreed's Keep. They'll decide what's to be done about it. In the meantime, Werask will lock it down."

I nodded and then asked him where I might find a member of the Guild.

"We don't have a guild house here. Too small. The capital don't really care about us."

"I realize that. But you must have some mages here."

"Of course we do. Dalish Mor. Talagin. Old Felde."

"I need to speak to one of them."

"Come with me, then," Hanton said. "Old Felde spends a lot of time at the Iron Bell. It's on my way home."

Captain Hanton led me to the west side of town where the buildings stood closer together and the roadways were dirt instead of cobblestone.

"He's mostly deaf, you know."

"Felde?" I asked.

"Yes. Best to stand to his left. Fairly close."

"Thanks for the advice."

With that, Hanton left me at the Iron Bell, a low sprawling tavern that looked like maybe it had once been a stable block. Inside it was noisy and crowded and smelled of grilled meat, ale, and sweat.

Hanton had told me that I would have no problem recognizing Felde, and he was right. Amidst the sullen and exhausted looking laborers, carters, warehousemen, porters, drovers, and teamsters was one man who stood out like a toadstool in a carrot patch. In fact he looked very much like an oversized toadstool, with a billowing embroidered linen doublet and a bright red broad brimmed hat.

I pushed my way through the noisy crowd and saw that Felde was beckoning to a barmaid. I intercepted her and asked her to get the mage another of whatever he was drinking and the same for me. And then I walked over to Felde. He was short and a bit doughy and looked up at me through squinty eyes. I had expected an older man, but the mage looked to be not much older than Wylla.

"You hear better on the left, don't you?" I asked.

"What?"

I shifted my position and spoke up. "Captain Hanton sent me."

"Hanton, eh? What does he want?"

"Hanton doesn't want anything. I'm the one who needs your help."

"What kind of help?"

"It's Guild-related," I said.

"Then go ask someone in Marston Hills. There's a guild-hall there." He turned away from me and tried to take a drink from his tankard, forgetting that he had already drained it.

I moved closer, towered over him. "My name is Bander, and I worked at the Imperial Ministry of the Axe. Red Shoulder Captain. I did a lot of favors for the Guild back in the day."

"Good for you," he said.

Despite his dismissive tone, I could tell I had piqued his interest. At that moment, the barmaid returned with a pitcher and an extra tankard. She refilled Felde's tankard and filled one for me. I thanked her and gave her some coin.

The mage took a swig of ale and stared at me for a moment. Then he said, "Make it quick. I have to piss."

I explained that I needed him to contact a mage in Vale named Perras Tul and ask him to come to Bexden.

Felde snorted. "You have many mages at your beck and call, do you?"

"Just contact him and tell him that Bander needs him to come to Bexden at once. I'll be at the Drover's Inn."

"I can do that," he said.

"Good."

"For a fee."

"I just bought you some ale."

"Let's consider that the down payment."

A bit of a queasy feeling welled up in my gut. It was the same feeling I got whenever I was about to make a bargain with a mage.

"And what of the balance?" I asked.

"A trifle," Felde said. "It won't take even an hour of your time."

I glared at him.

"And," he continued. "I will contact Perras Tul at once."

I sighed. "Tell me what you want me to do."

And so he did.

Chapter Nineteen

WHEN I RETURNED TO OUR ROOM AT THE DROVER'S INN, THE DOOR WAS UNLOCKED AND WYLLA WAS ASLEEP. She looked much younger when she was sleeping. And certainly more peaceful. I sat down on the edge of the bed and debated whether to wake her. But then her eyes opened.

"You didn't bolt the door," I said.

"It was too much effort to get out of bed," she said in a sleepy voice. "Mission accomplished?"

"Halfway accomplished." I told her about the city guards, Captain Hanton, and Felde the mage and his task.

"So what's this errand you have to run?"

I got up from the bed. "It's ridiculous."

"How so?"

"He wants me to intervene in a lover's spat."

"What?" Wylla sat up, fully awake. "Tell me everything."

"Apparently Felde had a relationship with a woman named Robie. They got into a big argument and now she is seeing another man. But Felde swears that he loves her and she him, but is now just acting out of spite."

"So you have to convince her to go back to Felde?"

"Not exactly. He wants me to have a word with his rival. A blacksmith, as it happens."

"And would this 'word' you're supposed to have require any fisticuffs?"

"I think that's the idea."

"Why you? I mean, beyond the obvious."

I shrugged. "I was the proverbial stranger walking into a tavern. Anonymous. From his perspective, it's perfect. The blacksmith is taken out of the picture, and there are no ties to Felde."

"You're not going to kill him?"

"No."

"Then what are you going to do?"

"I'm not sure yet."

Wylla stood from the bed and stretched. "Well, it seems like a lot of bother just to get word to some mage in Vale."

"It's beginning to look that way."

"Why do we even need him? Can't this Felde teleport us to Vale?"

"Theoretically, but a private portal is very expensive. Who knows what Felde would ask me to do in exchange. Maybe deal with ten romantic rivals."

"So this errand only buys you a message to your friend? Seems like a rather poor bargain to me."

"I could try to track down one of the other two mages in town, but that would slow us down even further."

"Well, since we have no choice, I guess I'm coming with you."

"Fine. Let's get this over with."

"After we eat."

We went downstairs to the dining room and sat at a long table with a bench seat that was set against the back wall in the corner. I prefer sitting in the corner of a tavern, situated so I can see of much as the room as much as possible.

Wylla knew what I was doing and teased me for being paranoid.

"Not paranoid, careful," I said. "I'm just being careful. I've always been a careful sort."

She moved over and sat down on the bench next to me. "Calm yourself. We will eat quickly."

A barmaid came over and I discovered that one of my favorite meals was being served tonight: turkey stew. We ordered food and ale and I looked at Wylla. The last time we were at a table together, she had a blade pressed to my inner thigh. Now her hand rested there. And she had a mischievous smile on her face.

"At least you get your turkey stew," she said.

"Don't mock me. That stew just might be the pinnacle of my day."

"Oh really?" She arched one eyebrow. "We'll have to think of something to top that."

"Like run a blacksmith out of town?"

"I've been pondering that," Wylla said. "What if we join forces with the blacksmith? Aid true love?"

"How do you know she's in love with the blacksmith?"

"Who wouldn't love a blacksmith?"

The barmaid returned with our food and ale. The stew was hot and although there were more chunks of turnip than turkey, the food suited me just fine. Wylla dug into her meal with gusto as well. We had both been starved for too long, so we didn't say much more. Just focused on eating.

After we finished and settled up, we went out to Alfrun Street. It was dark, but there was still a good amount of people moving about, looking for food and drink and maybe some companionship. Felde had told me, in great detail, where to find the blacksmith. So, after getting my bearings, I was able to lead us there. As we walked, Wylla asked if I wanted to hear her plan.

"Of course."

"Are you sure? It might make you feel a bit stupid. For not thinking of it yourself, that is."

"I'll take that chance."

"Very well, then." She took my hand and skipped a little as we walked—like a young girl. "It's all about timing."

"It usually is."

"This time tomorrow, we'll be in Vale, right? You still think your friend will show up and teleport us out of here?"

"I do."

"So all we need to do is make this Felde *believe* that you drove the blacksmith away."

"I'm not following your reasoning."

"That's what we do with the blacksmith. Reason with him."

"Reason with him so that he leaves town?"

"Yes. Exactly."

"That's your big idea? Talk with the blacksmith instead of breaking his leg?"

"Enlist his aid. Get him to play along. He'll pretend to leave town, Felde will be happy, *poof*, we'll be in Vale. Mission accomplished."

"The blacksmith will return," I said.

"Of course he will return. To be with his true love."

"Felde won't be too happy about that."

"Who cares? We'll be long gone."

I shook my head. "It won't end well for the blacksmith. Mages don't enjoy being deceived. Better the blacksmith just accepts his broken leg."

"What do we care about the blacksmith? Or Felde. As I said, we'll be long gone."

"Weren't you the one crowing about true love? Now you

just want to rope an innocent man into your deception and leave him holding the bag? Besides, what if we ever come back to Bexden? Felde would certainly hold a grudge."

"I'm never coming back here again. Once we kill the Dragon, I'm done with the south."

I didn't say anything, but I was encouraged by the fact that Wylla was thinking about the future. I had been very worried about her mood swings. Over the past several days, her disposition lurched from despondent to gleeful—often in the course of a single hour. That was never a good sign.

We arrived at the blacksmith's shop. It was locked up tight, but Wylla pointed out a little cabin set off in back of the workshop. The windows were lit up by candles, so someone was likely inside.

"Stay here," I told Wylla. Then I moved closer to one of the windows. I could hear voices. It sounded like the blacksmith wasn't alone. I knocked at the door.

"Who is it?" a male voice called.

"Bander of Rundlun."

"The shop's closed. Come back tomorrow."

"I have an urgent matter to discuss with you."

"Tomorrow!"

"I said, it was urgent."

A moment later, the door opened and a tall, wiry man stood in front of me, scowling. He didn't look at all like a blacksmith. More like an archer.

"Why, in Dynark's name, do you think you can interrupt a man's peaceful dinner?"

"Felde sent me." I stepped into the room.

His eyes widened and I could see what would happen next —even though it took less than two seconds. He grunted and snatched at something near the door. I saw him wrap his hands around an iron bar as thick around as a broom handle.

Then he jumped back and swung the bar like it was an axe and he was preparing to split a log.

I had defended myself against this type of attack thousands of times. I knew exactly what to do. Because it didn't matter if it was an iron bar, a club, or an axe. Any weapon that's swung won't do much damage if it's moving too slowly. The trick to defending against an attack like this is to step in quickly and make impact before the weapon gets up to speed.

So that's just what I did. I danced right in, leading with my shoulder.

The blacksmith's iron bar bounced off the slab of muscle at the top of my arm, but I just kept going.

I bowled him over and ripped the iron bar from his hands. Momentum is a useful thing.

The blacksmith toppled backward, crashing into a small table set with dinner.

I stood over him. At that point I had a few options. I could bash his head in with the iron bar. That would be easy enough. He was basically defenseless, sprawled on the ground.

Or, if I just wanted to intimidate the man, I could bend the iron bar with my bare hands right in front of him. The bar was certainly long enough to provide me with enough leverage to do so. And it would be an impressive show of my strength.

But I didn't do either of those things.

I tossed the bar away behind me and said, "I just want to talk."

Wylla appeared in back of me. I don't know why she decided not to stay where I had left her. I glared at her, but she ignored me.

"I want to talk as well," she told the blacksmith. "I have an idea for you."

~

I made one stop at a coaching inn on the south end of town, then returned to the Iron Bell tavern. It was even more crowded now, and a pair of lute players were entertaining the revelers with some bawdy tunes. Felde was still there. At his same table.

"You work quickly," he smirked at me. "You must've enjoyed it. Still, I hope you didn't hurt the poor sod too much."

"Well, there was a complication."

His face fell. "What kind of complication?"

"Were you able to contact Perras Tul?"

"Yes, yes. He'll be here in the morning. Tell me of this complication."

"I better show you."

We left the tavern, and as we walked, I explained that I had visited the blacksmith with every intention of running him out of town.

"Good, good," Felde said. He waddled quickly, trying to keep up with me.

"Not so good," I said. "It seems there's another party involved. The blacksmith is already out of the picture."

"He told you that?"

"Yes."

"Seems to me like a ploy to avoid getting thumped!"

"That's what I thought. But the man was quite specific. Told me that he had been discarded like an old boot. Robie has a new paramour, and they are planning to head west. Start some kind of farm."

"Nonsense. She would never leave Bexden."

"I was as suspicious as you. Until I saw what I saw."

"Tell me."

"I'd rather you see for yourself."

We didn't speak again until we arrived at Robie's shop, where she also lived. Light from candles shone through the narrow windows, casting a soft glow on the ketlyder shrubs which grew around the structure.

I motioned for Felde to be still and then I quietly moved to the window. I peered in and saw what I expected to see. Then I signaled for Felde to join me at the window.

He did his best to tiptoe over and then he squinted and looked inside.

I forced myself to appear impassive as I watched him react to what he was seeing.

Inside, on a silken divan were two women, locked in an embrace, kissing lustily.

Felde recognized Robie. He didn't recognize the other woman, a buxom redhead. But I did.

It was Wylla, of course. Carrying out her plan. Her second plan.

I tugged at the mage's cloak and motioned him away from the window. He had seen enough. We didn't speak until we were a few blocks away.

"I had no idea." Felde looked like he had seen a ghost.

"Obviously true love," I said. "From what the blacksmith said, they were paramours from way back. The redhead just got into town, and I guess they picked up where they left off."

The mage said nothing. He still looked flummoxed.

"I consider our transaction complete," I said. "I spoke to the blacksmith as you requested, but I have no intention of intimidating a woman."

"Of course not," Felde finally said.

"Good." I clapped him on the shoulder. "Don't worry. There are plenty of fish in the sea, and I'll wager that a distinguished gentleman such as you will have no problems landing another. Perhaps one even more beautiful."

"Perhaps," he said, looking down at the ground.

I said, "I'll walk you back to the tavern."

Felde nodded. It would be a lot for him to think about, but I had arranged a distraction in the form of a hired courtesan waiting at his table at the Iron Bell.

Back in our room at the inn, Wylla was once again stretched out on the bed.

She grinned at me. "My plan went well, didn't it?"

"Yes, but I daresay that it looked like you enjoyed playing your part a bit too much."

"What can I say? Robie is a masterful kisser. Better than you, probably."

I didn't say anything. Just stretched out on the floor and fell asleep.

Chapter Twenty

❦

"WE CAN'T BE SEEN TOGETHER," I TOLD WYLLA THE NEXT MORNING.

"Why? Do you have a secret paramour as well?" She grinned a mischievous grin, her face framed by her coiled auburn tresses, which were tousled by a night of sleep.

"I'm still concerned about Felde. I don't want him to discover our ruse." I stretched my body, which was stiff and cramped from a night on the floor.

"Fair enough," she said. "I'll stay in bed and amuse myself. Maybe you would be so kind as to fetch me some aebol or a meat pie."

"Certainly, my lady." I mock bowed at her. "Perhaps you could ready yourself, though? We may have to leave quickly."

I went down to the dining room and asked the barkeep if anyone had asked for me, but no one had. I told him that I was expecting a visitor and would be in my room waiting. Then I convinced him to fix me a tray of bread and smoked meats, which I brought up to Wylla.

She was dressed and ready to go, but she also was very hungry. Between mouthfuls of bread, Wylla told me that she had been impressed by the way I disarmed the blacksmith.

"Brawling is one of the few things I'm good at," I said.

At that moment there was a knock on the door. I opened it and a tall, gaunt man stood in the hallway. He wore the robes of the Black Following. His eyes were light and his hair had more grey than when I had last seen him. But at least he didn't look angry.

"Perras Tul," I said. "Thank you for coming."

He glanced over at Wylla, who was still finishing up her meal.

"Am I interrupting something?" the mage asked.

"Not at all good sir," Wylla said. "Bander, will you not introduce us?"

I did so and quickly explained our situation.

When I had finished, Perras Tul said, "That sounds like a bad business. We need to alert Guild Master Herron."

"We're ready to go whenever you are."

"No time like the present then." Perras Tul pressed his hands together. He closed his eyes and whispered a single word.

Suddenly, I felt the temperature in the room drop. A glowing portal swirled into existence. Tendrils of magical energy twisted like vines around the shimmering magical doorway.

Wylla took a step back, awestruck. She probably had never witnessed a teleport spell before.

"It's fine," I told her. "Perfectly safe."

"Are you sure?"

"Quite sure, my lady," Perras Tul said.

She looked at me again, for reassurance.

I took her hand and led her into the light. I felt a momentary loss of balance, like stepping on a stone that rolls under your feet. But then we were through the portal and into a large wood-paneled hall, presumably 400 miles away from Bexden.

"Welcome to Vale," Perras Tul said from behind us.

Wylla gripped my arm to steady herself. Her eyes darted around the hall which was quite a bit larger than the room we had just left.

"Your first time teleporting?" Perras Tul asked.

"Yes. Is it that obvious?"

"Nothing to be ashamed of," Perras Tul said.

"Better than riding for a couple of weeks," I said.

"I may have to vomit," Wylla said in a quiet voice.

"That's a common reaction," Perras Tul said. "Let's get you some fresh air."

He guided us through the hall and then along a corridor which led outside to a small square paved in cobblestones. All around us rose ancient three and four story stone buildings adorned with statues, iron gates, and decorative details. We were in the Pinney District near the old Keep on the west side of Vale, a sprawling capital city on the southern edge of the Rangelands. Most of the other buildings in Vale were timber-framed structures with slate tile or thatched roofs, but this wealthy neighborhood was filled with stone temples and estates that were at least five hundred years old.

I looked back at the structure we had just left and asked, "What is this place?"

"The former guildhall," Perras Tul said. "Now it's used as barracks and storage, mostly. Let us make our report to Herron. It's not far."

He navigated through twisting alleys and narrow streets that were certainly not designed to accommodate wagons or carts. I guessed that, back when this quarter was being built, the privileged few might have had an aversion to dung carts rolling past their opulent mansions.

We continued to walk, and I saw the towers of the Keep

rise over the other buildings in the Pinney District. Even this early, the air was hot and dry and dusty. I was glad to walk in the shade.

Before long we arrived at what was presumably the new guildhall. It was a converted temple, with spindly towers nearly as tall as the Keep's. An ancient statue of Hovend still stood in front of the old temple. The antediluvian god of the plains sat astride a rearing Valer steed and glared down upon his minions.

Wylla looked visibly impressed by the scale of the statue.

"Have you ever been to Vale?" I asked her.

"Once. But not to this part of the city."

We were ushered into a dark reception hall, lined with bench seats. Intricate tapestries hung from the walls, and ornate free-standing candelabras provided the only light. Perras Tul approached the clerk on duty, a young acolyte wearing the robes of the Black. Wylla and I sat down while Perras Tul conferred with the clerk. Then the acolyte gestured in the air. There was a brief crackle of energy and then a glowing blue ring the size of a dinner plate material- ized in the air in front of the clerk. I recognized this as a farspeech spell, which allowed the mage to speak to another mage wherever he or she might be located.

Wylla clutched my arm. "I think I've seen just about all the magic I care to," she whispered.

The clerk spoke into the flowing ring for a minute or two, then dismissed the spell.

"The Guild Master will see you."

I stood up, but then the clerk said, "Pardon, good sir. I meant that the Guild Master will see Perras Tul. You may remain here."

Perras Tul glanced at me knowingly then passed through a pair of double doors on the far end of the hall.

I sat down back next to Wylla. This was typical Guild

bureaucracy. They needed me or Wylla to provide them with all the details of what had happened with the rogue mage, but they were going to take their time asking us.

In truth, I didn't mind waiting here. The bench wasn't too uncomfortable. And air in the large dark stone room was a pleasant temperature. But I could tell that Wylla was getting more and more anxious. After a quarter hour, she stood up and told me that she wanted to walk around outside.

"I need to stay here," I said. "Once I brief Herron, I'll consider our obligation to have been fulfilled."

"I'll come back in an hour or so, then."

"Stay out of trouble. And stay on the west side of the city."

She smirked at me. "Yes, father." Then she left the guildhall.

I leaned back against the cool stone wall, stretched my legs out, closed my eyes, and waited.

It was a half hour later when Perras Tul returned with another acolyte.

"The Guild Master to ready to receive you now."

"Let's get this over with then."

I followed the two mages through the double doors and into a warren of corridors. We ascended a tall staircase and made our way up to the top floor of the guildhall. There we entered a very large, very opulent office. As I walked through the carved linnaewood doors, I immediately smelled the strong scent of darilla, which probably came from the scented oil which was burning in two large cressets on either side of the office.

The office itself was elegantly appointed with various tall-backed chairs, sturdy-looking bookshelves, blocky linnae-wood furniture decorated with gold inlay, and a large Myssian carpet laid over a finely polished wood floor. Just inside the doorway, a battle mage stood guard with a dour expression on his face. On the other end of the office was Guild Master Herron, giving instructions to another aide. The Guild Master looked up at us and motioned us closer. He gave some final instructions to the aide, dismissed him, and then strode over to us. Herron was a tall, thin man and he moved like a bird.

"Bander of Rundlun," he said. "Your reputation precedes you."

"I'm honored, Master Herron."

"May I offer you something?"

"Thank you, but no."

"Right, to business, then. Please sit down. I would like to ask you more of this Dragon person."

We sat around a large hexagonal table which matched the rest of the furniture in the office.

"I don't know too much about him—just what the nurse-maid Wylla witnessed."

"Which was what?"

"Some sort of bargain between this rogue mage and the mistress of Lockwell Farms in Hytwen. Her name is Ellia Lockwell."

"And what was the nature of this bargain?"

"Wylla wasn't sure, but it might have involved one of the children. Perhaps going into service for the mage."

I had to speak very carefully. I needed to disclose the fact that Jillen Lockwell had been abducted by the mage, but I didn't want to reveal that the girl had any sort of magical abilities.

"The nursemaid wasn't certain of what she heard?" Herron asked.

"Ellia Lockwell sent all the servants away save Wylla, who was supposed to be attending to the children. But Wylla chanced to hear a snippet of conversation as she was passing in the staircase."

"Pity she didn't linger." Herron absentmindedly twirled a carved stone talisman hanging from a chain around his neck. "Still, I am confused about how a discussion about sending a child into service with a mage ended in the alleged destruction of an inn."

In order to protect Jillen Lockwell, I needed to embellish the story with some fabrications.

"According to a survivor of the fire, the child tried to run away at the inn which caused her new master to fly into a rage."

"So he burned the building down?"

"I saw the inn for myself. It had been utterly destroyed and it appeared to have been a magical attack."

Herron nodded and was silent for a time.

I wasn't sure what he was thinking, but there were certainly a lot of holes in the story I had just told him. Herron must have come to the same conclusion.

He said, "This entire affair perplexes me, Bander, as I'm sure it does you. Tell me again how you happened to be at this destroyed inn."

I told him that Wylla had feared for the child's welfare and asked my assistance in checking that the girl was safe.

"And so, the four of you all found yourself at this inn— somewhere east of Bexden? You, the nursemaid, the child, and the Dragon. Is that correct?"

He was toying with me, I could tell. But I really had no other choice than to stick with my story.

"Not quite, Master Herron. I was on the road, traveling to Bexden when I made the acquaintance of Wylla. She told me her story and I agreed to accompany her to the inn."

"And when you arrived, you found this inn destroyed by the mage?"

"Yes."

"But why would this Dragon and his new servant even

stop at an inn? Why would he not have simply opened a portal to their final destination? Surely, being an Imperial Investigator, you wondered the same thing."

"Of course," I said. "It was my understanding that he had some other business at the inn. And it crossed my mind that perhaps it was this other business that led to the destruction of the inn, not the child's disobedience."

"Perhaps."

"In any case, I felt the obligation to bring this matter to your attention, Master Herron. Now you know as much as I."

"Which is still not as much as I need to know."

"Indeed. But I must ask, are you familiar with anyone by the epithet of 'the Dragon?'" I asked.

"Not at all. Seems rather childish to me. Nevertheless, I will contact the Grand Guild Master and discuss how to proceed. But rest assured, this matter will be investigated."

I stood up and nodded at the Guild Master and Perras Tul in turn. "If you need me further, I'll remain in Vale for a few days."

"Thank you and go in peace, Bander of Rundlun," Herron said.

As I departed the guildhall, I wasn't sure what to think. Herron obviously had his doubts about my tale. But I had a feeling that he might follow up on the destruction of the Stag & Pennant anyway—if for no other reason than it would make him look good. Bringing a rogue mage to justice would certainly be a feather in his cap. But I had no expectations of any real assistance from Herron. The Guild moved slowly. Painfully slowly. Herron would need to confer with Vale's Magister of the Wand as well as Savar Ossiline, Guild Master of Kreed's Keep before he even sent someone to investigate the site of the inn.

"Hold, Bander!" Perras Tul called. He had emerged from the guildhall a few moments after me. "That was quite a tale you told in there."

"I don't know what you're talking about." I kept walking even though I needed to stay in the vicinity of the guildhall in order to rendezvous with Wylla.

"Come on. You obviously know much more about this mysterious Dragon fellow than what you shared with Herron."

"Perhaps. But your Guild Master now has everything he needs to investigate. Believe me, the rogue mage is quite real, and I am certain he destroyed that inn—and murdered innocent people in the process."

Perras Tul said, "Well, you're certainly not making life easier for me."

"What do you mean?"

"I've been ordered to suspend my other duties."

"Why?"

"Why do you think? I'll probably get stuck with the task of traveling to that inn and investigating. And believe me, it won't be as easy as teleporting in and taking a quick look around. No one in the guildhall has linked there, so I'll likely need to spend a day or two in the saddle."

"We all have a job to do."

"That's a fine attitude."

I turned and clapped him on the shoulder. "If it makes you feel any better, your debt to me is almost paid in full."

"Almost?"

"A small amount of gold will wholly settle the debt."

He thought about that for a moment, and then asked, "Just how much gold are we talking about, you scoundrel?"

I named an amount which happened to be the rough cost

of a new pair of boots. Perras Tul sighed and fished out his purse.

"Why do I feel like I am getting the bad end of this deal?"

"You're not. I could have asked for gemstones."

I bid Perras Tul farewell and walked a wide circle through the Pinney District. I didn't want him to see me and Wylla together, and I certainly didn't want him to question her directly. Fortunately, I spotted her a block away from the guildhall.

"There you are," she said. "How did you fare? Will they help us?"

I hooked my arm in hers. "I will tell you once we are away from here."

We left the area quickly, heading to Market Way, which was one of the main thoroughfares through the city, and therefore crowded with all sorts of pedestrian, mounted, and wheeled traffic.

"Why the secrecy?" Wylla asked.

"I may have been less than forthcoming with the Guild."

She smiled at me. "Good man."

"We'll see. I don't expect any assistance from Herron. That means we need to find the Dragon all by ourselves."

"Fine with me. Let's get on with it."

"First, I need a pair of new boots. I'm not sure where we're heading, but the more I think about it, the more I think the Dragon has departed Vale. He'd be stupid to stay in the city after what he's done."

"What do you mean?"

"Once the Guild gets to the Stag & Pennant, they'll be able to learn all kinds of things—possibly even who cast the fireball spells that burned the place down. If it's one of their own mages, they'll know it."

Wylla had a million more questions, but I wanted to keep moving. So I took her arm, and we headed due east toward the Market District. Soon we joined a parade of tradesmen, carters, laborers, hawkers, and all manner of folk heading to the large central plaza to buy and sell all day long.

"Do you even know where you're going?" Wylla asked.

"Vaguely. There's some sort of cobbler alley around here."

No sooner had I uttered the words 'cobbler alley' when I felt a tug on my jerkin.

"Good sir, I know where every cobbler's shop in the city is, and even which is the best." A grimy street urchin still held a corner of my jerkin in his little hand. "I'll take you there!"

"Is that so?"

"Indeed. You want to go to Millican's shop. He's honest and makes the finest shoes." The boy was maybe six years old, maybe seven. I was a poor judge of children's' ages.

"I'm not looking for fine shoes," I said. "I'm looking for boots."

"Boots? Why didn't you say so? If it's a quality pair of boots you need, you must visit Blind Sittig."

"Is he a cobbler?"

"Of course."

"Is he really blind?"

"Yes, sir. He is indeed."

"And how does that work?"

The boy scrunched up his face. "He can see with his hands. Or just as good as see."

I was planning to telling the boy to move along, but Wylla intervened.

"Very well," she said with a smile. "Take us to this blind cobbler, and if he's as good as you say he is, there might be a coin in your future."

The urchin walked us over to Caveward Lane, which was lined on either side with makeshift wooden stalls covered with bright fabric designed to provide a little relief from the strong southern sun. A dizzying array of items were on display; everything from bolts of cloth, to bags and satchels, to ornamental knives, and spices tied in small squares of fabric. We ignored all of it and wound deeper into the Market District, dodging beggars, hagglers, chickens who had somehow gained their freedom, and even a rotund nobleman being carried in an ornately painted sedan chair.

Beckoning us to stay close, the boy slid between two stalls and disappeared into a rough stone tunnel. I took Wylla's hand, and we followed our guide into the darkness. I was ready for some sort of treachery, but the tunnel was merely a quick way through to another alley, which was far less crowded and filled with at least a dozen cobbler shops.

"Do not be swayed by what you see here, good sir! Blind Sittig's shop is at the end of Caidam Row here. We're very close."

We continued to follow the boy, but I thought to myself that if the cobbler he was promoting didn't look good enough, I'd have plenty of other choices right here. But finally we arrived at our destination. It was a ramshackle cabin that looked barely bigger than a woodshed. There was no sign, the one window was grimy with dust and spiderwebs, and the front door sagged on its hinges.

Wylla and I looked at each other, sharing our doubts with a glance. The boy tugged at my sleeve again and we all entered the cabin. My eyes struggled to adjust to the darkness, but I could tell that the cabin was significantly larger than I originally thought. It stretched away from the doorway for twenty or thirty feet, finally ending in shadows. There were all manner of shelves, work tables, and chests, over-flowing with dusty leather hides, covered pots, wooden blocks, tools, and other materials.

An old voice called out, "Who's there?"

"It's I, sir. Jory. I bring customers. An old warrior, by the looks of him. And his lady."

"And what may I do for you, sir warrior?" asked a brittle voice from the far side of the cabin.

I was barely able to make out the figure of a man rising from a chair. He walked closer, emerging from the shadows into a dim shaft of sunlight near the front door. The cobbler was over 70 years old, for certain, and thin as a scarecrow. His body was bent, and it looked as if he had a difficult time walking—most likely from spending his life hunched over a workbench. And as the light caught the man's face, I could see his milky, sightless eyes.

"I need boots," I said. "The boy told us you are the best cobbler in Vale."

"I am indeed, and the boots I make aren't cheap. My name is Sittig."

"My name is Bander and I can pay, but I need something today."

He waved his hands. "Impossible. It takes me the better part of two months to make a pair of boots."

"I'm not looking for a new pair. I'm looking for anything you can fit to my feet. I'll even take a dead man's pair. I'm not picky."

He said, "Take off the boots you're wearing now. You can sit on the bench."

As I sat down, I told him that the boots on my feet weren't made for me and didn't fit right.

"Well, we can start there," he said. "It much easier to fit an existing pair of boots than build new ones."

I pulled off the boots I had taken from Ortwen's marshal. He spent a few moments touching every part of the boots. Then he grunted to himself.

"Bring your feet over to me. I need to feel them."

Sittig had a surprisingly light touch, and a steady hand. Without speaking, he ran his fingers along my feet, pinching and probing like a sculptor. He also used an array of calipers and other measuring devices to record the size of my foot although I had no idea how he was reading the devices.

Finally, he said, "Leave your old boots with me. I can make them fit perfectly. They'll be better than a new pair. Much better."

"How long?"

"A day at least."

"I'll need them sooner."

He shook his head. "The leather needs to be steamed and stretched and worked. It takes time. Even for me."

Before I could protest further, Wylla asked, "What are those?"

I looked over to where she was pointing. A work table was covered with a half dozen pairs of children's slippers. They were old and worn, and some were barely intact.

"I'm afraid I don't know to what you are referring, my lady," Sitting said.

Wylla remembered she was speaking to a blind man and described the table of small shoes.

"Ah, those are for Vardagan," Sittig said.

"Are they for children?"

"I don't know what they are for. I sell them to Vardagan. He peddles them outside the city. That's all I know." He made his way over to a shelf on the other side of the workshop and felt around among the items stacked there.

"Don't you repair them?" Wylla asked. "They are barely more than scraps."

"Why do you ask? Are you willing to give me a better price than Vardagan?"

"I'm just curious who would buy such wretched shoes for their children."

Sittig continued to fish around the shelves. "I buy all sorts of worn and discarded shoes. Some I repair, some I use for pieces, others I sell." He pulled a pair of dusty sandals from the shelf. "Here we are."

"And who is Vardagan?" Wylla asked.

"A peddler on Chycott Street."

"I can take you to him," the boy chirped. "He sells all manner of goods."

Sittig gave me the sandals to wear until my boots were ready and told me to return at noon tomorrow. We settled on a price for the repair and left the shop with our young guide. I had no idea why Wylla was so interested in the peddler.

Chapter Twenty-One

VARDAGAN THE PEDDLER HAD LEFT THE CITY ALREADY. That's what his wife told us. I didn't hear much more than that because Wylla then sent me away to get some meat skewers. I could tell by her expression that she felt she'd have better luck with Vardagan's wife without my presence. So I decided to take a walk. I never found a food vendor. Wrong part of the city, I guess.

When I returned to the street outside Vardagan's home, Wylla was waiting for me, but the boy was no longer with her.

"Where's your new son?" I quipped.

"Jory's doing an errand for us. Let's find a pub. I think I may have figured something out."

A quarter hour later we were in a small tavern off Morland Cross. We sat around a corner table and I had my back to the wall—just the way I liked it. I told Wylla about my conversation with Herron and the story I had told him about meeting her on the road and being asked to help and then arriving at the inn which had been destroyed. I also admitted to the blunder of the tale and how Herron had asked why a mage would even stop at an inn when he could just teleport home with the child.

"And here I was thinking you were a crafty fellow who could actually think on his feet!" She shoved me playfully. "What did the Guild Master say to your story?"

"Not much, but Perras Tul was suspicious. That's why I wanted to get us out of the Pinney District. The last thing we need is the Guild interrogating you."

I took a swallow of ale. It was Beolute ale, but it tasted a bit too watery to me. Better than nothing though.

"Now tell me of this wild goose chase with the peddler," I said.

Wylla sat back in her chair. "I don't know. Something about seeing those small shoes at the cobbler's place made me think. What if they were for Jillen?"

"That's not very likely."

"Even if they weren't, think about the situation. The Dragon is living somewhere outside the city, is he not? You said so yourself."

"I said he wouldn't return to the city after what he did on the West Way."

"Yes, but why would he stay in the city to begin with? With all these people around, there would be a greater chance of him being discovered. I just get the feeling that his lair is somewhere more secluded."

I didn't say anything.

Wylla continued, "In Hytwen we had a fair number of peddlers visit us. Any place that's somewhat remote is in need of a peddler's goods. It made me think that if the Dragon lived out in the wilderness, he might do business with a peddler."

"So you think that Vardagan sells shoes to the Dragon, and can lead us to him?"

"No." She took a drink of her ale.

"No?"

"Not Vardagan. But maybe someone like him."

"You're speaking in riddles again," I said.

"Vardagan's wife told me that he sells those scraps of leather to a ranchman to the north who makes leather balls for his children. Toys. So Vardagan's not the right peddler, but I sent Jory to ask around. Maybe there's a peddler who has seen a mage living out of the city somewhere."

I finished my ale and smiled at Wylla. "It's as good a notion as any. Maybe you should be the investigator."

We left the tavern and headed to the north end of the city via Lean Gate Road. There were a number of inns there that were a slightly less rough than the ones to the south—which were closer to the caravan route. I picked one called the Lindsdown House which I may have stayed at once before. It was a familiar-looking tall stone building off the main road that appeared quiet and well-maintained.

Wylla appraised the inn. "Are you sure you can afford this?"

"I will after my next errand."

"You're not planning to rob criminals again?"

"No, but I'm telling you, it's not a bad idea. However I have another task to attend to."

"I'll come with you."

I shook my head. "This involves a long walk and you need to rest."

It was true. I could tell Wylla was still weak from her injuries. In fact, we really needed to find a healer. She didn't protest when I got her settled in an upper floor room. And she even agreed to bolt the door after I left.

"Just don't get killed. I don't want to have to finish this matter by myself," she said.

"I don't intend to."

I left the inn and inspected the sandals Sittig had given

me. They were considerably worn, but if I tightened them, they'd probably last for the several miles I needed to journey outside of the city. Fortunately I was fairly close to the Lean Gate. It led north along a major way which served as the caravan route between Vale and the Steading. Easy in, easy out.

Heading north along the highway I passed by a succession of ranches and farms. Every mile or so a country lane would intersect the highway. After an hour, the sun grew stronger. There was no shade along the road, just a sea of prairie, stretching out forever.

Eventually I came to a crossing marked by a cairn of sand-colored stones. I followed the west lane which was scarcely more than a wagon track. After a mile and a half I located a serpentine brook which brought water into the surrounding fields. I sat for a moment beside the shallow brook and tried to recall where I had concealed this particular cache. Over the past year I had hidden seven or eight sacks of coins and gems outside major cities. The trick was remembering exactly where I had hidden them.

I scouted along the brook to the north and then to the south and then I got lucky and spotted my marker, a particular arrangement of very large rocks I had positioned on one shore of the brook. Each rock was actually a small boulder, heavier than what most men could lift or even roll. So I was reasonably sure the marker would never be disturbed. But still, I didn't take any chances.

My treasure was not hidden beneath the boulders; it was hidden exactly eighteen paces back to the north—under a flat rock in the middle of the brook.

Out of habit I looked around to see if anyone had followed me. Once I decided that I was completely alone, I withdrew my oilskin pouch from beneath the rock. The pouch was dripping with mud and slime but it still contained enough gems to allow me to live in the city for a year should I choose. I only took enough for a few horses and some other supplies. Then I put everything back, checked again to make sure I hadn't been observed, and began the long walk back to the city.

By the time I returned it was late in the afternoon and my feet hurt. But at least I had some resources. Between my own gems and the gold Perras Tul had given me, I felt more prepared for whatever challenges might lie ahead.

Before I returned to the inn, I sought out a bath and a barber—who both were faced with the daunting task of cleaning me up. But eventually I was made to look presentable. At least I didn't smell quite so bad. I owed Wylla that after all she had been through.

I made one more stop at a shop on Paerchen Lane that sold used clothing. The shop was well-organized and smelled of lye, and I was able to find a clean linen shirt that fit me— just barely. It had been repaired and laundered and was much better than the grimy, sweat-soaked garment I had been wearing.

Feeling much more presentable and in fairly good spirits, I made my way back to the inn. But I found the door to our room unbarred and Wylla gone.

Chapter Twenty-Two

IMMEDIATELY I EXAMINED THE ROOM FOR ANY SIGNS OF A STRUGGLE. There wasn't any blood. Nothing was broken or out of place. Downstairs, I spoke to the barkeep, but he hadn't seen Wylla. Neither had his wife, who had been attending patrons in the dining hall.

I left the Lindsdown House and crossed the neighborhood, looking down alleys and in any shops that were still open. I checked pubs and taverns, but there was no sign of her. Vale was a large, sprawling city, and I had been away for at least four hours. That meant Wylla could be anywhere. Theoretically, I could walk the entire city, but it would be dark soon and I really had no clue where she had gone. For all I knew, the Guild was interrogating her.

Without any other good options, I returned to our room, stretched out on the bed and waited.

I must have dozed off because the next thing I knew, someone was kicking at my feet.

"Wake up. I'm hungry."

Wylla was standing at the foot of the bed.

Her hair was pleated, her eyes darkened with charcoal,

and she was wearing a new dress. She twirled in front of me and I caught a whiff of her perfume. I guess she had the same idea as me, about cleaning up.

"Nice shirt," she said.

"Nice dress."

We took our nicely dressed selves downstairs and ate roasted vegetables and turkey and drank wine. A lot of wine. Then we returned to the room and Wylla took off her new dress and I took off my new shirt. Her eyes widened at the sight of my body, marked by a web of heavy scars.

"You look like someone sharpened knives on your chest," she said. "Maybe the entire Cutlers' Guild."

I shrugged. "I haven't exactly led a life of comfort."

"I should say not."

"You, on the other hand, look very comfortable."

"I have marks of my own," she smiled. Then she turned and stretched facedown on the bed.

Upon her back was a large, intricate tattoo of an owl in flight. It almost looked like the bird was coming right at me, the detail was so remarkable.

I lay down beside her and traced my finger along the lines inked into her skin, from her shoulder blades down to the small of her back.

"You didn't tell me you were a druid," I said.

Tattoos were common among druids, shamans, and priest-esses, but not among nursemaids or marshal's wives.

"I'm not. But there was a druid who lived near Hytwen for few years. I paid her to mark me."

"Why?"

"It's a long story."

"We have all night," I said, brushing my fingers along the owl's talons.

"Do we?" She purred in pleasure.

"As long as you want."

Wylla told me that in the weeks after her husband left her, she got a strange visitor in the old ura tree near her cabin. It was a large white owl, and it stayed for weeks.

"I know this sounds odd, but I spoke to that owl," she said.

"Did it speak back?"

"Of course not. But its presence comforted me. Like someone was watching over me. Does that make sense?"

"It doesn't matter if it makes sense to me. I'm not the one with the owl on my back."

Wylla laughed softly. "Do you like it? Tell me truly."

"It has a ferocious look about it. Especially with those talons and that sharp-looking beak. It doesn't bite, does it?"

"No, but I might." She turned and pulled me close.

I awoke the next morning tangled in Wylla's hair. It smelled like flowers. After a time, she stretched and smiled at me. "That was fun."

"I'll never look at an owl the same way again."

She smacked me playfully with her pillow and demanded that I go fetch her some food from the dining hall. I dressed and made my way downstairs to find something to eat—and maybe a few mugs of moxa.

Back in the bed, after we had eaten and otherwise occupied ourselves, Wylla asked me what I thought about her peddler theory.

I propped myself up on one elbow. "It's a long shot, but if the Dragon is here, he's either to the north or the south. The north is prairie and ranches and a well-traveled road to Brecalle and then The Steading. Not the best place in the world to hide out."

"And the south is jungle. The Territories."

"Well, no more jungle than is around Hytwen. The jungle doesn't actually start until a few hundred miles south."

"You've been there?"

"Many years ago. Probably before you were born."

She hit me with the pillow again. "What? When you were seven?"

"Anyway, there's an old logging road that runs all the way down to the Malverton Trading Post. If it still exists."

"So we just need to find a peddler who travels into the Tengan Territories."

"Yes, if the Dragon's lair is anywhere around Vale, it would probably be down there."

Wylla dressed in her traveling clothes and we ventured out into the city.

"Where to?" I asked.

"We need to find Jory."

"Your son?"

"That jest is no longer funny, but yes. Let us return to where we first met him."

We headed south along Lean Gate Road, a wide, dusty thoroughfare that led to the Market District. The city was in a brief lull between the opening of business and the noon hour, but still there were plenty of people around. We returned to the central plaza along Market Way and retraced our steps to where we first encountered the lad. But he was nowhere to be seen.

We loitered around for a bit, and then I told Wylla that I wanted to check on the progress of my boots. So I found the tunnel that led to Caidam Row and we knocked on the door of Sittig's shop.

After a time, the old man opened the door. "Who's there?"

"It is me, Bander."

"The warrior with the big feet?"

"Yes. I'm here with Wylla."

"Your boots won't be ready today, I'm afraid. The leather is older than I thought. Too stiff. I need one more day."

I sighed. "Are you sure about that? I can pay more if that's what it will take."

"Leather is not swayed by gold, my friend. It only responds to hard work, boiling water, and time. Come back tomorrow."

"Very well," I said.

"But can you tell us where we might find young Jory?" Wylla asked.

"I'm surprised he has not found you," Sittig said. "He's a most enterprising young lad."

I said, "We just checked Market Way."

"Try the Alley of Night. He's often hired as a runner there. But be awares. That corner of the city can be quite dangerous."

We thanked Sittig and then departed the shop.

"The Alley of Night?" Wylla asked.

"That's where the harlots ply their trade. Not that I have any firsthand knowledge of that."

"Of course not." She bumped her shoulder into my arm. "I know what that place is. I just can't picture a young boy there."

I shrugged. "As the old man said, Jory's an enterprising young lad. Why do you need to talk with him?"

"He's been asking after the different peddlers in town. Gathering information about their routes. That could save us a lot of time."

We worked our way to the northwest corner of the city, jostling through the crowds along Belfrey Gate Road and trying to avoid being run over by wagons and carts. Eventually we found the Alley of Night. I had been here before, so I knew what to expect.

The Alley of Night was not a single alley, it was a maze of alleys and passages, running a third of a mile from east to west. None were marked by street signs. You had to know where you were going, or you would find yourself hopelessly lost. And this wasn't the kind of place you wanted to get lost in.

The buildings were packed together like rotten teeth in a jaw—tight but canted at odd angles. The spidery structures stretched so high that they blocked out most of the light, creating dark narrow canyons. As my eyes adjusted to the shadows, I saw men and women silently lurking about in doorways and passages. But no sign of any children.

I took Wylla's hand and drew her closer.

"Watch yourself," I said. "The old man was not exaggerating."

"I can't believe Jory would be here."

I didn't say anything. Just led Wylla forward like I knew where I was going. Her boot-steps echoed off the cobblestones. Eyes followed us, and probably a few blackguards did more than stare. I'd wager we were being tracked.

We walked along a narrow passage, rounded the corner, and found ourselves in a small, dingy courtyard with a lone tree in the center, spindly and starved for light and water. An ornamental iron fence surrounded the tree—installed way back when, but now damaged and bent in several places. Maybe this had been a nice area a hundred years ago. Or maybe the fence was more recent. An attempt to mimic the poshness of the Pinney District.

Around the fenced tree were doorways and shuttered windows. No shops. No taverns. Everything was shut tight.

"Are you lost, good sir?"

I turned to see five men, forming up in a semicircle. Blocking our exit. Thugs, all of them. Most of them were skinny and weaselly. No weapons visible, but that didn't mean anything.

The man who spoke was a little older and a little shorter. Less scrawny, but he had a cunning look in his eyes. The leader for sure.

Wylla moved behind me at the same time I stepped forward.

"We're looking for a boy. Jory. He's doing some work for us," I said.

"No Jory here, friend."

The men moved in easily. Confident. Like they had done this a million times. Which they probably had.

I looked at each of them in turn. Marked their rhythm. Who moved first. Who moved quickest. Who moved least. It would all come in handy.

"Well, I guess we're in the wrong place," I said.

"That's for certain," the leader said. He stopped and nodded at the man to his right, the tallest of the bunch, but still maybe a half head shorter than me. Lanky, but with some muscles on him. He had pinkish skin and a wispy blond beard. It looked like he was having trouble growing it. Maybe he was second-in-command. Maybe he was their point man. But to me, he looked like a sacrificial lamb. A sacrificial lamb who had just pulled a long knife from the folds of his tunic. He started moving towards us.

I whispered to Wylla to stay back and then took a step forward to meet the tall thug halfway. My eyes darted from opponent to opponent, sizing them up one last time, and rehearsing my moves in my mind.

"I hope you two are worth it," the leader sneered.

"We're not," I growled. "We're most certainly not."

The tall thug grinned at me and danced in close, feinting with the knife. A showy slash in the air. Just to test the waters.

I stood my ground and waited for him to make a real move. Which he did a second later. And much faster than I expected.

It was another feint, but this time, it was with his left fist. A sharp jab at the bridge of my nose.

I jerked back, and when I did, the tall thug spun into me, backhanding the blade right at my kidneys. I tried to twist away, but was only partially successful. The blade sliced through my shirt and bit into my flesh. A bolt of pain shot up the side of my body.

I staggered back in disbelief. It had been a long time since I misjudged an attack.

The tall thug pressed his advantage, stepping in, keeping the bloody knife close to his own body, so I couldn't deflect it.

He knew what he was doing. And he was fast.

But had been watching my eyes, which was a mistake.

You need to watch your opponent's feet. Because most people can't make a move without changing where they're stepping. Even a little bit.

Long ago I perfected the art of looking at one thing and kicking another.

So while the tall thug was watching my eyes to see which way I'd turn to evade him, I lashed out with a sweeping kick which could have done some real damage if I had been wearing boots, but did a fine job of knocking him off balance.

The thug stumbled enough so I could grab his tunic and then we both went down. Me on top. Just how I planned it. More than 250 pounds. Slamming into his back.

At the very least he got the wind knocked out of him, but I thought I heard some ribs break. I didn't waste time thinking about that. I grabbed a fistful of his thin blond hair and slammed his head into the cobblestones, fast, like someone knocking on the door, *bang, bang.* By the third *bang* his head was partially mush, so I let go and staggered to my feet, breathing deeply, but trying not to gasp.

"Who's next?" I asked.

No one moved at first, but the other three men looked to their leader. Clearly, this was a new situation for them.

I decided to make their decision for them, by kicking the knife towards the closest thug, like I was being helpful.

He was a little ratlike man with bad skin. And when the knife skittered across the cobblestones, he looked down. He couldn't avoid it. Curiosity. Human nature. Or rat nature.

Which was fine because it gave me an extra half second to charge in fast. I hit ratman with a powerful right, driving out from my shoulder like a bolt from a ballista. My punch snapped his head back and maybe even snapped his spine. He went flying.

Two down, but I didn't stop or even pause, or even take a breath.

I barreled right into the next thug, turning hard and fast, elbow spinning and slamming full force into the bridge of his nose, which exploded into a splash of blood and bone fragments.

The fourth man watched what was happening in horror. I could see it on his face. It wasn't supposed to be like this.

I almost wanted to wait a minute so he could regain his composure. That would have been more sporting.

But to be honest, I don't have a sporting bone in my body. Besides, I could feel wetness on my side, which meant I was losing blood and couldn't afford a prolonged brawl.

So I shuffled forward and shot out a quick blow at his throat. There wasn't a lot of power behind the punch, but there didn't need to be. The throat is a pretty easy target. Soft and susceptible to a lot of things. Like the larynx getting pulverized. Which was exactly what happened. And it happened so quickly that the man didn't even have time to cry out in pain.

The leader backed away. He didn't get to be the leader by being stupid. At least not as stupid as his underlings. He witnessed the carnage. He realized that it had been a mistake to follow us into the courtyard. And he knew the only way he'd survive was to run. Run fast and hope I was too injured to chase him down.

Which was a completely accurate assessment and a reasonable course of action.

And he would have escaped, too, if Wylla hadn't snatched up the knife and threw it, point blank, at the small of his back.

She needed more practice, or a better balanced knife, or a stronger throwing arm, because the blade didn't bury itself up to the hilt in the thug's back. But it stuck in maybe an inch or so, cutting through skin and muscle, and some blood vessels. Not enough to kill him, But enough to slow him so I could take him down. Which I did. With vigor.

"Are you okay?" Wylla asked.

"I will be."

My body was still in a post-combat state, buzzing like a hive of bees. But I needed to find a healer quick. She helped me bind the cut in my side, and we quickly relieved the thugs of their purses. At least three out of the five no longer had use for earthly possessions. I wasn't sure about the other two.

As I limped out of the Alley of Night, I told Wylla, "Let's not do that again."

We found the closest healer, and he ended up costing a bit more than we took from the thugs, so it was a net loss. But he was able to minister to Wylla's old injuries as well my fresh ones. At the end of the day, we both felt better than we had any right to feel.

I was tired, so we returned to the Lindsdown House and I crawled up to our room and flopped down on the bed.

"So we're just going to give up?" Wylla asked. She didn't look inclined to join me in the bed.

"A strategic pause while we develop a new plan of attack."

"What does that mean?"

"It means that maybe our old plan shouldn't have depended so heavily upon a street urchin." I shut my eyes.

Wylla didn't say anything, but I felt her lay down beside me. Who could resist me?

But I didn't do anything about it because twenty seconds later I was asleep.

Chapter Twenty-Three

W HEN I AWOKE, I WAS ALONE. But it was still light.

I sat up and carefully probed my side where the thug had carved out a good chunk of flesh. The healer had put a healing salve on it, stitched it up, and laid his hands on the wound. I was actually surprised that it didn't hurt more. I tried to stretch, but I was sore all over. Especially my hands and shoulders. My mouth was dry and my head hurt, but it could have been worse. Much worse.

I looked at the door and wondered where Wylla had gone. Maybe off to a baker's getting me a tart. Maybe she was getting her hair perfumed again. I just hoped she wasn't wandering through another dangerous corner of Vale.

Since there wasn't much I could do, I laid back down, closed my eyes, and fell asleep again.

I dreamt I was in a big stone building—a castle or a fortress—that was on fire.

I was looking for someone, but I didn't know who. A friend or someone I was supposed to save.

All around me flames danced from floor to ceiling. Tapestries burned on the walls.

I ran through a long corridor. Behind me, parts of the ceiling collapsed, as flaming timbers crackled and exploded like logs in a campfire. I kept opening door after door, but every room was empty. And with each passing moment, the inferno grew in power.

Smoke choked my lungs, and I could barely see. Finally, I made it through a pair of glass doors on to a balcony overlooking a courtyard. I was on the third story and below me were crowds of people who had already escaped the building.

They were screaming at me, trying to warn me. Men pointed up, and women wailed in horror.

And then a dark shadow covered the balcony. I felt the rush of wind and looked up into the sky.

There was a colossal dragon.

Not a dragon from fairy tales, but one who looked as alive as any other beast that you might find in the forest or plains. It had a massive head and jaws bigger than a wagon. Each of its teeth was as long as a broadsword and dripped with blood-tinged saliva. Its eyes were each bigger than an archery target and shone with alien malevolence. As the dragon swooped closer on colossal leathery wings, I could see every scale on its body. It was clad in a marvel of natural armor. And it was coming for me.

But I had nowhere to escape.

Behind me, the fire blazed. Even though I was backed up to the edge of the balcony, a good half dozen feet from the door, I felt the heat from the fire sear my skin and hair. Below me was a thirty foot drop. And above me, the dragon turned and dove, like a hawk going after a mouse. I fell to my knees, and closed my eyes, and—

Wylla was there above me, her arms on my shoulders, trying to steady me.

"You cried out in your sleep. Are you in pain?"

I didn't answer right away. I was trying to shake away the shackles of the dream.

"I'm sorry I left you alone," she continued.

I took a deep breath and tried to calm myself. "I'm fine. Just a nightmare."

"Not about me, I hope." Wylla smirked.

"No, I was being attacked by a dragon. A real dragon. Wings, fangs, the whole thing."

"A real dragon?"

I sat up. "Yes."

"And this wouldn't be your mind sending you a message, would it?" she asked.

"I'm not sure what you're saying."

Wylla sat down next to me and took my hand. "Dragon? Come on. We're hunting a mage who goes by that name. Surely you see what's happening here."

"I don't believe in omens, if that's what you are insinuating. It was a dream, plain and simple."

"Maybe," she said. "Maybe not. Besides, I made some progress while you were here napping like an old woman."

"You located the boy?"

"I did."

"And?"

"And Jory found a peddler whose route runs down south along that logging road you mentioned."

"Tell me."

"The peddler's a man by the name of Kaderly. He departed this morning on his route."

"And he's sold to someone who fits the Dragon's description?"

"I have no idea. All I know is that this Kaderly is gone for a few weeks at a time, and he trades in just about anything. He also has a reputation for keeping his mouth shut."

I nodded. "Well, even if he hasn't done business with the Dragon, he might know the lay of the land down there. Well done."

Wylla smiled. "Thank you. Someone had to pick up the slack while you were lounging about."

"Speaking of which, how about you join me in a little lounging?" I pulled her close.

"I thought you'd never ask."

Our lips locked together, and I felt her mouth with my tongue. She kissed me back long and hard, and then it proceeded the usual way. I had nothing to complain about. Nothing at all.

Afterwards, I held Wylla and I fell into a deep dreamless sleep. Late at night or early in the morning, I woke up and Wylla was awake too.

"What are we doing here?" she asked, sitting up.

"I thought that was obvious."

"I mean, with the Dragon and Jillen."

"I don't know what you are talking about." I could tell that one of her black moods had come upon her.

She sighed. "Me neither. I just wonder if it is all in vain. I mean, who am I to go up against a mage. What makes me think that I can be some avenging angel?"

"You won't be facing him alone," I said.

"Really? That's what you have to say?"

"What do you want me to say?"

"I want you to say that you can best the Dragon. I mean, if it comes down to it, you and him. One on one. Can you?"

"Probably."

"Probably? Have you ever fought a mage before? A powerful one?"

"Plenty of times."

"And you're still here. That's something, I guess."

"Well, I have died several times in my life. Sometimes at

the hands of mages. But I've been pretty lucky. And my size affords me some natural protection against magic."

"How does that work?"

"I have no idea. All I know is that some spells cast against me just fizzle."

She folded her arms and said, "I've seen you fight. You need something more than just a haphazard magic shield."

"Thank you for your confidence. Truth be told, I wasn't at my best this afternoon."

"Well, you need to be at your best. When we find the Dragon. Which we will. I hope."

I didn't say anything and eventually we both fell back asleep. I feared that I might have another nightmare, but my sleep was deep and uneventful.

Chapter Twenty-Four

W E SET OFF EARLY THE NEXT MORNING. Our first mission—after we had eaten—was to visit Sittig's shop. The old man beckoned us inside with a smile on his face.

"I'm ready for you. The boots will fit like a second skin. Mark my words."

And he wasn't exaggerating. The boots fit like they had been made exactly for my own feet. He had also reinforced the soles. All in all, I was very happy. So I paid him a little extra.

"Did you ever find that scamp Jory?" Sittig asked.

"I did," Wylla said.

"Well, if you see him again, tell him that I have a coin for him."

"Well deserved," I said. "He practically dragged us to your doorstep."

With that, we took our leave and went to secure horses and supplies, which we did without any problem. That's one of the benefits of being in a large city like Vale. You can find just about anything you need—at any time you need it.

"Will you be fine to ride?" Wylla asked, as we set off.

"Yes, I was going to ask you the same question."

"The healer did well by me."

We rode south through the Belfrey Gate and then increased our pace once we crossed the West Way on to the old logging road that led to Malverton. Unlike the well-maintained highways and Imperial roads, this road was not much more than a packed dirt track, barely wider than a wagon. On either side, tall alor trees grew, providing a good amount of shade. Within two hundred miles, the alor would be crowded out by snake-like pampa which made up the Tengan jungle. But hopefully we'd locate the peddler well before that.

From time to time, we stopped so I could check the pattern of wagon tracks in the dust. I wasn't a ranger by any means, but I had a rudimentary knowledge of how time and weather could degrade a mark. So far we were on the right path because at least one wagon had traveled in this direction over the past day or so.

"I've been thinking about the Dragon. And one thing puzzles me," Wylla said.

"Just one thing?"

"It may be the most important thing. I keep asking myself, what would a mage want with a child?"

I had thought about that very question myself and came up with several possibilities. But none of the answers were good. Over the course of my many years, I've encountered many, many depraved people. People who would hurt children, torture them, or worse. I feared that this Dragon was one of these deviants. But I didn't want to cause Wylla more anguish. It was clear that Jillen Lockwell was like a daughter to her.

Maybe Wylla could tell that I was reluctant to speculate about Jillen Lockwell's fate, so she offered her own hypothesis.

"Do you think it's possible that he seeks an apprentice?" she asked.

"Outside of the Guild?"

"Yes."

"For what reason?"

"I don't know. Power?"

"I'm not sure how an apprentice could strengthen him."

"What if he needs another mage for something? Maybe he forces Jillen to assist him."

I shook my head. "First of all, from what you described, I wouldn't call Jillen Lockwell a mage. Not by any means. She might have some latent magical abilities, but mages train for decades. She just wouldn't have the control necessary to do much. At least, what a mage might need an apprentice for."

"I don't know," Wylla said quietly. "It was a thought."

"Well, don't stop thinking. You're turning out to be a much better investigator than me."

We rode in silence for a while. After four or five hours I spied the first turn off from the logging road. I dismounted and inspected the dirt around the turn.

"What do you think?" Wylla asked.

"Hard to tell. The wagon definitely went down this path. I just can't tell if it came back out yet."

She dismounted and started pacing around in the dirt beside me, stooping intermittently to get a better look. After a few moments, she discovered something.

"Here we go." She pointed to some tracks arcing from the side path to the logging road. "These are fresh and definitely are coming back out."

I nodded. "Good work."

"I just can't tell exactly how fresh."

I picked up a bit of dirt from the wheel ruts and felt it between my fingers. I knew plenty of people who could look at what I was seeing and not only be able to tell when the tracks were made, but also how fast the wagon was going, which direction it was going, and even how much it weighed. But I was at a loss. Instead I thought about the timing.

"If the peddler left yesterday morning, and this was his first stop, it makes sense that he'd still be ahead of us. We need to figure out at what point do all his stops and detours add up to a day's worth of delay."

Wylla said, "Don't forget that we're not pulling a wagon, so we're moving a lot quicker than Kaderly. That should figure in your estimations."

"True."

We continued onward, and it turned out our guesses and calculations were mostly accurate. We caught up with Kaderly the peddler towards the end of the next day.

Chapter Twenty-Five

THE PEDDLER DROVE AN ANCIENT FARM WAGON WITH A CANVAS COVER ON THE BACK. As we rode closer, I saw that he wasn't alone. A young man holding a small crossbow sat beside him. There also could have been more men in the back of the wagon, but I doubted it. Kaderly would want to keep as much space as possible for his merchandise.

"Hail!" I called.

We rode up in front and to the side, so Kaderly could get a good look at us and see that we didn't have any weapons. He was a stocky bald man with a thick red beard. The youth next to him was about twenty years old and had the same red hair, but on the top of his head instead of his face.

"What do you want?" Kaderly called back, without slowing the wagon.

"We want to make a purchase."

I guess that's what he wanted to hear, because he reined the horses to a stop. Wylla and I rode in front of the wagon and dismounted.

"You are Kaderly the peddler, right?"

"That I am, and who might you be? I'm not accustomed to selling to strangers who simply ride up next to me."

"My name is Bander, and this is Wylla."

Kaderly climbed down from the wagon and stretched his legs. "Well, you already know my name—and this is my son Milnan. He's better than a fair shot, so I wouldn't advise trying anything untoward."

"Of course not."

"Now that we have made our pleasantries, what is it that you're looking to buy?"

I stepped closer, keeping him between me and the son with the crossbow. And even though I stood nearly a foot taller than Kaderly, I tried not to tower over him. Keeping the mood friendly was a big part of the negotiation.

"I'm looking to buy information," I said.

His eyes narrowed. I'm sure he would have rather heard that I was interested in blankets or tools or whatever he had the most of in the back of his wagon. But to his credit, Kaderly remained professional.

"What kind of information?"

"I need to know about a man named the Dragon. He's a mage."

"We don't know any mages, do we, Milnan?" He glanced back up at his son who was still in the wagon and still holding the crossbow. "And we never heard of anyone with the name Dragon. What kind of name is that?"

"We think he lives down here. We think you sell to him."

"Well, you're mistaken. There are no mages living down here in the wood."

"He's a tall man, maybe your age," Wylla said. "Very thin, gaunt even. Thin hair, big forehead. Narrow eyes set close together. A severe-looking man."

Kaderly looked down at the ground. I could tell that he knew something.

Finally, he said, "What do you want with him?"

"I want to talk to him."

"You're going through a lot of trouble to talk to someone you don't even know. I need a better reason than that."

I withdrew a sack of gold coins and tossed it to Kaderly.

"Here are a whole lot of reasons. Now tell me what you know of him."

Kaderly licked his lips, like he wanted a drink. "There's a man who fits that description—"

"I knew it!" Wylla said, beaming.

"He's not a mage, though. He's a scholar. Studies plants. Herbs. Stuff like that. And his name isn't the Dragon."

"What is it?" I asked.

"Haddon Fane."

I didn't recognize the name. "Where does he live?"

"In an old lumber mill. Down in Ripton Valley."

"How far?"

Kaderly shrugged. "I don't know. Maybe twenty miles. There's a track to the east. Winds down to a little river. The old timers call it Ripton Valley."

"And there's a mill down there?" Wylla asked.

"Used to be a mill, way back when. Now it's mostly ruins. A bunch of old buildings. The water wheel still turns though. Haddon Fane fenced in part of the compound and added some sheds and a barn. He has a substantial garden."

"For his studies," Kaderly's son Milnan added.

"Some's for eating," Kaderly corrected. "He traded us some hinkleberries once. Sweet as honey."

"Does he have children?" Wylla asked.

"Children? Out here? No. It's just him. Lives by himself as far as I know. Right, Milnan?"

"Aye."

Wylla asked, "So you never sell him anything for children? Shoes, clothes?"

"Course not. We bring him some tools, rope, tinctures, foodstuffs, jerky—nothing out of the usual."

I thought for a few moments. If this man Haddon Fane was indeed the Dragon, and he was living out here in the wilderness, why would he risk doing business with a peddler? From what Kaderly had said, Haddon Fane lived no more than a day's ride from Vale. He could get his own wagon and make a trip into the city every month or so. That should be more than adequate for supplying himself with all the larger items he might need. And the smaller items, like spices, could be teleported in on his person.

"Haddon Fane is a good customer," Kaderly said. "If you mean him harm, I think we'll have a problem, you and I."

I admired the man's mettle, so I decided to tell him what we knew of the Dragon. I told him of Jillen Lockwell and our fear that she had been abducted. I told him about the Stag & Pennant and Leshea and how we found everything burned to the ground.

"And you really think that this man, this Dragon, is Haddon Fane?" Kaderly asked.

I said, "He very well could be."

"And what makes you so certain?"

"I'm not certain at all. That's why I need to talk with him."

Wylla asked, "Are you going there now? To Ripton Valley?"

Kaderly looked surprised. "I have one more stop. A crystal mine a few hours to the south. Why?"

"I have a proposition for you," she said. Then she turned to me and told me to give Kaderly a bit more gold.

≈

Wylla's plan was simple—and very smart. We'd all ride together to Haddon Fane's homestead and then, a mile away, she'd wait with the horses and Kaderly's son, while I'd ride with Kaderly as his new guard.

I could tell that the peddler was still somewhat skeptical. I didn't blame him. If someone had come to me with this story of abductions and attacks on inns, I doubt I'd believe them. But Wylla was persistent and Kaderly reluctantly agreed. But he wanted to make his next stop at the crystal mine and proposed we head to Ripton Valley in the morning.

"If you are to be my new guard, you might as well earn your keep," he said.

So we rode with Kaderly and his son to the mine which turned out to be a family operation. The patriarch was a hefty man by the name of Lyd Whelch, who bargained with Kaderly for an assortment of merchandise, ranging from pots and pans, to tools, clothing, and even a stack of blank ledger books. After the transaction was complete, Lyd Whelch invited us for some bread and ale in his bunkhouse.

Kaderly introduced us as family friends who were riding along to learn the business.

"You're not retiring, Kaderly, are you?" Lyd Whelch asked.

"Of course not," Wylla interjected. "My husband and I will take the northern route. That is if he can get off his rump and earn enough money for the wagon." She elbowed me playfully.

Lyd Whelch laughed a big booming laugh and poured us more ale. Then he asked about recent news of the Empire. I guessed that this was a common request. People living down south in the Territories were even more isolated than most.

"Do I look like a herald?" Kaderly asked, with a smile. But he then proceeded to recount what was going on across Harion as well as some recent news in Vale. I was interested to hear the news myself since it had been more than two weeks since I had been at a tavern with a herald.

After about an hour, I could tell that Wylla was getting impatient. We had learned that the Whelch family dug for pelidod, a dark greenish crystal that wasn't particularly valuable as a gemstone, but was sought after by some craftsmen as a material used for inlay work. I'm always interested in how different people earn their keep, but Wylla was fidgeting and yawning like a child.

So I clapped Kaderly on the shoulder and said, "We'd best let our host get back to his business and us to ours."

Then I shook Lyd Whelch's hand and thanked him for his hospitality. He wished all of us luck and bade us farewell.

Once we were back on the road, Wylla said, "I thought we'd never get out of there!"

"What's your hurry?" I asked.

"I don't know. I just feel like we're wasting our time."

I shook my head. "We're making progress."

"Are we?"

"We'll see in the morning."

She stared at me with a sad look in her eyes. "This all could be for naught, couldn't it?"

"That's the nature of investigation. You come up with a hypothesis and then you try to prove it true. Your hypothesis is that the Dragon is living down here in the Territories. Tomorrow we'll prove that or disprove it."

"You're wrong," Wylla said.

"What?" I was a little surprised at her bluntness, although I probably should have been used to it by now.

She looked annoyed and I could see her stiffen in her saddle. "How many people do you think are living south of Vale?"

"What do you mean?"

"Within two days ride. Down here in the Territories. How many?"

"That's a question for the peddler. I have no idea."

"That's my point. Kaderly might do business with a dozen homesteads, but there could be fifty more that have no use for his goods because they go into Vale once a month for themselves."

"I'm sure that's true."

"Don't you see? For every Haddon Fane that we learn about through Kaderly, there could be five more that he doesn't know about, and therefore we don't know about."

I could tell that she was working herself into an agitated state again.

"The thing to do is continue asking questions," I said, trying to calm her. "If the man turns out to be a scholar, we ask him if there's anyone else he knows down here who keeps to himself. And then we ask that person..."

"That could take forever!"

"Yes, that's why most investigators tend to have a patient disposition. You might want to work on that."

She sighed, but didn't say anything more on the subject.

We rode in silence until nearly dusk and then Kaderly pulled his wagon off the road to a narrow meadow by a stream. The meadow looked like it had been frequently used as a campsite. Some of the trees had been cut down so that the grass could grow. There was a stone fire pit and even some old firewood stacked up.

After we looked after the horses, Kaderly approached me with a pair of axes. He handed one to me and said, "I daresay you'll be more skilled with this than Milnan."

Then he led me to the edge of the meadow where we set to work clearing trees and chopping more firewood. By the time we finished, it was dark and Wylla and Milnan had prepared a mutton stew for us.

We ate and spoke about everything except our plans for the next day—even though I could tell that Wylla could think only of our mission. When it was late, we all retired to our bedrolls. Wylla kept her distance from me. And some time during the night, it started to rain. We all crawled under the wagon and I slept uneasily for a few more hours.

Chapter Twenty-Six

ARLY THE NEXT MORNING THE RAIN STOPPED. And by the time we arrived at Ripton Valley, the sun had burned off any remaining moisture and the air was thick and steamy.

"Here's where we part ways," Kaderly told us. "If you're still intent on your plan, that is."

"We are," I said.

"His homestead is close?" Wylla asked.

"Less than a mile away," Kaderly said. "Down the hill and to the east, by the brook."

"More of a river than a brook, father," Milnan said. "But it is indeed nearby."

I took Wylla's hands in mine and looked her in her eyes. "I'll investigate and if Haddon Fane's our man, I'll come back for you."

"Don't get killed," she said.

"I don't plan to."

Kaderly said, "I don't know what you two are worried about. The man is as meek as a mouse. He's a scholar, for Dynark's sake!"

"We'll see about that."

I took Milnan's seat in the wagon and his crossbow too, and then we set off down the hill. The road curved down into a valley choked with dense bushes and low trees. After ten or fifteen minutes, I heard the sound of a river and spied a group of thatched roofed structures.

"That's the place," Kaderly said.

"What do you usually do once you get here?"

"Just pull the wagon up near the gate. Haddon Fane's almost always nearby. He comes out and we get down to business."

"Very well. Just proceed as usual. Once I get a look at him, I'll let you know if I want to speak with him."

Kaderly nodded and drove the wagon towards a compound of old buildings beside the river. There was a sawmill with a water wheel. Beside it was a long, open air storage shed to keep cut lumber dry, and several other buildings in various states of disrepair, including an old bunkhouse. The perimeter of the compound had been fenced in and a handful of chickens wandered about.

We climbed down from the wagon and I looked around. Haddon Fane did indeed have a sizeable garden on the north side of the compound. It was framed by a tall fence of rough-hewn poles to keep animals out.

"Hello!" Kaderly called out.

I walked over to the sawmill. It was an impressive wooden structure that sat atop a ten foot tall stone foundation, perched on the bank of the noisy, splashing river. The wheel still turned, but from what I could see, the saw blades and other machinery had either been removed or had rusted away.

I joined Kaderly at the gate.

"No sign of him," the peddler said. "Maybe he's out picking berries."

"Keep calling for him," I said.

We spent another ten minutes wandering the property, but Haddon Fane was nowhere to be seen.

"He doesn't keep dogs, does he?" I asked.

"Not that I have ever seen."

I opened the gate and made my way towards the bunkhouse. Kaderly reluctantly followed.

"This is where he lives, I'm guessing."

Kaderly said, "I've never been inside."

It was a long, low building with a covered porch and it looked like it had been standing there for a century or more. I pushed open the door and Kaderly and I stepped in. The inside of the house was much grander than the outside. Even in the gloom, I could make out finely carved furniture, rich tapestries and artwork, and cabinets filled with books and curios.

"Not bad for a lowly scholar," I said.

Kaderly looked around in wonder. "I had no idea."

The bunkhouse appeared to be just a single large room, with a stone fireplace along the back wall and a long trestle table along the north wall. Between them was another table used for food preparation. I checked the fireplace.

"Cold," I said.

"Maybe he went into the city."

I moved over to the south side of the bunkhouse which was Haddon Fane's sleeping area. It was dominated by a large four poster bed that looked like it belonged in a Lord Governor's mansion. The bed had been slept in, but I couldn't tell how long ago.

After checking a few other things, like the wash basin and the cooking pot, my best guess was that Haddon Fane hadn't been home for a few days at least. We walked back out to the wagon, and I told Kaderly I wanted to return to where Wylla and his son were waiting. The peddler seemed eager to leave Haddon Fane's compound, so he didn't offer any objections.

When we arrived, we saw Kaderly's son dozing under a tree and Wylla brushing one of the horses.

"Well?" she asked.

"He wasn't there," I said.

"What do you mean?"

"I mean, we looked around, and we didn't see him. Best I can tell he hasn't been home for a few days."

"Were there horses around?"

"I didn't look. I assumed you'd want to see the place for yourself."

"Of course I do. Let's go."

Kaderly turned to me and said, "We need to be on our way. We're already behind schedule."

"That's fine," I told him. "I appreciate your help with this."

Wylla and I gathered our bedrolls, packed up the horses, and got ready to ride.

"I hope you find what you're looking for," Kaderly called after us.

"Me, too," I muttered to myself.

I led Wylla down the hill and into the valley. Once she caught sight of the old mill compound, Wylla shook her head.

"I admit it. This doesn't look like a place that a mage would call home."

"No it doesn't. At least on the outside. But wait until you see the bunkhouse."

"Let's ride around the property," she suggested.

We started on the north side and rode past a shed, the garden, and then the barn. There was no sign of horses, nor of any other animal except the chickens in the interior yard. On the east side of the property was another shed and the bunk house. And then the river and the saw mill on the south end. In the center of the compound was the dilapidated lumber storage barn which had a partially collapsed roof.

After backtracking to the main gate, we tied the horses up near the fence, and then went in.

"It was an old lumber mill," I said.

"Obviously."

"Haddon Fane!" I called, even though I didn't expect anyone to answer. The sound of the river partially drowned out my voice.

"Let's move away from the saw mill," I said. "I can't hear myself think."

Wylla wandered over to the barn and I followed her. It was a two-story structure with walls of exposed timbers and wattle and daub. I pulled the door open, and we let our eyes adjust to the darkness. Inside there were a number of empty stalls and a pile of old hay.

"Moldy," Wylla said as she picked through the hay. "No horses have been kept here for a long time."

There was a tack room, but it contained nothing of note. No saddles. No reins, bridles, blankets.

"So he didn't keep horses," Wylla said. "Don't you find that odd? Especially in such a remote place."

"It would be odd for you or me," I said. "But not for a mage who can teleport."

Wylla raised an eyebrow. "You're right."

We left the barn and checked a large storage shed near the bunk house. It was packed with dry goods and provisions. Barrels of flour and grain. Kegs of ale, and casks of wine. Dried meat and fish. There must have been enough to keep a work crew of dozen men fed and supplied for a half a year. And it was all relatively fresh.

"This is strange," I said. "The bunk house has been converted into a cabin and there's only one bed in it."

"So you're wondering where Haddon Fane's men dwell?"

"I am."

Wylla shaded her eyes from the sun and surveyed the rest of the yard. "What's that building to the west?"

It turned out to be another shed, filled with farming tools. And it definitely was too small to house a dozen men.

Even though the last two structures did not have walls, we examined the saw mill itself and the lumber storage barn. I pointed out to Wylla that the saw mill was missing its blade and someone had boarded up the area where the blade protruded from the foundation. Other than that, the building was empty.

The lumber storage barn was a different story. It stretched a good sixty feet long, but the last third of the roof had collapsed. Neither one of us wanted to chance walking beneath the remaining roof, but we circled the structure and I was able to make out a heap of broken furniture stacked in one corner.

"Do you see what I see?"

Wylla nodded. "Cots. A lot of them."

"I bet they used to be in the bunkhouse."

"I need to see this bunkhouse for myself," Wylla said.

So we walked across the yard and I showed her where Haddon Fane dwelt. Inside, Wylla checked some of the same things I had checked earlier: the fire, the cooking pot, the bed—as well as a tall wardrobe which was filled with clothes. She went through Haddon Fane's garments, one by one. As she examined them, she made little noises of frustration. She wasn't finding what she was looking for.

I looked through the cabinets, checking for anything that would lead me to believe that a mage lived there. But there were no grimoires, talismans, thader crystals, potions, scrolls, or anything resembling a magic item. I saw books of poetry and histories, candles, a key, carved figurines and other small objects of art, pone dice, an ornamental dagger, a jeweled box filled with a few old coins from Gadmark, some dried out inkwells, and a rolled up piece of parchment, upon which was sketched a plan of the sawmill. I started to return the items to their original locations when Wylla called out.

"This cloak! I recognize it!"

She held up a finely stitched cloak made of satin and embroidered with silver-gilt. It was the color of blood.

"Are you certain?"

Wylla hesitated. "I only got a quick look at him, but he definitely was wearing a red cloak."

"This red cloak?"

She put the cloak down and sighed. "I don't know. Maybe."

I continued to look through the bunkhouse, but didn't see anything else of interest.

"Let's leave this place," Wylla said. "If Haddon Fane truly is a mage, he could teleport back at any moment. And I don't think we want to be sitting on his bed when he gets back."

"Why not? I told you I can best him."

"If I recall, you said you probably could best him, didn't you?"

Wylla returned the cloak to the wardrobe, and we left the bunkhouse. Outside she leaned on the fence and gazed over to the river, lost in thought.

"We can—" I stopped myself. Something had caught my eye.

It was a footprint in the dust outside of the gate, under the eaves of the sawmill. But not just any footprint.

A small delicate footprint. Like a girl might make.

Chapter Twenty-Seven

✾

"I CAN'T BELIEVE IT," WYLLA GASPED.

"Could one of these footprints be Jillen's?" I asked. I had to raise my voice because of the sound of the river.

There wasn't just one set of footprints. There were several. It was tough to tell exactly how many since most of the footprints had been wiped away by last night's rain. But there was a three foot wide strip of dusty dirt protected by the sawmill's overhanging roof. That's where we saw the footprints. Made by bare feet. Smaller than Wylla's for sure. Some looked like they were from a very young child. Others could be from older children or even small adults.

"There's no way to tell," Wylla said. "Maybe."

We also couldn't easily see where the footprints led, but we could determine where they came from. I traced them back to a secret door, cunningly cut from the stone foundation of the sawmill. The stones had been set in an iron frame and mortared into place. And then the whole assembly had been perfectly balanced on heavy hinges. It had been extremely well engineered. The only way that I could tell there was a door there was because it was slightly ajar.

I pushed the door open wider and stuck my head into the room. A blast of cold, damp air hit me—as well as a horrible stench that made me gag.

"What is it?" Wylla shouted from behind me, over the loud grind of the water wheel gears.

"I can't tell yet. I can't see a thing. My eyes need to adjust. But there's something foul in here."

"Don't move. I saw a lantern in the bunkhouse." She left to retrieve it and I took another step inside, pulling my shirt up to block my nose and mouth from the smell.

The chamber was about fifteen feet wide and very long. I couldn't tell how long because after about twenty or thirty feet it was just pitch black. But on the edge of the darkness I could barely make out what looked to be a wall of floor-to-ceiling iron bars sealing off the front part of the chamber. It was like a prison.

There was another door leading south, maybe to the mechanism that was supposed to power the saw.

I looked back at the iron bars and took a few steps closer. There were tables and shelves along the north wall, filled with crates and other assorted junk. A storeroom of sorts.

It was hard to see, but I made my way to the iron bars. As my eyes adjusted further, I could see that the prison area extended farther back into the darkness. I tested the door and found it unlocked.

"Hello," I called. "Anyone there?"

The chamber was silent. But I didn't have a good feeling about this. The strong odor here seemed more and more like it came from a dead body.

I heard a noise from behind.

"I'm back," Wylla shouted, as she handed me a lit lantern.

I held it up high, and the lamp illuminated most of the chamber.

"Dynark's blood! What is this place?" Wylla cried.

It was indeed a prison. There were at least six cells beyond the barred wall—all no more than eight feet by eight feet and filled with refuse, scraps of cloth, straw sleeping pallets, and human waste.

"That's where the footprints came from." Wylla pointed to the dirt floor. There were indeed small footprints in dirt inside the cells and in the hallway. And the cell doors were all open.

"Stay back," I told Wylla.

I pulled open the door and walked through the corridor. The six cells were all against the north wall and there was another barred wall to the west with a door.

As I moved closer, I saw the source of the stench: a dead body. It was on the other side of the door, sprawled in a pool of black congealed blood and thick with buzzing flies.

The first thing I guessed was that the body was Haddon Fane's. And then once I got closer I became completely sure it was him. His head had been bashed in and his brains oozed from his shattered skull. There was a dark mass of flesh and blood on the wall beside him. If I had to guess, I'd wager he had been slammed against the stone wall with considerable force.

Wylla choked a sob from somewhere behind me. She clearly had not remained where I told her to.

"Calm down," I said. "Whatever killed him is long gone. I hope."

I moved closer to examine the body, but then I caught sight of something on the west wall, at the very end of the chamber.

It was a free standing archway made of carved wood, and it stood nearly up to the ceiling. Big enough for a man to pass through. I moved the lantern closer. Runes or symbols of some sort were etched into the wood. As I examined them I noticed that a shimmery light danced along the engraving. It was almost like sparks from a blacksmith's hammer. A wave of cold air issued from the archway, chilling me.

"Back!" I said, but my voice now sounded strangely muffled. I also found it difficult to move—like I was wading through a river. Fear clawed through me. This was bad.

With all my strength I staggered back, chancing one last look at the dead man's face, and then pulled Wylla from the chamber.

Outside, we both took several moments to recover.

"What in the blazes was that?" Wylla finally said.

"I have no idea, but whatever it is, it's magical."

"And that corpse...?" she asked.

"Haddon Fane. The Dragon, right? Did you recognize him?"

"I... I think so. But what happened to him?"

"Hard to say. Magical misadventure? Maybe he summoned something he shouldn't have."

"Summoned?" Wylla asked. "What do you mean?"

"It doesn't matter. We need to get back to Vale. Tell the Guild. They'll be able to make sense of it."

Wylla pushed the hair away from her face and stared at me. "Those footprints..."

"I know. I saw them."

"They could be Jillen's. She could have escaped. She could be alive." Her eyes flooded with tears and she fell into my arms.

I held her tight and didn't say anything.

After Wylla had calmed down, we tried to trace the foot-prints from the sawmill. They were mostly wiped away by the rain, but I found some partial tracks at the edge of a grove of big old pampa trees about forty yards from the compound.

The pampas' fan-like leaves had shielded the ground from the rain and preserved the prints. Wylla saw the tracks too and squatted down on the ground to get a better look.

"More than one child, for sure," she said. "Could be five or six. And different sizes. Where do they lead?"

"Further into this grove."

As we pushed into the trees, the tracks became more distinct, and it was much easier to follow them. We continued for fifteen or twenty more yards but then the tracks just vanished.

At first, we thought we had missed something. Maybe the children had taken a turn. But after we walked a large circle around the grove, we were convinced that there were no other tracks leading out.

"I don't understand," Wylla said.

"Me neither."

It looked like the children had gathered in an area and then just stayed there. Or vanished. Maybe they had been teleported away. But I didn't see any larger footprints that would indicate the presence of an adult. I didn't know what had happened. But I did know that this was something I wouldn't be able to make sense of on my own.

So we returned to the compound, and I carefully closed the secret door to the chamber under the sawmill. Just as I had suspected, the door fit perfectly and there was no way anyone would be able to discover the chamber. I felt reasonably sure that nothing would be disturbed until we returned.

Then we saddled up and rode like the wind back to Vale.

Chapter Twenty-Eight

I T TOOK US TWO DAYS OF HARD RIDING, BUT WE FINALLY MADE IT BACK TO THE GUILD-HALL IN VALE. This time the clerk escorted us directly to Herron. Maybe he could see the desperation on our faces.

We didn't waste time on niceties. I introduced Wylla and then told Herron what we had discovered: the secret chamber, the cells, the dead body, and the magical archway. I told him about the footprints and the grove and our thought that the children somehow vanished.

Herron listened to all of this quietly, looking down at his desk, not meeting my gaze.

When I had finished my narrative, he began to ask questions. A lot of questions. He wanted to know the detailed location of the compound, and the arrangement of the structures within it. He called for a wax tablet and asked me to sketch everything in as much detail as I could recall. He asked me about Kaderly and Milnan and even Lyd Whelch. Then he turned to Wylla and asked her the same things.

When our answers differed—even the slightest bit—he asked more questions. At the end of it, we were exhausted.

Herron stood up. "I think we have what we need. Thank you. Both."

Wylla clenched her fists. "What do you mean, 'thank you?' That's it?"

The Guild Master stared at her as if she was a child who spoke out of turn. "The Guild will investigate. I'll dispatch a team in the morning."

"We'll go with you," I said. "We can direct you there."

"That is impossible, Captain. We both know that."

Wylla regained her composure a bit. "Guild Master, with all due respect, we need to know what happened to Jillen Lockwell. I've cared for her since she was a small child."

"I cannot make any promises, but return here in a few days and I'll let you know if we discovered anything about the girl. But right now my concern is that body and the object you described. If it is indeed magical, we will need to secure the area at once."

"I have no doubt about the magic," I said. "I just need to know what transpired in that chamber."

"That makes two of us," Herron said. He stood at his desk with an impassive look on his face. Clearly we were dismissed.

Outside, Wylla turned to me. She was furious.

"How can they deny us like that?"

"That's the Guild. I knew they wouldn't allow us to return there. Whatever went on in that chamber, they need to keep it secret."

"So is that it? How are supposed to find Jillen now?"

"I'm working on that," I said. "In the meantime, we need someplace to sleep."

We made our way back to Lean Gate Road and back to the Lindsdown House. Fortunately the innkeeper had space for us. We were both so exhausted by the long ride, we collapsed into the bed and slept like the dead.

The next morning, when I awoke, I was alone. Again.

I should have been getting used to Wylla's early morning disappearances, but I wasn't. I splashed some water on my face, left the room, and went downstairs to the dining room.

There I found Wylla with a cup of moxa and the crumbs of some aebol.

"Couldn't sleep?" I asked.

She tilted her head. "It's nearly noon. I was getting worried about you."

I took one of her aebol remnants and ate it. It was good. Not too greasy.

"So now that you've slept on it, what's our plan?" she asked.

"Ask me again after I've had some more nourishment," I grumbled.

We were quiet for awhile. The serving girl brought me some moxa and bread and fish and more aebol. Once I had finished, Wylla looked at me questioningly.

"Okay, you're not going to like this," I said.

"I already don't like it," she countered. "I don't like the tone of your voice."

"We need to leave the city again. There's someone who might be able to shed some light on this."

"Who?"

"I can't say."

She looked at me quizzically. "Is he a bounty hunter? Please tell me he's a bounty hunter," she said.

"No. He's a mage." I took a drink of my moxa. "Well, actually, it's more that he *believes* he's a mage. A rather important one at that."

Wylla rolled her eyes. "You're jesting."

"He may be able to tell us things that the Guild won't. In

his own way, he's brilliant. But—there's no other way to put it —he's also quite mad."

"Now I'm curious. Very curious. Why won't you tell me his name?"

I took a deep breath. "It's not that I won't tell you. It's that I can't."

"You're forbidden?"

This would be hard to explain. There was something about the man I was thinking of that was unworldly. It could be a type of magic which obscured him from the thoughts of others. Even now that I was thinking of him, it took me a lot of effort to even picture his face and where he lived. It was like something was resisting me.

"Are you okay?" Wylla asked.

"What?"

"You looked strange for a moment. Well, stranger than usual."

I smiled at her. "Thanks."

"So at least tell me where this pretend mage lives, won't you?" She took my last aebol and popped it into her mouth.

I thought about that and struggled to answer. But I kept at it. Trying to picture his home. It kept slipping around in my mind like a slimy fish. Eventually I got a brief flash of something. "Hamwick," I said. Yes, it was definitely Hamwick.

"And how are we supposed to get all the way to Hamwick?"

"Well, if I spend everything I have, we can teleport there."

Wylla looked pale.

"Teleport? Again?"

"Yes, there's a public portal here."

"I know. But isn't it just for the wealthy?"

She was right in a way. Most people could not afford to

use a public portal. Portals were for successful merchants and diplomats who needed to travel quickly and did not care how much such travel cost. But every once in awhile, even the common folk would travel by portal. I had just enough in gems to get us to Hamwick.

We left our horses at the stable since I wasn't sure when—or if—we'd return. And then we departed Vale via the Green Gate to the southwest and walked for seven minutes until we reached the waystation.

It was a sprawling low stone building with eight sides, made of large stone blocks. Inside, polished stone columns were arranged in various alcoves. Between these pillars, red-robed portal mages would open their gateways to the waystations leading to other cities. There were a fair number of merchants and nobles milling about, waiting for their destinations to be called.

I spoke to the clerk and checked on the schedule for Hamwick. We would have to wait an hour, but that was certainly better than a couple of weeks on horseback. He looked at my clothes and appearance a little dubiously, but my gems were as good as any other man's.

After I paid, we were admitted through a gate into the main room where we sat on a stone bench and waited.

"I never thought I'd be wealthy enough for a portal," Wylla whispered to me. "Look at these people."

The men wore embroidered doublets with jeweled buttons and velvet hose. Some sported caps decorated with jewels and feathers. Many of the women were dressed in the latest fashion of the day: gowns of velvet with puffed sleeves and collars embroidered with blackwork or trimmed with lace. Their hair was twisted and tucked into jeweled cauls.

Wylla touched her own hair self-consciously. It was thick and untamed, and to me, much more attractive than the noblewomen's hair.

"Have you ever been to Hamwick?" I asked her.

"I've never been west of the Meredel."

"Why's that?"

She shrugged. "Not everyone is a vagrant like you."

"Wanderer."

"Whatever you say."

"You might like Hamwick."

"Why?"

"It's a big market city. Where the north and south meet, as they say. Lots of wool. All manner of garments. Artful architecture. Interesting people."

"I don't pay buildings much mind and I've had enough of interesting people in my life."

I wasn't sure what she meant by that.

We sat in silence and watched travelers until the clerk announced that the Hamwick portal would be opening in a few minutes. Then we joined a handful of well-dressed people and began to make our way to the appropriate pillars. Another clerk counted the travelers going to Hamwick and then nodded to the portal mage, who spoke a few words and began to conjure the portal.

"Am I going to feel sick again?" Wylla asked.

"Possibly. But even so, it will be nothing. You have to go through hundreds of portals in order to actually feel any ill effects."

"That's not very comforting."

Even twenty feet from the mage, I felt the air grow cold. A shimmering portal swirled into existence between two of the pillars. Magical energy glowed in waves, almost like layers of sheercloth stretched between the pillars. One at a time, all of us travelers trudged through. Wylla squeezed my hand nervously, and I held her tight as we walked through together.

We came out in another large octagonal chamber with red-robed mages, clerks, guards, and well-dressed citizens.

Only this time, the air felt drier and cooler, and there was a faint odor of jantim. I looked over at Wylla. She didn't appear ill at all.

"You feeling all right?"

"Yes. It was... strange, but no sickness."

"I told you. You get used to it."

We left the waystation and walked out onto the road to Hamwick. Like all the waystations, this one was built about a half mile outside of the city gates. Hirbo Thrang once told me a long time ago there had been magical accidents in the portals, so the Guild now made sure that the waystations were located a safe distance away from any city.

"We're not actually going into the city," I told Wylla.

"What? After all the things you said about it? You got my hopes up."

"We need to go west," I said. "Probably."

"What do you mean, 'probably?' Don't you know?"

The fact was, I didn't have a clear idea of where my friend lived. I had a faint recollection that it was on some estate west of Hamwick, but whenever I tried to recall the name or exact location, my mind became foggy.

I told Wylla, "He doesn't want to be found. Even by those who know him."

"I don't understand."

"Me neither. But it must be some sort of spell. It affects me less than most people, but it still affects me. That's why I can't remember his name, or exactly where he lives."

She scrunched up her face. "So how are we supposed to find him?"

"I think I can get us there. It will just take some effort. And if I can get us close enough, it will all come back to me. I know it sounds crazy, but it's worth a shot."

I took a deep breath and tried to clear my mind. Then I pictured what I thought he looked like.

It didn't work. Not even close. I couldn't even recall his image, let alone where he lived. Maybe I had made the whole thing up. Maybe he didn't even exist at all.

I pushed away my doubts and tried a different approach. Instead of trying to force myself to remember exactly where he lived, I attempted to recall just one detail.

The door of his house. That's what I focused upon. What did his door look like?

An indistinct image came into my mind: a set of wide stone steps made of river rock. Leading up to the door. There were thick vines framing the door and climbing up the side of the house.

Then, all of a sudden, I was able to picture the door.

It was stained the color of rust. Carved wood. Intricate iron hinges and hardware. Some type of image sculpted into the wood.

A man's face. Peering out of the forest. And then it came to me.

A green man on a red door.

I exhaled and told Wylla, "I know where we need to go."

Chapter Twenty-Nine

TWO HOURS LATER, WE STOOD IN FRONT OF THE ACTUAL DOOR, CONNECTED TO THE ACTUAL HOUSE, ON AN ACTUAL ESTATE. It was exactly as I had pictured it.

"So you just forced yourself to remember?" Wylla asked.

"Not really. I tricked myself into remembering. It was a phrase, like a line of a poem, that I committed to memory. His magic, or whatever it is, was able to obscure my recollection of him and where he lived, so I focused instead on a small—but very memorable—detail."

"The green man on the red door," she said, visibly impressed.

"Exactly."

"I'll have to remember that if I am ever in the position of having my memory tampered with."

"You never know," I said.

The house attached to the red door was a former hunting lodge for the estate, a tall, blocky stone building with two main floors and then an attic space with dormers. It had a generous amount of tall narrow windows on the first two floors although some were nearly obscured by the vines which grew on either side of the door. The rest of the shrubbery surrounding the structure was carefully tended and trimmed. Likely by my friend himself.

The structure wasn't enormous, but certainly offered much more space than one person needed.

"Well, we've come all this way," Wylla said. "Are you going to knock?"

"Just be patient with him," I said. "And try to behave yourself. He can be a bit... eccentric."

"What do you mean by—"

Before she could finish the question, the red door was yanked open and a man about my own age scowled at us. And it all came back. All my memories of him. Every one.

"Hello, Valthar," I said.

"You're late. Come in."

Wylla and I exchanged glances and followed Valthar into the old lodge. He shuffled along with a cane and escorted us through a dark entrance way with doorways on either side leading to a parlor and a library. Both rooms were piled high with crates and books and stacks of other furniture in a chaotic mess. Valthar ignored those rooms and pushed through a set of double doors at the end of the corridor.

"Come along! Stop dawdling!"

We found ourselves in the great hall, a long room dominated by a stone fireplace large enough for me to lay in. It was flanked by two pairs of tall windows which let in a fair amount of light. Three old chairs had been pulled up close to the fire.

"Don't just stand there. Tend to the fire, Bander," Valthar said.

He sunk into one of the chairs and then turned to Wylla. "I don't know your name lass, but you have an evil look about you. Mind yourself!"

"She's a friend," I said as I poked at some logs. "Her name is Wylla. Late of Hytwen."

"From the looks of her, she's more than a friend, I'd wager. If one has the coin, that is."

"How dare you!" Wylla hissed.

"Careful, Valthar," I said. "Wylla's not one to be trifled with."

He cackled, "I'm just a feeble old man. Pay me no mind!"

Wylla looked at me. I knew what she was thinking. Valthar appeared to be younger than me. His eyes were bright and his face was barely marred by lines. The odd thing is that he acted like a man a quarter century older than he actually was.

"How are you, my friend?" I asked.

He gave a dismissive wave. "Bah, this frail flesh confounds me at every turn. I can't sleep more than an hour at a time. My hips and back ache like someone's been pounding me with a cudgel, and half the time I walk into a room and can't remember why I'm there."

"I'm sorry to hear that," I said.

"Oh, you're sorry? Is that why you never visit me? Or are you too busy saving the Empire to look in on an old man from time to time?"

"If I recall, I was here last spring. I caught you that big red stag. We feasted. Played a lot of pone. That was you, wasn't it, Valthar?"

"Now you're mocking me, you oaf."

I grinned at him. "Besides, with whatever spell you cast on me to erase my memory, you're lucky that I found my way back here at all."

He nodded at Wylla. "Does she know about that?"

"I shared a bit," I said. "Truth be told, I don't even know enough about it to explain it to anyone else."

"As it should be," he said. "Besides, the whore doesn't need—"

Before he could finish his sentence, Wylla flew at him and slapped him hard enough to knock him from his chair.

"My name is Wylla," she said, standing over him, trembling with fury. "Best for you if you remember that."

There were a few moments of tense silence and I wasn't sure what would happen next.

But then Valthar threw his head back and erupted into peals of laughter which eventually gave way to a severe coughing fit.

"Very well," he gasped. "I deserved that. Now help me up, Wylla." He extended his arm and Wylla hesitated just for a moment before pulling him to his feet.

"Gods, you're strong," he muttered.

"I think we all need some wine," I said.

"Or something a bit more potent," Wylla said.

Valthar eased himself back into his chair with a quiet groan. "I've got a cask of fine uskbow from Laketon. Eresthar sent it. Fetch us some from the cellar, Bander, and then I'll tell Wylla here my tale."

"Don't kill each other while I'm gone," I said. Then I made my way to the kitchen and then down into the cellar. It was stocked with crates of vegetables, dried meats, at least a hundred dusty wine bottles, and several casks. After searching through the room for several minutes, I finally found the uskbow cask and then carried it up to the kitchen.

It took a while to tap it and then find a carafe and some goblets, but eventually I managed to serve Valthar and Wylla, who were deep in conversation. Polite conversation, thank Dynark. I guessed it took that one strong blow from Wylla to knock some sense into Valthar, but I was happy that he was behaving himself. I fetched myself a goblet of uskbow and returned to the great hall.

"Pardon," Wylla leaned closer to Valthar. "Did you say the year 711?"

"Indeed. The year of my birth," he said.

"That's over a thousand years ago!"

"Yes it is—which is what makes my tale especially noteworthy." He took a swig of uskbow and then grimaced. "Eresthar has no taste in spirits."

"So you are a thousand years old?" Wylla asked with a smirk. "That's odd. You don't look a day over 500."

"To be precise, I was born a thousand and two years ago, but I'm not exactly sure how old I am. The chamber I was trapped in altered time. At least, that's what I believe happened." He raised his goblet to me. "If it hadn't been for Bander here, and his friends, I'd still be trapped in there."

Wylla looked at me, eyebrow raised.

"That part's true," I said. "We found him in an old Tengan temple. Must have been thirty years ago—"

"Twenty seven, you cur! Don't make me out to be more doddering than I actually am."

"Twenty seven years ago, then. Perhaps we should have left you there."

"No, I'm happy to have been freed. Although I would greatly prefer living in my own time. These days, everything is too tamed and regulated. You've wrung all the wildness out of the world, all the adventure."

"There's plenty of wildness in this world, old friend. And you don't even have to go looking for it. Sometimes it finds you."

"Nevertheless, I intend to find my way back." He turned to Wylla. "It's my life's work, you know."

"And how do you intend to go back in time?" Wylla asked.

"It's probably well beyond your mental capacity to understand, but I plan on orienting on a temporal marker. Once I can locate one, that is."

I explained, "Valthar fancies himself a mage."

"I am indeed a mage. One of the most powerful in this age and any age."

"And yet, I've never seen you cast a single spell."

His eyes twinkled. "What about the cloud that obscures your memory?"

"I'm not sure that is actually your doing."

"Shall I polymorph you into a snail? Hmmm? Would that suit you?"

Wylla laughed at me. "A snail? I think that should suit you very well. The pace of your wanderings might suffer a bit, but—"

Valthar turned to me. "You're not still doing that, are you? That useless pilgrimage?"

"Yes, and it's not useless. And it's not actually a pilgrimage."

We drank and chatted some more. I noticed that Wylla seemed much more at ease. Probably due to the uskbow.

Finally, Valthar said, "So tell me the purpose of your visit. And be quick about it, I'm getting hungry."

"I can prepare some food," Wylla offered.

"That would be most kind," Valthar said. "But I would fear that you might attempt to poison me. Would you?"

"That depends."

"Oh?"

"Yes, it depends on whether or not you can help us." She winked at him.

"Oh, in that case I am most confident I shall live to see another sunrise," Valthar said. "There's bread and cheese and even some fermented vegetables in the larder. Bring out whatever you can find."

Wylla rose a little unsteadily, swept over to me, and gave me a little kiss. I could smell the uskbow on her breath and wondered how much she had imbibed.

"Tell him everything," she whispered. Then she smiled and skipped towards the kitchen.

"Are you sure she isn't a tart?" Valthar asked.

"Steady, old friend. You don't want me slapping you next. I hit a bit harder than the lady."

"Fair enough." He took another drink of uskbow. "Now tell me your tale of woe and confusion."

Valthar was one of the strangest men I knew, but I felt I could trust him completely. Maybe that was the effect of his magic again, clouding my mind. But I didn't care.

I went ahead and told him exactly what had happened, in complete detail, starting from when Minch met on the West Way and I explained about Jillen Lockwell—back when I was shoeless and half dead from being poisoned.

I told him about Arno Lockwell and his mercenaries and Ellia Lockwell and her odd detachment at the disappearance of her simple-minded ward. I told him about Hytwen and Ortwen and their history. I told him about Alford Platt, the farm steward, and the money troubles Lockwell Farms faced and the new cobblestones and renovation of Lockwell Manor. I explained who Creagar Skenn was and the bad blood between the Lockwells and the Skenns. And I shared how the Lockwells seemed convinced that the Skenns had taken Jillen Lockwell.

I was in the middle of recounting my midnight raid on Ortwen when Wylla returned with a tray piled high with bread and dried figs and nuts and cheese and even pickled cucumbers and carrots. We ate and then Wylla took over the story, telling Valthar about Jillen Lockwell's abilities and how her mother discovered them.

For the first time, Valthar interrupted with a question.

"Did you actually witness the girl teleport? With your own eyes?"

"I did," Wylla said. "Several times. I have to admit I was terrified."

"Was there a portal?"

"What do you mean?"

"When she teleported, did she step through a glowing door?"

Wylla thought for a moment, and then said, "No. She just vanished. Suddenly. And then she would reappear across the room."

"Blinking," Valthar muttered, half to himself.

"She called it 'walking through walls.'"

"How old was this girl when you first saw her teleport?"

"This all happened about a year ago, so Jillen would have been eleven years old."

"Fascinating," Valthar said.

Wylla went on to explain about Jillen's invisible friend, Norrah, the girl who lived in the walls of Lockwell Manor and told Jillen things. And then Wylla got to the part about the Dragon.

"I thought dragons are extinct in your time?" Valthar asked.

"There's no such thing as dragons," I sighed. "It's an alias: 'the Dragon.' We believe his real name was Haddon Fane."

"Haddon Fane, eh?" Valthar looked as if he was mulling the name over in his mind, but after a time he shook his head and asked Wylla to continue.

She told him all about Jillen Lockwell's fear that the Dragon was coming to get her. And then she shared her plan to help the girl escape.

Wylla continued, "Jillen predicted the day when the Dragon first came to Lockwell Manor. And she predicted when he would return for her. But our plan worked and Jillen made her escape."

"Well, it worked to a point," I said. "Wylla enlisted my aid to travel to the coaching inn where she and Jillen Lockwell had planned to meet. But when we arrived, the inn had been destroyed and there was no sign of the girl."

"Didn't you know that the mage would simply track the girl?" Valthar asked.

"I did not," Wylla said. "Obviously." Sadness clouded her face. "I sent Jillen to her doom."

"We don't know that," I said. "There's a good chance she escaped. Judging by what we saw at the mill."

"What mill?" Valthar asked.

I picked up the narrative and told of our journey to Bexden and then Vale and then Wylla's idea to check peddlers who might ply their trade to the south.

Valthar said, "It all seems like a rather oblique way to track the mage down. Why didn't you just go back to Hytwen and confront the girl's parents? You're both brutes. I'm certain you could have forced the information out of them."

He had a point, but it was one I had considered already.

"As far as we know, the mother was the one who made the arrangement with Haddon Fane. And we didn't think she knew much about him."

"Other than the fact that he was eager to buy Jillen," Wylla added. "She also convinced him to help them attack Ortwen."

"And did he?"

I said, "We're not sure. We haven't been back there."

Valthar raised one bushy eyebrow. Clearly, he did not agree with our plan of action. But then I told him about Wylla's hunch that Ellia Lockwell had met the Dragon in Vale and then our idea that the mage was living somewhere outside the city. I relayed how we tracked down Kaderly the peddler and eventually found our way to Haddon Fane's compound.

"That was very lucky of you. Very lucky indeed." He had a strange look in his eye when he said it.

"Our luck continued." I told him about the small footprints in the dirt and the chamber beneath the mill building, the cells, Haddon Fane's body, and the symbol-covered archway that emanated magic.

"You're certain he was dead?"

"Yes."

"Did you check the body?"

"I know what a dead man looks like."

"Did you happen to notice if he was wearing any sort of amulet?"

"I didn't see anything like that." I turned to Wylla. "Did you?"

She shook her head. "What sort of amulet?"

"It would look like a small silver crescent. Almost the shape of a crescent moon. Did you see anything like that? In his hand maybe?"

"No," I said. "What's the significance of the amulet?"

"It's nothing. Something I've been studying for another matter. I always ask when I hear a story involving some unusual magic. Never mind. Please proceed."

"There's not much to tell after that. We left the chamber as quickly as we could and then scoured the area for more footprints. We found what looked to be a trail of child-sized tracks leading into a wooded area. But then they vanished."

"Vanished?"

"Yes," I said. "We circled the grove and there were no other tracks in or out."

"Could the children have climbed the trees and then swung from branch to branch to obfuscate their trail?"

"We're talking about children, not monkeys," Wylla said.

I said, "Besides, the trees in that grove were pampas." Pampas didn't really have branches. They had one thick rubbery trunk with a crown of leaves at the top. Not ideal for swinging.

I finished up the tale by explaining how we shared our discovery with Herron, the Guild Master in Vale, and that he planned to dispatch a team of mages to investigate. I thought Valthar might bristle at this, as he had little love for the Guild.

He rubbed his eyes, lost in thought. Finally he said, "I'm tired. I need to retire for the evening."

"It's barely dark," Wylla said.

"I am an old man. I need my sleep."

He got up and shuffled towards a back room.

"What about us?" Wylla called after him.

"There are five bedrooms upstairs. The last one at the end of the hall has blankets and not that many rats. I'm somewhat hard of hearing, so feel free to make as much noise as you want when you rut. You won't be disturbing me."

With that, he waved a hand dismissively and exited the room.

I looked at Wylla. "Sounds like a plan to me."

Chapter Thirty

WHEN I AWOKE THE NEXT MORNING, WYLLA WAS SPRAWLED OUT BESIDE ME, SNORING. I was relieved to see that she was still in the bed with me. I had started to suspect that she was a vampire or some other nocturnal creature.

It was cold outside when I used the privy and when I returned, Wylla was awake and brushing her hair.

"I wish I could brush the pain out of my head," she said.

"Too much drink?"

"You could say that." She gave up on her hair and flopped back on the bed. "I think this is another waste of time."

I didn't say anything.

She frowned at me. "I mean, where did you find this fellow?"

"You heard the story."

"I heard it, but I don't believe it. A thousand year old mage trapped in time. It's like a story my grandmother would tell me when I was a young girl."

"You didn't hear the best part. Valthar is the son of Klothar."

She convulsed into laughter. And then held her head in her hands. "Stop. You're making my head hurt even more."

"I'm serious. Ask him yourself."

"The son of Klothar? Is he also Dynark's nephew?"

She laughed for a while more and then pulled me back into the bed and kissed me.

"You're a strange man, Bander. And you have strange friends."

We dozed for an hour more. And then Wylla dragged herself from the bed and announced that she was thirsty. "What do you think the chance is that Klothar's son will offer us moxa?"

"Excellent," I said. "Especially since I smell it brewing."

"Really? I can't smell anything."

We made our way downstairs and discovered that Valthar was indeed in the kitchen preparing some food. As we greeted him, he gestured to a kettle of moxa.

"Help yourselves. I have no servants here."

He used a long-handled paddle to remove some fresh-baked pebble cakes from the stone oven.

"I trust you slept well. Or whatever it is you did up there."

"Very well. Thank you," Wylla said.

We brought the moxa and pebble cakes out into the hall and I built up the fire.

"As much as we enjoy your hospitality, we need to find Jillen Lockwell and lay this matter to rest," I said.

"I can't help you there," Valthar said.

Wylla's face fell.

He continued, "But I have been thinking about what you found at that mill and I have a few conjectures."

"We'd appreciate anything you could tell us," Wylla said.

Valthar sat back in his chair and took a sip of moxa. "How much do you know about portals and the planes?"

"Nothing at all," she said. "I only traveled through a portal for the first time a week ago.

"Well, I will try to keep this simple," he said. "At its core, all magic involves the transference of energy from one plane to another, specifically between ormgaerd, the world around us, and ungaerd, the elemental plane."

Wylla shook her head. "I have no idea what a plane even is."

"You're lucky I'm in a good mood this morning. I shall enlighten you. A plane is simply another word for world."

"There's more than one world?"

"There are many."

"Possibly," I interjected. "But there are only two worlds that we actually know of."

"That you know of!" Valthar said. "I happen to know that there are others beyond ormgaerd and ungaerd."

"And you can travel between worlds?" Wylla asked.

Valthar chuckled. "Not between those two. You wouldn't last a second in ungaerd."

"Tell her about demon summoning," I said.

"They are not actually demons. That's an old wives tale. They are elementals."

"Might as well be demons," I said, even though I knew Valthar was correct. I had seen a fair amount of elementals conjured from ungaerd. They were all horrific monstrosities often with burning appendages. They could topple buildings and easily wipe out a squadron of guards. The only good thing about them is that they, too, were not able to survive for more than a few minutes away from their natural plane.

Valthar continued, "Let us get back to the matter of tele-portation and portals—"

"What's the difference?" Wylla asked.

"If the two of you could refrain from interrupting for but a few moments, I shall tell you." He sighed and looked at each of us in turn, daring us to speak. Then he continued. "Both spells are in the Changing school and both facilitate instantaneous travel across any distance. Teleportation, in itself, involves the transport of the caster, whereas a portal allows transport of anyone who steps through it. Are you following?"

"I think so," Wylla said.

"The third variation is called a 'gate.' It's similar to a portal but the teleportation spell is generated by the magical item itself, not by a mage. Although often the gate needs some sort of trigger."

Confusion played across Wylla's face, but Valthar continued with his lecture.

"I believe that archway you discovered was some sort of magical gate—a magical gate that required more than one mage to trigger it. And if it was true that Haddon Fane was a rogue mage, he couldn't exactly enlist the aid of other Guild mages to help him open the portal."

"That's why he needed the children," I said.

"I don't understand," Wylla said.

Valthar said, "He was probably scouring the land for children like your ward—children who had some magical abilities but who, for one reason or another, had escaped notice of the Guild."

"There's more children like Jillen?" Wylla asked.

"Undoubtedly," Valthar said.

It all became clear, but the thought turned my stomach. Valthar was correct. There had to be more children like Jillen, but not many more. Haddon Fane must have been looking for years to find enough to open the gate. And that meant the very first prisoners had been there for a long time.

"So what happened?" I asked. "The children were gone and Haddon Fane was dead. Did something come through the gate and kill him, but allow the children to escape?"

"I can't say without examining the site which is now impossible with the Guild there."

"But you think they could have escaped?" Wylla asked.

"You didn't see other bodies there, did you?"

She didn't reply, just stared into the flames of the fireplace, lost in thought.

"I suggest that you go back to the girl's home," Valthar said. "If she did escape, might she not try to find you there?"

We left an hour later. I asked Valthar if he would open a portal to Vale for us, but I knew he wouldn't—or couldn't. Instead he handed Wylla a small pouch.

"What's that for?" she asked.

"Buy yourself transport in Hamwick. You can go wherever you want."

She opened the pouch and gasped. "There's a fortune in here!"

"Yes, tarfets, clouds, and lemuells. Four of each."

"That's extremely generous," I said. And it was. Wylla could live the rest of her days in luxury with those diamonds.

"But... why?" Wylla asked, her eyes still wide.

Valthar sniffed. "Consider it an apology for my rudeness yesterday. Come. I will walk you to the edge of the garden."

We pushed through the red door of the lodge and stepped out into the sunshine.

"I can't convince you to come with us?" I asked. "We could use your expertise."

"I'm far too old to travel, you know that." He tapped the side of his head. "But that reminds me. I have something else to give you. Bander, escort me to the kitchen."

He gripped my arm, and we tottered back inside, leaving Wylla in the garden to marvel at her diamonds. In the kitchen Valthar gave me a half dozen pebblecakes wrapped in a cloth.

"This is what you wanted to give me? I thought it might be a ring of protection or something."

He leaned in close and whispered a sentence in my ear. His expression was deadly serious, but even so, I dismissed his warning as nonsense. But five days later, after almost dying, I realized he was right.

Chapter Thirty-One

W E RETURNED TO VALE THE WAY WE DEPARTED IT, JUST IN REVERSE. This time Wylla paid. But even the cost of a public portal didn't appreciably diminish her fortune.

"Maybe see a gem trader," I suggested. "You don't want to be carrying those diamonds around."

She nodded, but didn't say anything. She was probably still awed by Valthar's gift.

It was too early to return to the guildhall. I was certain that Herron's investigators were still in the Territories. But I looked forward to hearing what they discovered. It would be interesting if they came to the same conclusion as Valthar.

To me, it made perfect sense: imprisoned children forced to use their magical energy to help Haddon Fane open a gate. I knew that summoning mages often worked in teams. Apparently certain types of portals took a massive amount of energy to open. But to what end? Was Haddon Fane trying to summon something? Or was he trying to go somewhere?

"There's a gem trader," Wylla said, pointing.

I shook my head. "Not here, so close to the gate. His rates

are probably high because of his location. Unwary travelers just choose whoever is most convenient. We'll do better in the market district."

We wandered for a half hour or so, and I examined a number of establishments before settling on one right off of Morland Cross. I liked the look of their security. A half dozen guards, alert and positioned well. Inside there was a faerling perched on a bookcase. It looked well cared for, which was another good sign.

"Have you ever seen a faerling?" I whispered to Wylla.

"Not close up."

Faerlings were semi-intelligent ape-like creatures which had a unique ability. They could sense human thoughts and would become agitated in the presence of those who were planning a deception or had other dishonest intentions. The size of a small child and covered with shaggy fur, faerlings came in all sorts of colors but all had distinctive black mask-like markings on their faces. Often, their owners would dress them in children's clothing, although I never understood why. This one looked down at us placidly while Wylla changed one of her diamonds to coins and gems and deposited the rest.

She looked up and smiled at the faerling. The creature just blinked at her.

I was extra alert as we left the gem trader's shop. Thieves often targeted departing customers, sometimes following them for a mile—using teams of trackers—before striking. It was almost impossible to guard against, but we were not far from the guildhall, so that's where I led us. We stuck to Morland Cross, a wide, well-traveled street, for most of the way there, and didn't encounter any trouble. But that didn't mean we weren't being followed.

Inside the guildhall, I spoke to the clerk who recognized me from the other day.

"Guild Master Herron expected your visit, sir. However

he asked me to inform you that the expedition has not yet returned."

"I wondered as much."

"Where are you lodging? We will leave word if and when we have something to share."

I told him we were staying at the Lindsdown House near Lean Gate Road and he seemed to recognize it.

"Is there anything else I might help you with, sir?"

"Actually, yes. We may have thieves on our tails."

"Indeed?"

"Yes. I was hoping we could take sanctuary here and wait them out."

He thought for a moment and then said, "Since you are a friend to the Guild, I believe I have a better idea. If you would be so kind as to follow me."

Wylla looked at me, but I gave her a reassuring glance, and we followed the clerk through an archway and into a back hallway. He called to another acolyte to take his place in the reception hall and then guided us down a spiral staircase into a narrow stone hallway lined with doors.

"This is part of the original temple," the clerk explained. "It goes down another two levels, although our destination is right here at the end of the hallway."

He strode over to the last door at the end of the doorway and pulled it open.

Light spilled out and I felt a wave of cool air. It was a portal.

"Where does it lead?" I asked.

"The north side of the city. Iblan's shop up near the Keep. You'll be free of your pursuers for certain."

"Iblan?"

"He's a bone carver, sir. Quite skilled. The thing is, you need to say the password the moment you arrive. The word is 'sceptre,' by the way."

"What happens if we don't say the password?" Wylla asked.

"Let's just say that Iblan has been known to carve more than bone."

We thanked the clerk and stepped into the portal, Wylla tightly clutching my arm.

A moment later we found ourselves in a long storeroom lit by wall sconces. Three of the walls were covered with floor-to-ceiling shelves packed with bones of every shape and size. The back wall had full skeletons of both a urus and a cliff lion mounted on it. There was a pair of double doors at the end of the storeroom.

"Are you okay?" I asked Wylla.

"Yes. Barely felt anything that time."

"I told you."

While she gawked at all the bones, I took a few steps towards the doors. Immediately a bell rang on the other side of the door. I had probably tripped some sort of ward.

"Do we wait for the proprietor to come here or should we depart?" Wylla asked.

"Probably safer not to burst out of the storeroom," I said. "Besides, we're standing on a pit trap."

She looked down and saw what I had spotted already: a four foot by eight foot rectangle etched into the wooden plank floor. It served as the covering for the pit. The way these things usually worked was that something activated a series of latches which would release the covering, dumping whoever was standing on top of the cover into a deep pit.

I stepped outside of the rectangle and motioned for Wylla to do the same.

"Just in case," I whispered.

"Who goes there?" a voice called out.

"Sceptre," I said in a loud voice.

"Say again."

"Sceptre!"

I heard a clicking sound, and the door opened. A tall man with red hair stood in the doorway, sheathing a pair of white bone knives.

"Welcome to Iblan's," he said.

"Thank you," I said. "My name is Bander, and this is Wylla. Are you Iblan?"

"Indeed I am. This way, if you please."

We followed him down a corridor and around a corner and soon found ourselves in the front room of his shop. There were various displays of figurines, statues, and other artwork—all carved from bone.

"And what's your story, friends?" Iblan asked.

"We were targeted by thieves, so we sought sanctuary in the guildhall," I said.

"And they sent you here."

I nodded.

"Well, I can offer you some very reasonable prices on some statuettes if you're interested."

"Do you have any weapons?" Wylla asked.

Iblan seemed surprised by the question. "A few."

"Like what?"

"Arrowheads," he said. "I don't do the full arrows, but Rachin the fletcher does exceptional work using my arrowheads."

"I don't know how to shoot," Wylla said. "I was thinking more of a dagger or knife. Something discreet."

"Boneblades, eh? Are you a battle mage then?"

"What?"

"Metal interferes with spell casting," I explained. "Battle mages usually wield weapons made of bone or even polished obsidian."

Iblan clucked dismissively. "Obsidian's too fragile. Bone's what you want."

"What are these?" Wylla wandered over and began to scrutinize a shelf of small carved images.

"Pendants. Intricately crafted. All one of a kind. Here's a beautiful doe."

"I like this one." She held up an owl pendant.

"I bet you do," I said. "And if I had any gold remaining, I'd buy it for you."

"I can buy my own baubles."

"You offend me, mistress," Iblan said. "These are no mere baubles. Each one takes me over a week to carve."

"No need to tout your wares to me, sir. I'll purchase this owl."

"Very good, mistress. The detail work is exceptional, as you can see."

"And a stiletto."

"What?"

"You heard me. I wish to purchase a stiletto. Something thin. Small. Ladylike."

Iblan did not hesitate at all. "I have just the thing."

A quarter hour later we left the shop with Wylla's purchases and found ourselves on Cranwell Lane, not far from Lindsdown House.

"We weren't obligated to buy anything from him, you know," I told Wylla.

"Better to spend my money at the bone carver's than have it stolen."

"Perhaps."

"In any case, I want to give you the gold."

"That's not necessary."

"I insist."

"Really," I said. "I can always get more."

"I'm sure you can, but this is for appearance's sake."

"What do you mean?"

"I don't want to call attention to the fact that I have gold. I'm just a woman, after all."

I smiled at her. "You're not 'just' anything, so stop playing at it."

"Then you'll take the gold?"

"You make a good point, so yes."

She leaned into me and kissed me. At the same time, she slipped me a pouch full of coins. It was a well-orchestrated move. And it made me wonder if Wylla had ever been a professional pickpocket—although this was like a reverse pick-pocketing.

"That's better," she said. "It was getting too heavy, anyway."

"You still have the gems?"

"Of course."

I secured the pouch inside my jacket.

Wylla said, "Now that we're all settled, let's go to the market. There are some things you can buy me."

"What? Poison for your new dagger?"

"Not what I was thinking, but that's not a bad idea." She grinned at me.

We ended up spending the next several hours going from shop to shop. Wylla got some new traveling clothes and various notions and spent time having her hair washed and styled. She offered to buy me whatever I wanted, but I told her that the only thing I really care about is a good pair of boots and the ones that Sittig had fixed for me were serving me well.

"What about that blood stained shirt?"

I had forgotten about that. The stain wasn't readily visible under my jacket unless I turned a certain way. But she was right, I did need a new shirt. So we bought one for me though it took a while to find one big enough to fit me.

Eventually we made our way back to the Lindsdown

RANDY NARGI

House, ate a meal, drank several bottles of wine, and staggered back to our room, where we tore off each other's
clothes and fell into the bed, laughing.

Many hours later, I finally started to fall asleep. I thought
to myself that these past two weeks with Wylla were the best
I had experienced in a long time. This was something I could
certainly get used to. We made a good team, too. The vagrant
and the owl woman.

Chapter Thirty-Two

T
HE NEXT MORNING WYLLA SUGGESTED
THAT WE VISIT THE BATHS. I felt exhausted
and my head was pounding. And she looked groggy
as well. I didn't know if soaking in a vat of hot water would
make us feel better or kill us. But I couldn't argue with the
fact that we both needed to wash. So we trudged over to the
Pinney District and sought the Aldhelm Baths, which catered
to the same sort of people who could afford a portal.

Wylla gaped in awe as we passed through the gates into
the main courtyard of Aldhelm. The bath house was an
immense old Tomirian edifice with arches and pillars and a
vaulted hall that rose nearly a hundred feet over our heads. I
paid our bathing fee and then took Wylla's pouch of gems for
safekeeping.

"The women's chambers are over there to the left. You
can steam and wash and then we'll meet in the Great Bath.
I'll see you there."

She nodded and wandered away, looking stunned by her
surroundings.

I walked over to the men's chambers, a series of rooms

with benches and cots where nobles and wealthy merchants were scrubbed and oiled and massaged. There were steam rooms and dry heat rooms and cold baths and attendants everywhere offering drinks and food and laundry services. I ignored them all and made my way to the Great Bath. It was a colossal pool, maybe fifty feet long surrounded by a cloister with niches and benches, and the whole area was crowded with bathers. I managed to find a small section where no one was sitting or lounging and I stripped off my clothes, being careful to wrap the two pouches of valuables in my shirt. Then I quickly slid into the heated and scented water up to my neck. I didn't particularly want to show off my scars, and... then I remembered Wylla's tattoo and cursed myself.

She would certainly attract attention with that owl on her back. At the very least, people would think she was a druid and wonder why a druid would be visiting a public bath.

I snatched up my clothes and rushed towards the hallway to that led to the women's chambers but there was an attendant blocking the entrance. She would certainly call for guards if a naked man tried to enter. I had no choice but to wait for Wylla to exit the women's chambers, which she eventually did after a half hour. She was wearing a robe, thank Dynark.

She beamed at me. "I could stay here forever! I mean it. I could live here. It's so nice—"

"We have to leave."

"What? No."

I steered her over to a quiet alcove and whispered, "Your owl. It will attract too much attention."

She laughed at me. "Who cares?"

"What do you mean?"

"I mean, who cares if someone notices me—or you for that matter? The Dragon is dead. The Lockwells are hundreds of miles away. We're not wanted criminals. I'm tired of running about, looking over my shoulder."

"That's known as being cautious. And it's generally a wise thing to be."

"Maybe for you." She shrugged out of her robe and eased her naked body into the pool.

I quickly looked around to see if anyone noticed. There were dozens of people around us. Someone must have seen her back.

"Wylla," I said, as I entered the water beside her. "There are other bath houses. More private ones."

"You said that this was the nicest."

I didn't reply. We just sat on a submerged step in the pool, warm water swirling around us. Wylla leaned back with her eyes closed and was obviously enjoying the bath. I just waited, glaring at anyone whose gaze settled on her.

I didn't really know what to do. Wylla was right in a way. I led a certain kind of life and being in constant danger was something I was accustomed to. But she wasn't. And now it was taking a toll on her.

"Take your time," I finally said. "Just please do not try to float on your stomach."

"Agreed."

We stayed for another couple of hours. As I anticipated, Wylla's tattoo attracted a fair number of curious stares, and maybe people thought she was some sort of notable druid and I was her bodyguard. Who knew? We were just lucky that no one tried to ask her any questions. I credit that to my hulking presence.

Clean and more relaxed, we spent the rest of the day strolling through the Pinney District, admiring the gardens and statues and old buildings. We didn't talk about the Dragon or Jillen Lockwell or the Guild. And Wylla was right.

It was nice not to have to constantly look over your shoulder. But I knew it couldn't last.

As night began to fall, we wound our way through the city towards the Lindsdown House and our soft bed. But when we arrived, Perras Tul was waiting for us.

"The investigators have returned," he said.

"Quicker than I thought," I said.

"Herron wants to speak with you. Now."

"You're not even going to tell me what they found?"

He shrugged. "Not my place. Herron will do the talking."

Perras Tul did not look like he was happy about this whole thing. Or maybe he just wasn't happy about being an errand boy. We didn't speak during the entire walk back to the guildhall.

The same clerk was on duty in the reception hall. Wylla smiled at him and quickly showed off the owl pendant, but not her new stiletto. And then we made our way to Herron's office.

He had been waiting for us and got right down to it.

"Everything was as you described," he said. "My men found the chamber beneath the mill. They found the cells, and that wretch's body."

"Do you know who he is?"

"No idea. The body was too far gone for any sort of resurrection."

"And the archway?"

"That's the troubling thing."

"Don't tell me," Wylla said. "It was a gate."

Herron looked genuinely surprised. "Yes, madam. Yes, it was."

"What kind of gate?" I asked.

"We don't know. Yet. But its very presence is disturbing."

We all sat and then Herron looked right at me and asked,

"How sure are you that this missing girl had been imprisoned there?"

I could tell that he wanted to know about Jillen Lockwell. Things I didn't want to talk about.

"Not sure at all," I said. "All we know is that there were small footprints. They could have been from a young woman."

The Guild Master nodded. "The investigators saw them as well. But they also detected residual magic in the cells. There is a very good chance that the prisoners were mages, or had some sort of magical ability."

That fit with Valthar's hypothesis. Haddon Fane needed others with magical abilities to help him open the gate.

"Can you determine if the gate had been opened?" I asked. "Did something come through and kill Haddon Fane?"

"No, we don't believe so. This type of gate requires a considerable amount of channeled energy to trigger it. It was close to being opened, but thankfully, more mages are needed to activate it it. We locked the artifact down and it's now en route to the Esoterium. We have experts there who will be able to unlock its secrets, I'm certain of it."

"Then what killed Haddon Fane?" I asked.

"You saw it for yourself," he said. "The man's head was smashed against the wall. I'd wager his assailant was someone large and brutish." Again, he looked directly at me. "Someone quite like you, Bander."

There was a tense silence for a few moments, and then Wylla laughed out loud.

"Well, I think I might have noticed him using someone's head as a battering ram."

"Of course," Herron said. "I'm not implying that you yourself had anything to do with his death, but Haddon Fane could very well have had an associate who turned on him."

"Or a master," I said. "Someone who might not have tolerated failure."

Herron nodded. "Indeed."

I leaned back in my seat. There were things that didn't add up. In fact, this entire meeting was very unusual. The Guild was normally very secretive. I had no idea why Herron was sharing this information, especially if the gate was some sort of unknown artifact.

Herron said, "We need to find out more about who this man was and if he had been working alone or with others."

"Could you use scrying to track whoever left the chamber?" I asked.

"My men tried that. The trail is too cold."

It occurred to me that we hadn't noticed any larger footprints leading to the grove, but I kept that fact to myself.

Herron continued, "It turns out that we require your assistance."

That's why he had been so forthcoming. It all made sense.

"What type of assistance?" I asked.

"We're trying to track down anyone who might have had contact with Haddon Fane—if that is indeed his name. One of my men has located the peddler you mentioned. Others are interviewing shopkeepers throughout the city. But I need you to return to Hytwen."

"That's not a good idea," I said. "We're not very popular there. Why not just send a Guild representative to interview the Lockwells?"

"Of course, that's our intention, but this is a delicate situation," Herron said. "As you know, the village is outside of the Empire's borders."

"Yes," I said. "Technically it falls within the Tengan Territories."

"And as such, we cannot just march in and demand cooperation. It is outside of the Guild's jurisdiction."

"But for all intents and purposes Hytwen is part of the Empire," Wylla said. "We trade within the Empire, our coin is the Empire's, and everyone not born in the village came from the Empire."

"I understand, good lady, but you must know that the Guild adheres to the rule of law quite precisely. We cannot and will not operate outside Harion's borders. It would set a dangerous precedent, to be sure."

Herron was not exaggerating. There were those among the Empire's elite who would like to see the Guild dissolved. Any hint that it was somehow above the law would doom it.

"What will you have us do?" I asked.

"You told me that that there had been some sort of bargain struck..."

"Yes, the Dragon—or Haddon Fane—was to aid Hytwen in their conflict with Ortwen," I said.

"If that aid was actually rendered—if someone used magic against citizens of the Empire—even if they were beyond the border, we'd be able to send mages in. Legally."

It seemed like a technicality to me, but I understood the Guild's position. "So we'd return and see if Ortwen has been destroyed?"

"You will investigate whether magic had been used during this conflict. We'll provide you with an open waypoint gem. I trust you know what that is."

I nodded. Waypoint gems allowed mages to open a portal to whatever location had been locked within the gem. Open waypoint gems made it possible for mages to open a portal to wherever the gem was located. It was a very valuable item and not deployed lightly. I was surprised that Herron would actually trust someone outside of the Guild with such a thing.

He said, "We can get you as far as Bexden, then you'll have to ride the rest of the way. Make your inquiries and activate the gem. Perras Tul will then join you and either begin inquiries of his own or simply return you here, depending on what you discover. Is that clear?"

"It's clear enough," I said. "I'm just not sure it is the best idea, since—"

Wylla interrupted me. "We'll do it."

I continued to protest, but she continued, "It may be the only way we figure out what happened to Jillen."

"Exactly, good lady. This is like a tangled skein and we must unravel it. Thread by thread."

"Very well," I said. "When do we leave?"

Chapter Thirty-Three

I T DIDN'T MAKE ANY SENSE TO TRAVEL AT NIGHT, SO WE RETURNED TO THE GUILD-HALL THE NEXT MORNING. Perras Tul met us and we discussed logistics for a few more minutes and then he escorted us to another room where Wylla and I waited alone for someone to bring the waypoint gem.

"This will be dangerous. You should stay here in Vale," I said. "I'll go alone."

Wylla jumped to her feet. "Absolutely not! If anything, you should be the one to stay. You're the one who has a price on his head."

"I doubt Arno Lockwell would go to the trouble."

"It's not him I'm worried about. Ellia Lockwell is the vindictive one. And once you cross her, you've made an enemy for life."

"I'm not afraid of either of the Lockwells."

"Good. Neither am I. That's why I'm going. Besides, I know the village better than you. I know how to get in and out without being seen. And I know where to hide."

"I don't plan on do much hiding."

At that moment, Perras Tul walked in. "This is a fact-finding mission only. Remember Herron's instructions. Gather information. That's all. Do not try to take things into your own hands."

I didn't reply, but Wylla nodded in agreement.

The mage brought out a small metal box, opened it, and withdrew an orange-colored gem strung on a length of leather cord. I was surprised by how small it was—not much bigger than a pigeon's egg. The waypoint gem glittered in the light of the torches that lit the room. If you looked closely, you could see what appeared to be a swirling flame dancing deep within the crystal.

"It's beautiful," Wylla said.

"Well, don't get too attached to it. I'll be taking it back once we're done," Perras Tul said.

He showed us both how to activate the gem and then handed it to me. But Wylla snatched it from my palm. "Better if I hold it. Especially if you end up in the Lockwells' dungeon."

"They don't have a dungeon."

"Metaphorically speaking."

Perras Tul fastened the cord to Wylla's wrist and checked it several times.

Wylla turned her hand and showed off what now looked to be a bracelet. "It looks really good on me. Are you sure I can't keep it?"

Perras Tul frowned and ignored the question. "I'll be monitoring this constantly, so whenever you activate it, I'll be there."

He gave us a small pouch of coins to buy horses and then opened a portal to Bexden.

"Keep your head down and use the gem once you find out one way or another if a mage interfered there," he said. "And don't get killed!"

"I rarely do," I said, and then we stepped through the portal.

We emerged in a grove of scrubby trees. The wind was blowing hard here, kicking up dust. Wylla pulled up her scarf to cover her face. I looked around to get my bearings. It appeared that we were north of Bexden, not far from Market Street—also not far from the ranch where we sold our original horses.

"Maybe we can buy them back," Wylla shouted, trying to be heard above the howling wind.

We trudged north. Thankfully the wind died down by the time we arrived at the ranch. The horses we took from Minch were still there, so we bought them back—although we paid a bit more than what we sold them for. I wasn't sure if the animals recognized us or not, but Wylla made a fuss over them.

Next we rode into town to buy some food and supplies. If I remembered correctly, it was at least 90 miles to Hytwen. Maybe a little more. Even if we rode quickly, we'd be on the road for at least two days. Probably two and a half. We needed supplies.

"Let's be quick," I told Wylla. "And keep your face covered. I don't want to run into the mage Felde."

She grinned. "I forgot about him. And Robie. She was nice."

Fortunately we didn't see either of them. Just bought our provisions and headed down to the West Way, past all the caravans and wagons. Then we started riding east. Back towards Hytwen.

We rode hard for the whole day and covered about twenty five miles. As dusk approached, I found us a clearing by a brook, just south of the highway. It looked to be a well-used campsite, with a fire ring and even some makeshift beds of piled boughs.

"It'll do," Wylla said.

After tending to the horses I made a fire. We ate our bread and dried meat in silence, which was fine with me. I'm not naturally garrulous, but over the past two weeks I learned that Wylla was more than able to talk the hind legs off a donkey. But tonight she was unusually quiet.

"Tired from the ride?" I asked.

"I suppose."

"You're not still in pain from your injuries?" The last time we rode on the West Way she could barely stay on her horse and we covered only half as many miles in a day of riding.

"No. I'm fine."

Clearly she wasn't. Maybe the stress of this entire ordeal was catching up with her. But I didn't want to badger her. Instead I decided to inspect the perimeter of the campsite before it became completely dark. I walked around the area and checked on the horses. Then I found an area out of sight of the entrance to our camp and just sat on my haunches and waited. I was good at waiting and sitting motionless in the bushes for a half hour was a tried-and-true way to determine if brigands were planning to raid your camp.

But all was quiet.

After a time, I returned to the fire, but Wylla was already asleep. I lay down next to her. Within a minute I was asleep as well.

At some point during the night, Wylla jostled me.

"What?"

"Are you awake?" she asked.

"I am now."

"Me too. I can't sleep."

"Why not?"

"I can't help wondering, is there something you're not telling me?"

"What?" I was still half asleep.

"You're keeping something from me," she said. "Aren't you?"

"I don't know what you're talking about."

"Yes you do."

"Wylla, I really don't." I propped myself up on one elbow.

"You are an expert investigator." It was more of a question than a statement.

"Says who?"

"You act as if you are baffled by this whole thing. I just don't believe it. You're too canny for that."

"You think I've figured it all and am keeping it to myself?"

"Yes, I do. I really do."

"Well, I'm not."

"I just want the truth."

"I know as much as you."

"Maybe," she said. "But maybe you have some ideas that you aren't sharing."

"Why would I do that?"

"Perhaps you're trying to protect me."

I turned and moved closer to her. "If I really wanted to protect you, I wouldn't have let you talk me into coming along."

"That's not what I mean."

I sighed. "Here's what I know. A rogue mage took Jillen Lockwell and probably kept her prisoner. There's a good chance it was because of her magical abilities. He was trying to open a gate for some reason that no one knows. He died; she escaped. Probably teleported away. And now we're going back to her home to see if she returned."

"There's got to be more." She fought back tears.

I held her close. "If there is, we'll discover it together."

Chapter Thirty-Four

WE WOKE EARLY THE NEXT MORNING. It was still dark, and it was cold. Wylla didn't say anything about her outburst last night.

I didn't even bother making a fire. No sense. We ate quickly, saddled up the horses, and set off.

At about noon we passed the ruins of the Stag & Pennant. We didn't stop.

By the end of the day, we had covered forty miles or more. We were close to the crossroads, but I could tell that Wylla was exhausted from the long ride. So I found us another place to sleep south of the highway. We'd arrive tomorrow fresh and alert.

The night passed quickly and without incident.

A few hours after setting off the next morning, we reached the crossroads with the wide road leading south to Hytwen and Ortwen.

We didn't really need to rest at this point, but I wanted to stretch my legs, so we dismounted and walked the horses off the highway. Wylla stared at the sign that announced that Hytwen and Ortwen were less than twenty miles away.

"I thought I'd never be back here," she said quietly.

"Maybe this will be the last time."

"I hope so. I really do." Her mouth was set in a hard line.

A few hours later we found ourselves at another crossroads, which was more of a fork in the road on the north shore of Lake Teagh. Hytwen was to the right and Ortwen was to the left.

I thought for a moment and then steered my horse to the left.

"Wrong way," Wylla called.

"I have an idea."

"What kind of idea?" She rode closer.

"We may not even have to go to Hytwen at all. Maybe we can find out everything we need in Ortwen." I explained that if there was evidence of a magical attack in Ortwen, that's all we would need to summon Perras Tul.

"What do you expect to find?" Wylla asked. "The whole village burned to the ground?"

I didn't answer, but in the back of my mind, I had considered the possibility.

Within an hour we arrived at Ortwen's guardhouse on the outskirts of the village. It was manned, which I took as a good sign.

"State your name and your business," one of the sentries asked. He was a lean man with close-cropped blond hair. He kind of looked like a Dwen, but thinner. Another man stood off to one side. He held a crossbow ready. There might have been more inside the guardhouse.

"My name is Bander, and this is Wylla. We wish to speak with Creagar Skenn."

"About what?"

"An important matter."

"What kind of important matter?"

"We have some information about Hytwen. For Creagar Skenn's ears only."

The guard shook his head. "Creagar Skenn don't meet with folks he don't know."

"He'll want to meet with me."

His eyes narrowed. "Will he now?"

"I'm the one who took his son."

Wylla tried to jerk me away. "Are you crazy?"

The blond sentry and the crossbowman looked at each other. I could almost see their brains working. Then they made a decision.

Sixty seconds later I was in manacles and being marched into town along a narrow canyon road that twisted and turned between tall rocky ridges. It was like walking through a natural maze. I remembered Minch telling me that the lapp needed to be barged out of Ortwen because the large wagons couldn't make the tight turns on this main road.

Wylla walked behind me, muttering about how stupid I was. I didn't care. I had a plan.

After a quarter mile or so, we arrived in Ortwen. It looked different since the last time I was here. In the daylight, the village appeared a bit more homey and less forbidding. I noticed flower boxes and small gardens and painted doors. There were people on the street including children. Thankfully nothing I saw made me think that this place had been attacked by Arno Lockwell. But I needed to find out for sure.

The sentries took us to the marshal's office in the northwest part of town. I remembered the structure, a narrow stone building. The two men dragged me up a couple of wooden steps, calling for the marshal. No one replied and as we made our way inside I saw that the office was empty.

They shoved both us into the cell that wasn't being used as the marshal's sleeping quarters and locked us in. Then the blond sentry ordered the other man to find Dorson, who was probably the new marshal.

I looked around the cell. There was a single narrow cot and a chamber pot. Nothing else. Not even any blankets. The floor was packed dirt and walls were made of solid stone blocks, like most of the other buildings in the village. Probably 45 years old. And maybe would last another 500 years unless Ortwen was hit by an earthquake.

I asked Wylla if she wanted to sit down on the cot, but she just glared at me. I didn't blame her.

"Everything will be fine. Trust me," I said in a low voice.

She turned away, remaining silent. I sat down on the edge of the cot and stretched my legs. We stayed like that for a good twenty minutes. Then the other sentry returned with two men, both in their fourth decade. One was short and stocky, with a square, weatherbeaten face. The other was taller and had thinning hair, but bright eyes. His arm was in a sling, but it didn't seem to slow him down. He strode right up to my cell.

"Well, well, well," he said. "I understand you were looking for me."

He was Creagar Skenn.

I stood up. "Thank you for coming. We have a lot to discuss."

"Oh, I didn't come because we're going to have a discussion. I came to see how tall you were so we could build the right size gallows. You're a big one, that's for sure."

"I need to know a few things."

Creagar Skenn snorted. "Oh really? Me too. Let's start with your names."

"My name is Bander, most recently of Rundlun. And this is Wylla."

"The Lockwells' maid," he said matter-of-factly.

"Nursemaid," Wylla said. "I looked after Jillen. No more, though."

I said, "I need to know if Arno Lockwell tried to attack Ortwen."

"As one of his sellswords, I would think you would know the answer to that question."

"I'm not one of his sellswords and you know it."

Creagar Skenn shrugged. "Perhaps. I probably would have remembered seeing you. But even if you are not a sellsword, you are a spy. That much is obvious."

"I'm not. What kind of spy marches up to your front gate?"

"A stupid one."

"Just tell me if they attacked."

His eyes narrowed. "They tried. Dynark knows, they tried. But we drove them off. Destiny of the righteous. Now how tall are you? Eighteen and a half hands? Nineteen?"

"It doesn't matter."

"Of course it does. We can have your feet hitting the ground when we're trying to hang you. That would be bad form."

"You're not going to hang me."

"That's what we do to spies. And besides, if we're being honest, you are worse than a spy, aren't you? You're a murderer. You snuck into the village. You killed Roffey. You abducted my son."

"I didn't kill your marshal. Lockwell's men did. And I didn't harm a hair on your boy's head. I came for answers about Jillen Lockwell that night. That's all."

"You came to murder and spy," Creagar Skenn said. "You came to gather information for an attack on my village. It didn't do any good, though, did it?"

"That's not why I came. Listen, just tell me if there was a mage among the attackers."

"A mage?"

"Yes. A man by the name of Haddon Fane."

"I didn't stop to ask the names of the men I was driving out of my village."

"I think you'd know if you were fighting a mage."

"I suppose I would."

"So there was no mage with Arno Lockwell?"

"No. Not that I could tell. But you know that already. What kind of games are you playing at?"

So Haddon Fane hadn't honored his part of the bargain. That was good for Ortwen, but bad for the Guild. They had no cause to enter Hytwen and interrogate the Lockwells.

But I didn't think the Lockwells were done here. Not by a long shot.

"Arno Lockwell will be back. With more men," I said.

"Thanks for the warning, but I figured as much. He seemed to give up too easily for a man with that much hate in his heart. But what about this mage?"

At least I had provoked his curiosity. "I think he's out of the picture. Let us free and I will tell you everything."

He squinted at me. "How about you tell me everything and I'll decide whether or not I'll let you free."

So I told him. I told him about Jillen Lockwell. And how Ellia Lockwell sold Jillen to the mage Haddon Fane. I told her that the girl's abduction had been faked. And, from the start, Ellia Lockwell planned to blame Ortwen and use the deception to justify an attack. I told them that I thought it came down to gold, pure and simple. Lockwell Farms wasn't doing well, and they wanted Ortwen's contracts. And I told them that I was certain that the Lockwells would come again.

"Now will you release us?" I asked.

"I'm still deciding."

"I can help you deal with the Lockwells for good."

"And why would you do that? What's your stake in all this?"

Wylla spoke for me. "You really have to ask? After what they did to Jillen Lockwell? Selling her into slavery?"

"I could see why you might have a soft spot for the girl, but what's his reason?"

"I have a soft spot for Wylla," I said.

He didn't say anything for a while. Then just turned and left. The sentries followed him out, but the stocky man stayed. Not the result I was hoping for.

"You Dorson?" I asked.

"Shut up."

So I did.

They left us there all day and all night. I tried to engage Dorson a few more times, but he ignored me. So did Wylla. But eventually she got tired of standing and joined me on the cot. It was a tight squeeze, but she was cold, so she used me for my body heat.

Chapter Thirty-Five

✥

THE NEXT MORNING, WE WERE GIVEN SOME FOOD. Two bowls of some kind of cold porridge. I offered mine to Wylla, but she told me that she didn't want it. At least she was talking to me this morning.

When we were done, Dorson commanded me to push the bowls through the bars and I did so.

"Now step back."

I did what he said.

He gathered up the bowls and left us. Before he exited the office he said, "Don't go anywhere."

It was supposed to be a jest, but what he didn't know was that I was reasonably sure that I could bend the bars enough to allow Wylla to escape.

Once Dorson was gone, Wylla said, "We need Perras Tul. I'm going to summon him."

"No."

"What do you mean, no? You think Creagar Skenn is going to let us out."

"Maybe."

"We're wasting time."

"Give me one more day. Then you can contact Perras Tul. But if we don't have any evidence for him, he won't be happy."

Dorson returned and so did Creagar Skenn. This time he brought his son, Fenton Skenn. The boy looked me over, but he seemed more curious about Wylla. I nodded to the lad, trying to appear friendly.

"Is this the man?" Creagar Skenn asked his son.

"Yes."

"And you're sure about this?"

"Yes, father."

Creagar Skenn turned to Dorson. "Let them out."

Without a word, the marshal unlocked the door and stepped aside.

"Thank you," I said.

"Thank my son. If it were up to me, you'd be marched to the gallows."

Fenton Skenn said, "He wasn't mean to me, father."

"Thank you, Fenton Skenn," I said. "This is Wylla."

She curtsied politely.

"Is she your wife?" the boy asked.

I looked at Wylla, but didn't say anything.

She smiled at Fenton Skenn and said, "No, I'm not his wife, but I am his friend."

"Will you be my friend too?"

"Of course, young sir. I would be honored."

"Walk with me, Bander," Creagar Skenn said.

We left Wylla and Fenton Skenn at the marshal's office and made our way towards the entrance to the village, walking in silence.

Finally Creagar Skenn said, "It's no big revelation. I know

Hytwen will attack again. I knew it the moment we drove them away the first time."

I didn't reply.

"But next time, that won't happen. They won't leave alive."

He waved his good arm like he was signaling.

Above us, on the ridges that ran along the main road, a half dozen archers emerged from hiding—three on each side.

"Smart," I said. "Is this the route they used last time?"

"Yes, they hit us at dawn. We were unprepared. They overpowered my guards and got as far as the square. But we beat them back. Since then I've posted additional guards in the village and the gatehouse."

"That's good, but they may try to attack from the lake. That's how I got in."

"We'll be ready for them. I've got men patrolling the shore all night long, as well as my best archer—Tawley—ready with flaming arrows."

"It's not easy to hit a skiff with a flaming arrow."

"He's been practicing."

I asked Creagar Skenn to escort me around the perimeter of the village. I wanted to see it all in the light of day. As we walked, I asked how many trained fighting men he had in Ortwen.

"Trained? Not many. Less than a dozen probably. We're farmers, not warriors. But I've got nearly forty able-bodied mudders ready to defend what's theirs."

"And how many invaders were there last time?"

"Hard to say. It was very chaotic. Ten or twelve at most."

That made sense. Mercenaries are very expensive—especially if you have to bring them in from a hundred miles away. And if Arno Lockwell expected to have a mage fighting alongside him, he'd think that a dozen hired swords would be enough. But they weren't. Not against an equal number of fighting men plus forty more standing behind them. I shared my suspicions with Creagar Skenn.

"I wondered about that," he said.

"When was the attack?"

He thought for a moment and then said, "About two weeks ago, maybe a day or two more. Why?"

I ran through the timetable in my head. After he licked his wounds, Lockwell had to travel to Marston Hills and raise a small army. At least thirty men. Then he had to get them back to Hytwen. Would it take two weeks? Possibly. It might even be longer if he couldn't find the men in Marston Hills. If that were the case, he would have to go all the way to Kreed's Keep.

"He's gathering more mercenaries," I said. "That's why he hasn't attacked again. It's taking time, but he plans to overpower you."

We walked back towards the marshal's office.

Creagar Skenn looked away. "Then I need to hit them first. Before the mercenaries arrive."

"You don't want to do that. Hytwen's got mudders too. They'll defend their village, same as your folks. And unless you've got mercenaries of your own that you haven't mentioned, you just don't have the manpower."

"Then what am I supposed to do? Just sit around and wait for them to come?"

"I may be able to get us some help. But we need to find out for sure when Lockwell plans on attacking," I said.

Creagar Skenn looked at me expectantly, like he could tell that I had a plan. Which I did.

I told him that I knew the marshal in Hytwen. "Minch. He's a good man. And he has no love for the Lockwells. He'll know what their timetable is."

"And he'll tell you?"

I nodded grimly. "One way or another, he'll tell me. I'll leave at midnight."

~

I knew Wylla would have a problem with my plan. And she did.

"I'm coming with you," she said. "It's non-negotiable."

"Everything's negotiable."

"Don't be an ass. We've come this far. I need to see it through."

"And you will. From Ortwen. Besides, I'm just going to talk to Minch. Find out what Arno Lockwell's timetable is. We need to know that information."

"Then what?"

"Then we summon Perras Tul."

"But everything has changed."

She was right. There was no mage involved in that first attack. And Haddon Fane was dead. There'd be no justification for the Guild to intervene—even if Lockwell attacked again.

"Admittedly, this is a long shot," I said. "But if we time it correctly and summon Perras Tul as Lockwell's force enters Ortwen, he'll be compelled to act. Even if it is in self-defense."

Wylla crossed her arms. "And how do you think your mage friend will feel once he's realized he's been deceived?"

"He won't care, because the Guild will have all the reason it needs to start investigating the Lockwells. Anyone attacking a one of the Guild's own will provoke them to action—no matter where it happens."

I could tell that Wylla was still skeptical, so I continued. "The Guild will send battle mages and maybe even some Shielders from Kreed's Keep. The Lockwells will be taken away and interrogated. You and I will go back to Vale. Herron trusts us, so there's a good chance he'll tell us what he learned from the Lockwells."

"What about what Valthar said? What if Jillen went home? What if she's there in the manor with her parents right now?"

"Valthar was just guessing. And if she's there, we'll figure something out."

"If she's there, the Guild will take her. You said so yourself. Probably lock her up and throw away the key."

"We don't know that," I said.

Her eyes flickered with anger. "You knew that. And you told me so. Back when you were being honest with me."

I didn't say anything.

When people got like this, it was better to leave them be. Instead I decided to take a walk and let Wylla calm down.

I left her fuming and walked over to the market district, a circle of buildings in the heart of the village. There were all the types of shops you might expect: a tailor, dry goods store, a carpenter, general provisions, a cobbler, healer, barber, leatherworker, and weaver. Most of the buildings were two story stone structures which held several businesses. In the open area at the very center of the village stood a maze of wooden stalls for food vendors, including those selling meats and fish, vegetables, spices, and cheese. My stomach rumbled in hunger as the aroma of grilling meats and fresh-baked breads wafted through the air, and I pushed my way towards the closest source of food.

Everyone was staring at me, but I didn't care. I remembered what the courier had advised when he first told me about Hytwen and Ortwen: they don't like strangers in Ortwen. I guessed it was true. But they had no problem selling me a half dozen skewers of grilled meat.

I took my meal down to the shore of the lake and looked

out over Lake Teagh's mist-covered expanse. Somewhere to the southwest, a dozen miles away, lay Hytwen. As I tore into the skewers, I thought about Haddon Fane and Ellia Lockwell.

Luckily for Ortwen, the mage hadn't kept his end of the bargain. He didn't participate in the attack two weeks ago. That made me wonder what else Haddon Fane reneged on. There was a very good chance that the mage didn't pay Ellia Lockwell what he owed her for Jillen.

He probably showed up on the day Ellia Lockwell was supposed to hand over Jillen and saw that the girl was gone. Of course he wouldn't pay for merchandise not received. What was Ellia Lockwell going to do? Complain to the Guild?

All this meant that the Arno Lockwell might not even have enough gold to hire thirty mercenaries. That would be good for Ortwen, but not so good for my plan. We needed the pretense that would allow the Guild to investigate the Lockwells.

I walked around the shore, passing a good amount of huts and cabins which, from the looks of them, housed boat builders, net and rope makers, and other craftsmen. Dozens of men were repairing skiffs and nets, or making the corded line upon which the lapp grew. Up to the west, along the canal, stood a row of warehouses. Between them stretched a large pavilion with long tables.

As I got closer, I saw men and women sorting dried lapp on the tables. Children helped out as well, carrying woven baskets filled with lapp back to other long tables where more workers baled the dried lapp into parcels the size of a wine cask. The parcels were loaded on to a series of ramps which led to barges on the canal. It looked to be a very efficient operation.

I lingered around the area for a half hour or so, then made

my way back to the marshal's office. There was no sign of Wylla nor anyone else for that matter. I wasn't exactly sure how many more hours of daylight were left, but it was clear that I had plenty of time before midnight. So I stretched out on the cot and went to sleep.

Chapter Thirty-Six

I AWOKE WHEN WYLLA KICKED AT MY FOOT.

"It's almost midnight," she said.

I sat up, still groggy. I usually didn't sleep that soundly.

"Have you changed your mind?" she asked matter-of-factly.

"About what? Going to Hytwen?"

"About taking me along."

"No."

She nodded. "I thought as much. You're a stubborn son of a bitch."

I yawned, trying to wake myself up. "Maybe so, but I've done this sort of thing before."

"Yes, but that doesn't mean you should refuse someone watching your back."

"It'll be quicker if I do this alone."

"Stubborn," she muttered.

I didn't say anything. Just leaned back and stretched. My back was tight from sleeping in the narrow cot.

Wylla said, "I might not be here when you get back." Her face was tight and her voice betrayed no emotion.

I looked up at her and met her eyes. "I hope that you are. I really do."

She turned and left without another word.

I sat for a while, still groggy. Wylla had the right to be angry, I knew. But we were close to finishing this thing. I just needed her to trust me.

I stood up and walked outside, intending to continue the conversation.

Wylla was there, but she was flanked by Creagar Skenn, the marshal Dorson, and a tall man dressed in black leathers sitting on a large dark horse. The man's leg was bandaged. Another horse was saddled and looked ready to go.

Creagar Skenn motioned to the man on the horse. "This is my brother Borsus. He's going with you. Your lady friend's staying here. As an assurance that you'll return."

Wylla glared at me as if I had been conspiring with Creagar Skenn. This wasn't helping.

I turned back to Borsus Skenn and looked him up and down.

"He can ride to the edge of the village," I said. "But I'm going in alone."

"Suits me just fine," Borsus Skenn said. "I'm not doing much walking these days."

"What happened?" I asked.

"Borsus was injured in the attack. Same as me," Creagar Skenn said.

"Don't matter," Borsus Skenn frowned. "Lockwell will get his. Mark my words."

"Not tonight, though," I said. "We go in. I find out when they're planning at taking another run at you. We go out. Are we all clear about that?"

"Aye," Borsus Skenn said. For the first time I noticed he

had a double crossbow hanging from his saddle. Perhaps he was armed in case we ran into any patrols on the road. Or perhaps the crossbow was for me.

I told Creagar Skenn, "I'll be back before dawn. If I haven't returned by then, start worrying."

Next I turned to Wylla. I wanted to reassure her one last time, but she had just walked away—back into the office. The other men all picked up on her bitterness, but no one said anything.

I sighed and climbed on my horse, a chestnut mare. Then I motioned for Borsus Skenn to lead on.

It was slow going through the twists and turns of the main road, but once we cleared the guardhouse, we urged our horses into a trot and began to make good progress. The moon was bright, and the air was cool. I felt refreshed and ready for anything.

The journey took a little less than two hours. Borsus Skenn was not very talkative, but I did learn that he was a hunter—and he had been to Hytwen a few times back when the two villages were on better terms.

About a mile from the edge of Hytwen, we found a dark stand of trees off the road. I helped Borsus Skenn off his horse and he limped over to a large boulder where he could sit. I tied up the horses. He readied his crossbow and nodded to me.

"If you're not back within an hour and a half, I'll leave without you," he said.

"I understand."

"Do you also understand that your lass will forfeit her life if you don't return?"

I didn't say anything, just set off at a fast walk down the road. I wasn't much of a runner. I could move quickly for a few seconds, but that was it. But I had long legs, and I didn't get tired, so I could cover a lot of ground at a quick pace.

Keeping to the moon shadows, I made my way past the first pastures and cattle pens, but then I cut off the road and headed due south. It was the route Wylla had shown me to avoid sentries when we snuck out of Hytwen two weeks ago. And it worked. I didn't see a soul.

I slipped from shadow to shadow as I entered the village proper and found myself on the far end of Valley Road—which led to Queen Street, where Minch's cabin was. Hopefully, I'd find him there—probably drunk, maybe just asleep. If I remembered correctly, Queen Street was somewhere in the middle of the residential district which spanned less than a half mile along Valley Road. But I knew close to five hundred people lived here, so there was a good chance there would be at least some folks awake at this hour. Most of them on their way to their outhouses. And maybe Lockwell had instituted a roving night watch. Who knew? It all meant that I had to be extra careful.

After a quarter hour of moving very deliberately, I arrived at Minch's cabin. I had seen a few people out, but they hadn't seen me. At least I hoped they hadn't.

His cabin was dark and the front door was unlocked. Probably would look bad if the marshal felt he needed to lock his door. I eased my way inside and just stood there listening. Minch was a heavy breather, so after a few moments, I was able to pinpoint where he lay sleeping. My eyes eventually adjusted to the gloom and I could barely make out the marshal, sprawled on his cot. Carefully, I stepped over to him and shook his shoulder.

"Minch," I whispered.

He jolted awake. "Dynark's blood!"

"It's Bander. Remember me?"

"What are you doing here? I never thought I'd see you again." He sat up, and I saw that his chest had been bandaged.

"Keep your voice down. I need to know about Lockwell. When will the mercenaries arrive?"

He wiped his eyes. "What do you mean?"

"The attack on Ortwen. When is it planned for?"

"That happened already."

"Not the first attack. The second one. He's planning to attack again, isn't he? With more men..."

"Aye, and that's happened as well. What hour is it?"

"You're not making sense."

"They left at midnight."

My mind began racing with questions. How many men? Why didn't I see them on the road? A second later, I started figuring things out.

"They went by boat, didn't they?" I asked.

He nodded. "Just like we did. But they were going to land east of the docks and climb the cliffs."

"How many men?"

"Lockwell's hired two dozen sellswords from Kreed's Keep. Plus thirty of our own."

More than fifty men. This wasn't good. Creagar Skenn had fifty men, but only ten who were trained fighters. Lockwell had two dozen. It would be a rout. Especially if Lockwell managed to get into the village unnoticed.

I needed to go back and warn Creagar Skenn. But even as I bolted from Minch's cabin, I knew it was too late.

Chapter Thirty-Seven

BORSUS SKENN WAS RIGHT WHERE I LEFT HIM. He looked surprised to see me.

"That was fast," he said.

"Saddle up! Lockwell's attacking now!"

He cursed and hobbled over to his horse. I helped him mount, then I swung up onto my mare and we urged our horses into the night as quickly as they would go.

Borsus Skenn was a much better horseman than me and knew how hard to press the horses, so he led the way. I followed, and we rode swiftly for nearly two hours before we reached the guardhouse. Borsus Skenn called out, but there were no sentries there. The structure had been abandoned.

We pushed our horses into a hard gallop, racing through the twists and turns of the narrow entrance road. After a hundred yards or so, I began to hear the sounds of battle and smell the smoke of burning buildings. This was bad. Very bad.

As my horse thundered towards the village center, I looked up towards the top of the ridges. There were no sign of Creagar Skenn's archers, nor anyone else.

We raced around the final corner and I saw the village lit

up, with flames licking the roofs of at least a dozen buildings. Heavy smoke blanketed everything, and I could just barely make out small scattered groups of men battling with swords and clubs and pitchforks. I swung down from my horse into the fray, slamming my fist into the kidney of the closest swordsman. He staggered forward, and I accelerated the process by grabbing his tunic and pitching him forward. Mass, velocity, momentum. Once he was down, I stomped on his neck. Now I had a sword.

I ripped off some cloth and tied it around my face as a makeshift mask to keep the smoke at bay. But I didn't think it would really work. The smoke was so thick here, I could barely see ten feet in front of me. But even without the smoke, it was difficult to tell who the enemy was. Ortwen's townspeople looked the same as Hytwen's. I guessed I could concentrate on the men who had armor or expensive weapons like the swordsman I had taken down.

I heard a grunt behind me and, as I turned, a heavy shield slammed into me, knocking me back. I stumbled and lost my footing and my sword flew from my grasp. The big mercenary wielding the shield charged me, brandishing a wicked hooked battle axe in his other hand.

Laying there on the ground, I didn't have many options. I tried to kick out and knock him off balance, but he just laughed and danced back, breathing hard. I knew that the moment I tried to stand, he'd strike, so my plan was to scurry away from him, backwards like a crab. That didn't work.

He advanced methodically, huffing and puffing and swinging his axe like he was warming up for a session of splitting logs.

I kept inching back and then one hand bumped against cold steel. It was my sword. My fingers closed around the grip —and at the same time my other hand clawed a handful of dirt. I had an idea, but I had to time it just right.

There was some commotion behind the mercenary and I guess it was making him a little impatient because he cursed and then rushed in, pulling the axe back in a horizontal backswing level with my head. He made the mistake that even a lot of seasoned warriors did when fighting with an axe or a club. The tendency is to go for the biggest, most powerful blow possible—the kind of blow that could chop a man's head clear off. But those kinds of massive backswings take a lot of time for the weapon to travel—both back to gather force and forward into the target.

I took advantage of that delay to hurl a handful of dirt at his face. It didn't blind him or get in his mouth and choke him, but it did distract him for another second—which was all the time I needed to slash my sword around with all my strength and bury its blade deep into his thigh. He screamed in pain and crumpled backwards to the ground. At the same time I spun to my knees and launched myself at him. I felt his ribs snap as my 250 pounds landed on top of him. Then I choked the life out of him.

Staggering to my feet, I snatched up the axe. It was an impressive and expensive weapon with a nice heft to it. The axe's steel head was polished to a mirror-like gleam, and the blade was finely honed. I also retrieved the sword which was less fine, but certainly serviceable. Later I'd decide which weapon I liked better, but for now I'd use both.

Around me it had grown quiet. I turned slowly, straining my ears and trying to figure out where the main battle was. The smoke had cleared in this area and visibility was better, but sound was still distorted. I kept moving west, and saw a burning arrow arc across the sky, north towards the main part of town. After a few moments I heard a scream off to my left —towards the shore. I made my way through the alleys of Ortwen, evading roving mercenaries. But then my luck ran out.

Two men clad in thick leathers and armed with longswords turned a corner and spotted me. They looked at each other and then quickly strode towards me, murder in their eyes. Both of them were at least twenty years younger than me. The man on my left was as tall as me, but bone thin —all arms and legs. His companion wasn't quite as tall, but he was thick and heavy set with a scar that ran from above his left eyebrow down to the corner of his mouth.

"There you are," I called. "The square's all but mopped up. Where's Arno Lockwell?"

"Nice try, whey-face," the scarred man growled at me. Clearly, my ruse hadn't fooled him.

They held their blades loosely and moved towards me—relaxed and confident.

I switched the axe to my right hand and the sword to my left and held my ground. This would be interesting.

The thin mercenary continued to move left while the scarred man moved right. It was a classic flanking move.

I stood as still as a statue, breathing in deeply, both weapons at my side. I needed the mercenaries no farther than five feet away, which was a single pace for me. My body tensed like it always did before a fight. I felt the energy well up in my chest and then my shoulders, spreading through my body to my arms and my hands. Time seemed to slow, and I almost felt like I could hear every beat of my opponents' hearts and sense every twitch of their muscles.

The thin one moved first, driving towards me, sword straight out like he was going to skewer me.

I turned slightly to face him, but I kept the scarred man in my peripheral vision because my turn was just for show. Before the thin man got anywhere near me, I launched myself away from him—exploding right towards the scarred merce-nary. My axe drove back and up into the scarred man's crotch. The axe head didn't have to travel far—an arc of less than forty five degrees—and it didn't need a lot of force behind the blow because I had struck an extremely soft target.

The scarred man screamed like a banshee and pitched over, clutching at the fountain of blood between his legs.

I stamped my back foot down to arrest some of my motion, then snapped my sword up to block the thin man's attack. But I barely had to do anything. He was so shocked by what had happened to his partner that I easily swatted his blade away with my own. Then I brought the axe back forward and drove the end of it up into his face. *Crunch!* All kinds of bones and teeth shattered and the thin man crumpled to the ground like a dead spider.

Two more down. Maybe fifty to go. But the problem was that I didn't have the time to sit around and engage these mercenaries one-on-one.

I needed to find Wylla and discover what was going on.

Near as I could tell I was southeast of the marshal's office. What was the chance that Wylla had stayed there and holed up? Not very likely, I thought. But she was not a trained fighter, either. I couldn't see her going up against these mercenaries. I had to face facts. She could be anywhere. I just hoped she had activated the waypoint gem and summoned Perras Tul.

The sounds of battle echoed through the night—still indistinct, but closer. I passed a two story wooden structure blazing with flames that snaked high up into the sky. The fire lit up the area enough for me to see a knot of a dozen men fighting down by the shore, maybe fifty or sixty yards away. That felt like the epicenter of the battle and I had a hunch Creagar Skenn would be down there. Maybe Wylla too.

I rushed forward, but before I could get halfway there, something in motion—right in in front of me—caught my eye. I looked up to see a man hurtle through the smoky air twenty feet over my head. He screamed as he tumbled end-over-end through the night—almost as if he'd been savagely flung through the air by a giant. The man hit the ground hard a few yards from me in a tangle of broken bones and crushed internal organs. I ran over to him, but there was nothing I could do. He was burbling blood and convulsing. Then he died.

My mind was reeling. What in Dynark's name could have done that?

I sprinted onward. Coming up over a rise, I got a better view of the battle. And I finally laid eyes upon Jillen Lockwell.

Chapter Thirty-Eight

S HE STOOD WITH HER MOTHER ON THE SHORE END OF A PIER, FACING THE VILLAGE. Small for her age with a mop of curly red hair, and an otherworldly expression of rage on her face.

Arno Lockwell was there as well. And the three of them were ringed by mercenaries protecting them. It looked like some kind of last stand.

But as I moved closer, I saw that the Lockwells weren't defending themselves. They were slaughtering everyone around them.

And it was all due to Jillen Lockwell.

The girl was shrieking and gesturing with her hands and sending Creagar Skenn's men flying. Not just knocking them back. But throwing them high into the air and a hundred feet away—where they fell to their deaths. Jillen Lockwell was using her powers as a weapon—helping her parents destroy Ortwen.

I frantically looked around for Wylla, but there was no sign of her among the broken bodies around the pier. But from my vantage point I did spy Creagar Skenn. He was huddled behind an overturned skiff not far away. I crouched low and made my way over to him.

"You came back," he gasped. He was bleeding from a half dozen serious wounds and looked like he needed a healer immediately.

"Yes."

"No matter. All is lost. The demon spawn girl is destroying us."

"Where's Wylla?"

"She's fallen. She tried to reason with them—with the girl. But she was thrown out into the lake. Probably dead like everyone else."

"Hold on," I said. Then I left him and sprinted to the lake's edge. There were bodies scattered all around. And more floating in the water. I waded in and started pulling them to shore. Most were dead. Some were near dead. And then I caught a glimpse of red hair in the moonlight. It was Wylla. Her body was crumpled on the water's edge. She was face down on the shore and she wasn't moving.

I carefully turned her over. Her skin was cold to the touch, but she had a pulse—weak—but it was there. I moved her head to the side to make sure her throat was clear. Then I checked to see if she was breathing. She was—just barely. But it didn't look like she had much time left.

All I could think of was summoning Perras Tul. I checked Wylla's wrist for the waypoint gem, but it wasn't there. Then I checked her other wrist. It, too, was bare.

My mind was reeling. I had no way of contacting the Guild. We were on our own. This was very bad.

Frantically, I began to search through Wylla's pockets and pouches. Maybe she had taken the waypoint gem off her wrist for some reason. Stowed it somewhere else.

As I prodded through her clothing, Wylla began to stir. She groaned and her eyes fluttered.

"Wylla!" I helped her sit upright.

"I tried," she croaked.

"Are you injured?"

"She threw me. I feel like my head's split open."

"It's not. I checked. Where's the waypoint gem? We need Perras Tul."

She was fading.

"Wylla, the gem?"

"My own flesh," she muttered.

"Wylla, stay with me!"

"Bring me an enemy. Alive."

Every word was a major effort, but I didn't understand.

"You're not making sense," I said.

"Just do it. I can't hold on." She pushed at me weakly. "Bring me one of Lockwell's men. Or even one of Skenn's. Please. Go!"

I remembered what Valthar had told me as we were leaving his house in Hamwick. It seemed like the raving of a lunatic at the time, but now I wondered if it could actually be true.

As I staggered back towards the battle I saw that Ortwen's defenders were actually holding their own against Lockwell's forces. Jillen Lockwell was no longer using her powers. From what I could tell, the girl was sitting on the edge of the pier. She was either crying or resting. Her mother stood over her yelling something, but they were too far away for me to discern what she was saying. But I was guessing that Jillen Lockwell's magic energy had tapped out.

Up ahead I spotted a wounded man lurching away from the battle. He was clad in leather armor which meant that he probably was one of Lockwell's mercenaries. I snuck up behind him and clubbed him unconscious with the haft of my axe.

Then I threw him over my shoulder and dashed back to

Wylla. Even though I had a horrific feeling about what I was doing, I dumped the mercenary on the ground beside her.

At first I thought maybe Wylla had lost consciousness, or —Dynark forbid—died. But she pushed herself up on one elbow.

"Turn away," she said in a quiet voice.

"What?"

"I... I don't want you to see this. Please."

I did as she asked, turning my head and stepping away. But I knew this was wrong. Very wrong.

At first, all I could hear was her labored breathing. Then she let out an anguished cry. All of a sudden a glowing light shone from behind me, like a bright lantern. An unearthly keening sound filled the air. Then the light moved and rippled. Wylla groaned in anguish like a woman giving birth.

I almost turned, but then my axe blade caught the reflection of what was going on in back of me—and I couldn't believe what I was seeing.

A long, glowing tendril emerged from Wylla's mouth and undulated in the air. It almost looked like a gnarled tree branch, but it was insubstantial like smoke. I couldn't see clearly, but it appeared as if the tendril was adhering itself to the mercenary's neck. The man screamed in pain, instantly awake, and pawed at the glowing tendril. But his hand passed right through spectral appendage.

Wylla seemed to gain strength from the tendril as it pulsed and bloated. At the same time, the man began to convulse. His scream grew louder and more frantic.

"Wylla!" I yelled. "Stop this."

"Do not turn around!" Her voice was loud and strong now.

I couldn't believe it. Valthar had been right. The crazy old man had been right all along.

As we were leaving his home, Valthar had called me back

to the kitchen under the pretense of giving me some pebble-cakes. Wylla remained in the garden, distracted by the pouch of gems he had given her.

"Beware," Valthar had warned. "I believe your lady to be a theodrestre."

That's all he had said, but his expression had been deadly serious. At the time, I thought this was nonsense. I had heard of theodrestrae, of course. They were magical beings who could drain the life out of their enemies. But I had never encountered a theodrestre—nor the male counterpart, a theodrenca. Both were thought to be extinct. And even if they weren't, the idea that Wylla was one struck me as ridiculous. Up until now.

Wylla's voice snapped me out of my reverie. "It is done."

I turned to face her. She stood tall and looked completely healthy. In fact, she looked better than healthy. She looked vibrant. Energized.

"What are you...?"

Her eyes flashed. "I will explain it all later," she said. "Now we must stop my daughter."

"Your daughter?"

Even as the words left my lips, I realized the truth. It made sense, and the pieces were falling into place. Still, I had a million questions.

But they would have to wait. Wylla ran towards the Lockwells, screaming in fury. And I chased after her.

The pier was soaked with blood and surrounded by fallen soldiers. The Lockwells and a half dozen mercenaries still claimed it, but the last handful of Ortwen's defenders—including Creagar Skenn—were making one final push.

Swords clanged and men roared, but above it all, I could hear the voice of Ellia Lockwell. She was berating Jillen. "Kill them you little bitch! Kill them all!"

But the girl looked like she was half dead. She slumped

like a broken puppet. Ellia Lockwell tried to drag Jillen to her feet. She yelled some command at the girl then viciously backhanded Jillen, who stumbled and nearly toppled into the water.

Creagar Skenn instructed his men to fall back. He could barely stand on his own and needed to lean on one of his men. But that did not diminish his commanding voice. Raising his sword, he addressed Lockwell's half dozen mercenaries.

"This is over," he yelled. "Throw down your weapons. If you comply, you may leave now. Otherwise, your blood will darken the waters of the Teagh this night. Mark me!"

At the same time, Ellia Lockwell had grabbed Jillen by the shoulders and was now shaking the girl violently.

"Let her be!" Wylla yelled in a powerful voice. She charged towards the pier brandishing the bone knife she had got in Vale. Another piece of the puzzle.

I rushed to her side, but she pushed me away and addressed Arno Lockwell.

"Arno," she said. "Please. For Jillen's sake. Stop this—"

But Arno Lockwell just turned away, refusing to meet her gaze.

"Last chance," Creagar Skenn shouted.

"Never!" Without warning Arno Lockwell launched himself off the edge of the pier towards Creagar Skenn. But he didn't make it.

A flower of blood blossomed at his chest as a crossbow bolt slammed into him. A second bolt lodged itself into Ellia Lockwell's throat, knocking her back off her feet.

I looked behind me and saw Borsus Skenn on his horse, reloading his crossbow. But he needn't have bothered. Lockwell's remaining men dropped their weapons in the dirt and prostrated themselves in front of Creagar Skenn.

It was over.

Wylla pushed her way up on to the pier and pulled Jillen Lockwell into her arms. And seeing them together—both with their copper-colored curls and pale skin—provided another piece of the puzzle.

But it wasn't the last.

Chapter Thirty-Nine

I DIDN'T SEE WYLLA AGAIN FOR 24 HOURS. I spent every waking moment helping Creagar Skenn restore order. I rode to to Hytwen and explained to Minch what had happened. I brought Lynd the healer back with me to help Ortwen's healers minister to the injured. Finally I crawled back to the cell in Dorson's office and collapsed into the cot. I was asleep within seconds. I hadn't even bothered taking my boots off.

At some time during the night, someone kicked my feet to wake me. It was Wylla.

"We're going to need some time to get away," she said.

"Where are we going?"

She took my hand and spoke gently. "Not you and me. Me and Jillen."

Then she led me outside where the moon lit up the yard.

"You want to tell me what this whole thing was actually about?" I asked.

"It was about a lost girl. It was always about a lost girl. Everything I told you was true."

"You left out a few things."

"I did," she said. "Would you have helped me otherwise?"

I turned away from her. "I don't think you needed my help."

"You're wrong. I did. I really did."

"Are you a mage?" I asked.

"I don't know what I am."

"But Jillen's your daughter?"

"Yes."

"You told me you couldn't bear children. That's why your husband left you."

"That's what I thought. But nature works in mysterious ways. And it turns out that Unferd left me with a little farewell present. Once I started showing, I left the village and moved in with Ragenild."

"Who's Ragenild?"

"The druid. Who tattooed me. I would have stayed with her, but she passed away shortly after Jillen was born. She was very old and I think she was hanging on for as long as she could just to help me. Anyway, I knew I couldn't care for a baby living alone in the middle of the forest. So we went back to Hytwen, and I spoke to Arno. Persuaded him to take in Jillen and raise her as their own daughter. But I should have known better. Ellia Lockwell never really wanted her. And it just got worse."

"Did Jillen know that you're her real mother?"

"No," Wylla said. "She still doesn't. Not really."

"She inherited your powers," I said.

"I can't do what she does."

"But what you do..." I trailed off. The anguished sound of the mercenary being drained of his life still rang in my ears.

"What I do is vile. And I only do it when I have to."

"The Guild will hunt you. Both of you."

She looked straight ahead. "I know. But I don't know where to go."

I thought for a moment. "This is a big land. There are a lot of possibilities for us."

"Are you offering something?" she asked.

"Maybe I am."

"What exactly? Are you proposing that I be your fellow vagrant? And bring my daughter along for the ride?"

"Something like that."

She shook her head. "I'm done with wandering. We have to find someplace safe. Jillen needs me."

"What if I said that I need you too?"

Wylla shook her head. "That would be a lie. You don't need me. You don't need anybody."

I'm not sure how I felt about that, but I didn't say anything. Wylla moved close and pressed something into my hand. It was the waypoint gem.

"Give us a day's head start," she said. "Then you can summon Perras Tul."

"The Guild will be furious. I'm not sure what I'll be able to tell them."

"You'll think of something. And they'll be distracted by what they find here."

She was right about that. But I didn't think that would put them off for long.

"You need to find the Witches," I said. "The Witches of Melikti."

"I've never heard of them."

"They are like you. Women with powers. They live apart from everyone else. The Guild hates them. But that's who you need to join. They'll protect you and Jillen."

Hope shone in Wylla's eyes. "How do I find them?"

"That's the trick. They are extremely secretive. The location of their coven is always changing. I have had dealings with them myself in the past, but nothing good. I'd be a liability in seeking them out."

"Why?"

"It's a long, unpleasant story."

I thought for a moment. "I do know a mage who could help, but I haven't seen him in a long time."

"I've had enough of dealing with mages," Wylla said.

Then it came to me.

"Valthar," I said. "He might be able to find them."

Wylla wrinkled her nose. "He hates me."

"He gave you those gems. He will help you. I know it."

I could tell she was thinking about it.

"Perhaps," she said.

"Do you remember how to get there?"

She closed her eyes in thought. Then said, "No, I don't."

"It is his magic. Obscuring our memories."

"But I do remember a door. A red door. And a green man."

I smiled. She would do just fine.

When she left, I threw the waypoint gem into Lake Teagh.

Two days later Perras Tul showed up. I told him that the waypoint gem had been lost, Wylla had been killed in the battle, and Jillen Lockwell had teleported away. Creagar Skenn backed me up. After another day of questioning, Perras Tul and the other mages let me go. I think they were still suspicious, but they had much to sort through in Hytwen. There were a lot of unsolved mysteries as well. No one yet had determined who Haddon Fane actually was—and what killed him. Maybe that's something Wylla might learn from her daughter.

I said goodbye to Creagar Skenn and then went to Hytwen and bade farewell to Minch. These two men would have to repair all the damage and bring the two villages together. I promised to visit when I next passed through this corner of the Empire.

And then, late in the afternoon on a Spring day, I found myself alone at a crossroads on the West Way.

I could go east, backtracking to Marston Hills and Kreed's Keep. But only in theory. Because I knew I would never choose that path.

For the past year, my entire life had been about forward motion. And I knew I wouldn't stop now.

So I went west. Towards Bexden and Hryssan and Vale and even Hamwick where Valthar lived—if that's where I wanted to go.

Get a free Bander Adventure

Retired Imperial investigator Bander has put two decades of city life behind him and now wanders the Empire of Harion as a drifter. All he wants now is some peace and quiet. But when he takes a seldom-traveled trail through some of the roughest terrain in the Empire, he encounters conspiracy and murder in a remote mining village.

Visit randynargi.com/free-book

www.ingramcontent.com/pod-product-compliance
Lightning Source LLC
Chambersburg PA
CBHW061918130726
47908CB00017B/1879